Praise for

GILDA CARR'S TINY MYSTERIES

"The characters and setting of 1923 work perfectly here, and the story is one you want to keep reading along." —Red Carpet Crash on *Westside Lights*

"A masterpiece." —*Library Journal* on *Westside Saints*

"The harsh realities of Westside Manhattan are richly imagined and the diverse cast is expertly shaded. . . . Series fans will be gratified by this excellent outing." —*Publishers Weekly* on *Westside Saints*

"W. M. Akers's *Westside Saints* is inundated with death, but that doesn't keep it from being lively. . . . The constant presence of death does nothing to slow the frenetic pace of *Westside Saints*. Akers fills each chapter with action—often violent—and adds layers of mysteries with each step Gilda and Mary take." —Chapter 16

"The book is an instantly engrossing, clever, thriller/mystery that I couldn't stop reading. . . . I have no idea if there will be more books to come, but I certainly hope so. I'm going to keep Mr. Akers's name in my search bar at NetGalley just in case." —Lost in a Good Book blog on *Westside Saints*

"[In] W. M. Akers's superb debut, *Westside* . . . [his] research is excellent . . . his prose sharply crystalline." —*New York Times*

"Akers's debut novel is an addictively readable fusion of mystery, dark fantasy, alternate history, and existential horror. . . . It's like a literary shot of Prohibition-era rotgut moonshine—bracing, quite possibly hallucination-inducing, and unlike anything you've ever experienced before. . . . The illegitimate love child of Algernon Blackwood and Raymond Chandler." —*Kirkus Reviews* (starred review) on *Westside*

"Full of action and colorful characters, this genre mash-up is expertly done and will be enjoyed by fans of mysteries and fantasy alike."

—*Booklist* (starred review) on *Westside*

"*The Alienist* meets *The City & the City* in this brilliant debut that mixes fantasy and mystery. Gilda Carr's 'tiny mysteries' pack a giant punch." —David Morrell, *New York Times* bestselling author of *Murder as a Fine Art*, on *Westside*

"A fascinating, delightfully twisty mystery. *Westside* crosses Prohibition-era New York with the dark strangeness of *Neverwhere*. Fierce young detective Gilda Carr makes you believe that small mysteries hold the answers to everything." —Erika Swyler, bestselling author of *The Book of Speculation* and *Light from Other Stars*, on *Westside*

"A cast of meticulously developed and memorable characters as well as strong worldbuilding and atmospherics. . . . Fans of genre-bending fiction will relish this inventive mix of mystery and the paranormal."

—*Publishers Weekly* on *Westside*

"Akers's hugely enjoyable debut marries inventive alt-history with truly strange magic and a protagonist you won't soon forget."

—B&N Sci-Fi & Fantasy Blog on *Westside*

ALSO BY W. M. AKERS

Westside

Westside Saints

WESTSIDE LIGHTS

WESTSIDE LIGHTS

A NOVEL

W. M. AKERS

HarperCollins books may be purchased for educational, business, or sales promotional use. For information, please email the Special Markets Department at SPsales@harpercollins.com.

A hardcover edition of this book was published in 2022 by Harper Voyager, an imprint of HarperCollins Publishers.

FIRST HARPER VOYAGER PAPERBACK EDITION PUBLISHED 2023.

Designed by Paula Russell Szafranski
Map design by James Sinclair

Library of Congress Cataloging-in-Publication Data

Names: Akers, W. M., author.
Title: Westside lights / W.M. Akers.
Description: First edition. | New York, NY : Harper Voyager, [2022] | Series: Gilda Carr tiny mystery ; vol. 3 | Summary: "Akers takes a Manhattan that many readers will be familiar with and twists it into something darkly magical and incredibly compelling. In the latest sequel to the critically acclaimed Jazz Age fantasy series, Gilda Carr, detective of tiny mysteries, finds that on the New York waterfront, there is nothing more deadly than the past"— Provided by publisher.
Identifiers: LCCN 2021034690 (print) | LCCN 2021034691 (ebook) | ISBN 9780063043954 (hardcover) | ISBN 9780063043978 (ebook)
Subjects: LCGFT: Detective and mystery fiction. | Fantasy fiction. | Novels.
Classification: LCC PS3601.K482 W48 2022 (print) | LCC PS3601.K482 (ebook) | DDC 813/.6—dc23
LC record available at https://lccn.loc.gov/2021034690
LC ebook record available at https://lccn.loc.gov/2021034691

ISBN 978-0-06-304396-1 (pbk.)

23 24 25 26 27 LBC 5 4 3 2 1

For my teachers,

particularly Robin Smith

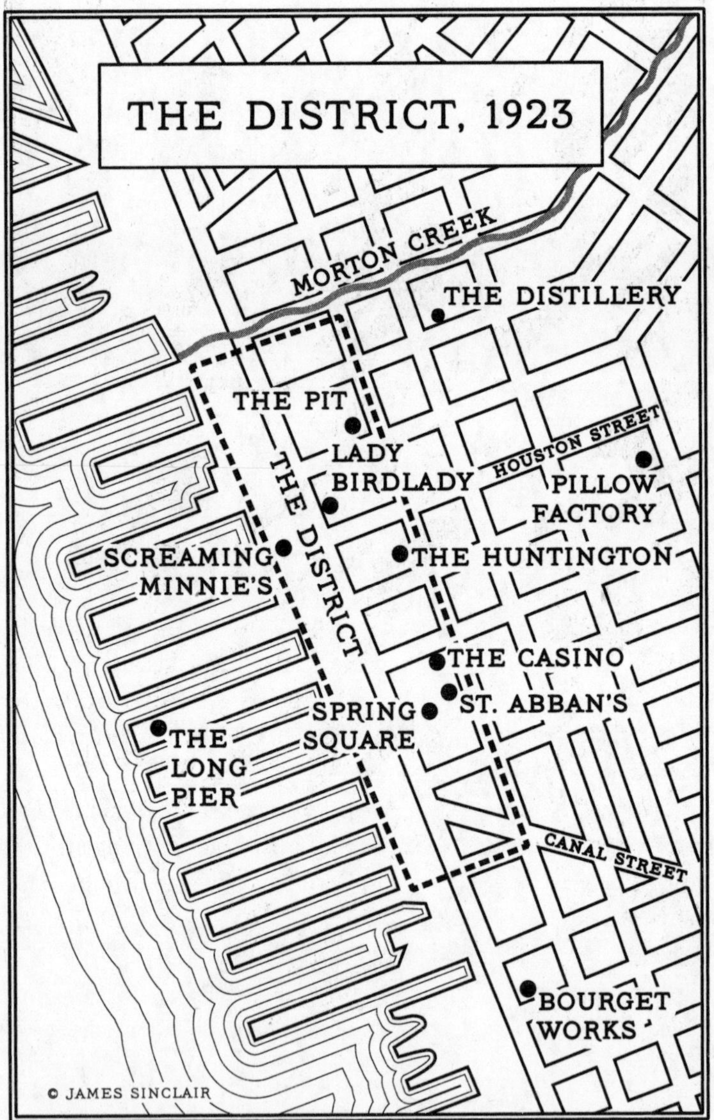
THE DISTRICT, 1923
MORTON CREEK
THE DISTILLERY
THE PIT
LADY BIRDLADY
HOUSTON STREET
PILLOW FACTORY
THE DISTRICT
SCREAMING MINNIE'S
THE HUNTINGTON
THE CASINO
ST. ABBAN'S
SPRING SQUARE
THE LONG PIER
CANAL STREET
BOURGET WORKS
© JAMES SINCLAIR

ONE

I lost the gull.

Or perhaps we lost her. We were the ones who found her, claimed her, fed her, and loved her, and we were there when she disappeared. It was 1923—a year when *I* sank into *we*. That summer, we did everything as one.

For a while.

The bird was a lazy old thing, a one-legged creature with wings so mottled they looked dirty even when she was fresh from a Hudson bath. She flew in half-hearted, sinking circles and squawked like she didn't care about being heard. She was a beautiful, useless thing, and we named her Grover Hartley in tribute to a comically handsome Giants catcher whom I doted on when I was younger, when the world was closer to sane.

She was the first pet I'd ever had. I'd never understood the urge to let wildlife into one's home, as I needed no help keeping my town house a perfect mess, but when Cherub and I began playing at domesticity, an animal seemed a natural addition. It could have been worse. She could have been a cat—or a child.

We hung a yellow fire bucket from the stern of our little boat and welcomed her with a feast of apple cores, chicken wings, oyster shells, collard stalks, and bread crusts. It was a pleasure watching the gull fatten on our scraps. If one of her brethren dared intrude on Grover Hartley's meal, we frightened them off by pelting rocks, singing off-key, and slapping stray bits of rope against the deck. She sucked down food like a vacuum cleaner—it was the only time she showed any effort—and when she flew off, belly dragging across the water, I knew that though we could never own her, she was ours.

On a day when the falling sun dyed the river orange and the breeze carried the first hint of fall, I went to dump our leftovers into the fire bucket and found it nearly full. I felt a sudden certainty that by choice or by tragedy Grover Hartley had deserted us, and that very likely we would never see her again. Some people would have allowed themselves a tear. I simply stood there, twisting a gristly chicken bone between my fingers, trying to decide if I was mourning the gull or the people she'd left behind.

New Jersey had nearly swallowed the sun when Cherub prodded a toe into my thigh.

"Something wrong?"

"The bird didn't eat."

"So?"

I put on a smile and turned around. He was where I liked him: sprawled across the cramped little cockpit with a cigar stub in his mouth and a pulp magazine folded in his hands, sweat glittering on his body like diamond mail. A year on the water had done nothing to harden his slack physique, but long days in the sun had darkened his complexion from light brown to something that verged on purple. He was as beautiful as the boat he lay on, and she was no hag. Her hull was bone white, her deck as smooth as good bourbon. She had been the jewel of the Hudson ever since the night he stole her from the Eastside docks and christened her in my honor: the *Misery Queen*.

I trailed my fingers across his gut. He hated being tickled, and so I did it every chance I got.

"Our pet is missing. You're not concerned?"

"Birds go. They come back or they don't. For all we know she winters in New Orleans."

I opened the bench where we stashed tangled rope and canvas. I shoved the mess aside and tried to hide my irritation when I didn't find what I required.

"Where's my bag?"

"What bag?"

"The sack where I keep my lock picks and notes and all the other junk that goes into my work. Where's it gone?"

"In the cabin, under the bunk. You weren't using it, so I put it away."

"I see."

He stood, leaving a gleaming patch of sweat on the bench. He smelled more powerfully of river than the Hudson itself. The closer he got, the easier it was to forget I was annoyed.

"Going back to work?" he said, the lump in his throat bobbing like the water beneath our feet.

"Just thinking of asking around after our gull."

"One of your tiny mysteries."

"Maybe so."

His eyes slid away from me. He drew a meaningful breath. I waited for him to gather the words I was forcing him to say.

"I was dreaming of flying," he said. "A year ago. More."

"I recall."

"Swooping around the skyscrapers up in Midtown, scaring the hell out of the working stiffs. I had these massive white wings."

"Sounds lovely."

"It was. And you shook me awake, you monster, tears in your eyes, and told me you were swearing off honest work. 'I'm going to pieces,' you said. 'I need a good, long break. No mysteries, tiny or otherwise.' You made me promise to hold you to it."

I had. For more than a year now, he had helped me resist temptation. When the coasters began disappearing from the saloons, I did not wonder where they'd gone. When scratching sounds were heard underneath the Boardwalk, I fought the urge to cut a hole in the wood and see what they were. I'd refused all requests to go hunting for lost wallets, watches, broaches, bracelets, and fiancées. Curiosity had nearly gotten me killed too many times. I was learning to resist its call. But when Grover Hartley disappeared, the little voice in my head screamed *why* louder than it had in a long time.

A dizzying sickness welled up in me. I was on a precipice, unable to decide which way to fall. There was no harm, I hoped, in letting him make my choice.

"Go ahead, then. Hold me to it."

"Let the gull take care of herself until after Labor Day."

"And what shall I do in the meantime?"

"Relax!" He threw his arms wide as he said it, flinging sweat into the current. Upon his shoulders sat the Boardwalk, the city, and the sky. It seemed impossible that anyone could want more than that. "Enjoy our happy retirement."

"We're too young to retire."

"Pretirement, then. We've earned it."

He was close enough for my eyes to trace every crack in his full lips. I slid my hand up his back and pulled him to me, kissing him until his knees buckled and we sank to the deck.

Relax.

There was nothing harder for me to do. But for him, for us, I would try.

I threaded my fingers around his. Light, dark, light, dark, light, dark. No matter how much sun he got, I grew evermore pale. I squeezed his hand until it hurt us both.

"I'll give it till Labor Day," I said. "I don't want this to end."

"It doesn't have to. The water's not going anywhere and neither am I."

If I'd been feeling petulant, I'd have reminded him the water *was* going somewhere all the time. But it was easier to let the bobbing ship and the booze drifting through my blood take hold. One more kiss and I sank halfway to sleep, forgetting this wasn't heaven, that my mind was elsewhere, that the closer we got to autumn the more I wanted to run away. But the itch had started. Our bird was gone, and I wanted to know where.

We had come to the river looking for happiness. To my surprise, we found plenty. Cherub was my oldest friend, my favorite lover, a retired gangster who had proposed marriage once or twice or more. In the spring of '22, I came as close to death as I ever had, and I decided the experience had earned me a little taste of life. Cherub had been dreaming of the waterfront, and I asked if I could come along. I expected it to blow up in a week or less, but he was easy to live with—even in the cramped confines of a stolen sloop—and the time melted by.

For work, for play, for everything we could dream of, we had the District—a tenderloin where slummers and drunks from across the city could choose from a menu that included raw liquor, cocaine, heroin, cheap sex, lewd dancing, boxing, wrestling, ratting, and the finest jazz north of Lake Pontchartrain. Thanks to lawful society's aggressive disinterest in the Westside—an overgrown paradise where nature reigned, where electricity faltered, where guns did not fire but murder was common, where modernity had no place—people could do whatever they wanted there. Cherub, myself, and the few thousand other natives of the Lower West had known that for years, even before the fence was built down the middle of Broadway.

Now, though, our secret was out.

The District was the result of a treaty struck between the self-styled emperor of the Westside, Glen-Richard Van Alen, and the Roebling Company, a publicly traded gang of corporate goons whose blandly indistinguishable foot soldiers were known as the Gray Boys. Van Alen owned the land, the Roeblings controlled the entertainment, and as long as not too many people died, the police and the Volstead enforcers were grateful to turn a blind eye. The District was meant to solve all the problems of both organizations, providing the Roeblings with a limitless audience for their ruthlessly cheap brand of vice and safeguarding Van Alen against a war that would have meant the destruction of the Westside. Like my time with Cherub, I'd expected it to crumble within a week, but the profits were astonishing, and money is a superlative glue. People filled the Boardwalk with gin in their stomachs and narcotics in their veins and music in their ears. Everyone was rich and good looking. Everyone was happy.

Even, occasionally, me.

I cannot clearly explain what brought us there. Even on the Lower West, where cold and hunger and the countless horrors of the night had left behind a population too preoccupied with survival to waste time on bigotry, love between a white woman and a Black man was only easy as long as we stuck to my town house and the deserted avenues that rolled lazily upward from Washington Square. Drawing attention to ourselves would mean anything from inconvenience to violent death. With that threat added to my inborn hatred of crowds, there was no reason for us to forgo the serene emptiness of our Westside for the suddenly thriving waterfront. And yet, when the District opened its rusty gates to the world, there we were, living on the river, returning to the town house only when nasty weather or a craving for Hellida's cooking drove us inside.

It would be simple to say that Cherub yearned for the water, and the docks in the District were less rotten than anywhere else on the Lower West. He also had a half-baked idea to use the *Misery Queen* as a ferry, charging wealthy fools a fortune to carry them around the Battery and, if he felt generous, bring them safely home again. But it would be closer to the truth to say that we were on the run. He had lost every friend he'd ever had in the gang war of 1921, and I had endured a particularly unsettling family tragedy in the bleak winter that followed. Along the way I had killed, maimed, and threatened, a streak of violence that was either completely at odds with my character or simply the person I had become. Truth was, there were too many ghosts on Washington Square. There were ghosts on the river, too, but when you were watching a one-legged gull circle lazily in front of the setting sun, they were easier to ignore.

The District would have died swiftly if it weren't for the genius of Ida Greene and Vivienne Bourget. Van Alen's chief deputy, Mrs.

Greene oversaw the charitable side of the empire of light. When a woman on Amsterdam Avenue gave birth, Mrs. Greene paid the midwife and, very often, cut the cord. When a boy on West Twenty-Third watched cholera claim his parents, she found him a new home. She was as precise as a scalpel, capable of making the miraculous seem routine.

Uncommonly kind and perfectly ruthless, there was no one else Van Alen would have trusted to provide the District's gin. At a distillery on Morton Creek, Mrs. Greene's women worked around the clock to produce a beet-stained liquor that, while not quite toxic, could strip the lining from your stomach and the worries from your soul. It was said the liquor caused strange effects—from soaring euphoria to hallucinations both chilling and divine—but those were the ravings of poets, lunatics whom I have the sense to ignore. But the Lower West has always had cheap liquor, and even though Mrs. Greene's gin seemed to get stronger every year, it was nowhere as novel as the Devices of Professor Bourget.

They arrived a few weeks after we did, in the soft perfection of June 1922. At first, there were nine of them: one at each intersection in the District and a bigger one perched in the middle of the flattened block between Spring and Houston that was already being called Spring Square. Later, we were promised, there would be more. For weeks they sat wrapped under canvas, guarded, like every valuable in the District, by the Peacekeepers—the District's version of law and order, whose patrols invariably paired one of Van Alen's rainbow guardsmen with a glowering Roebling man. Rumors spread that the Devices were instruments of surveillance or death, or advertisements for a particularly well-financed Broadway show. For those of a curious bent, like myself, the anticipation was torture. When they announced the unveiling, Cherub had no interest, but I couldn't stay away.

A whitewashed dais was thrown up before the largest of the things, and a hundred or so gawkers crowded around. Naturally, there were speeches. First came Van Alen, tall and thin and gray, his hands clenching the podium to keep them steady. Ida Greene was at his elbow, as always, ready to catch him if he should fall. When I'd met Van Alen, he'd been an oak. Now he was a splinter. It reminded me of my father in an especially unpleasant way.

His address was followed by a few short words from a representative of the Roebling Company, a Chinese man named Oliver Lee who was so at ease in evening clothes that it was rumored he'd been born in a tuxedo. In an organization whose soldiers prided themselves on being white, flabby, and dull, he was either an anomaly or the first of a new breed. I'd seen him around enough that he knew my name and what I drank, and I wasn't sure if I was flattered or scared. He enjoyed acting as though we were friends, even though we both knew that somewhere on one of his ledgers was a notation for how much it would cost to have me killed.

Bourget spoke last. She wore a heavy black dress that looked stolen from my wardrobe and a cap tilted so rakishly across her snow-white hair that I was surprised it didn't fall off. She looked impatient to reveal her marvel to the world, but she bowed to the occasion, making a short, hopeful speech about the majesty of technology and the glittering future of the Lower Westside. That's what I assumed, anyway. I was at the water's edge, where the wind was blowing in, and I didn't catch a word.

At last she tore away the covering to reveal a many-layered orb etched with lacy patterns, perched on a heavy iron pedestal. When the sunlight hit, its jagged steel and glass panels sparkled like they had been spritzed with morning dew. It was beautiful.

No one was impressed.

"The hell is it?" cried one of the crowd.

"It looks like a polished testicle," I said, and the woman behind me cackled.

I hadn't noticed her before. I don't know how that's possible. She was six feet tall, as thin as a switch, and perhaps forty-five, with unfashionably long, flat hair and a string of pearls that dangled past her waist. Her laugh poured out like acid. She clapped me on the shoulder—her touch was skeletal—and passed me a half-full bottle of champagne. I drank deep. The wine was so cold, it stung my teeth.

In a lifetime of Westside summers, I'd never tasted anything so well-chilled.

"Thanks."

"No trouble. Such a pleasure to meet a Westsider who sees this is nothing but a very expensive farce."

"Do you know what the machine is supposed to be?"

"Nobody does. I was at a demonstration last week for representatives from the local papers and weekly magazines. They showed off the whole thing from top to bottom but didn't dare turn it on."

Bourget reached into her pocket—you must respect a woman whose dresses have pockets—for a glittering crystal shard. She twisted it above her head, soaking it with sunlight, then slid it into a slot at the base of the machine. She turned a crank. Beneath her dress, muscle strained. The Device's plates began to whir, and the crowd oohed, though the machine appeared to be doing nothing at all.

"The professor gave us a little talk," said the woman in the pearls, "said that this whatever-the-hell-you-call-it was made from civic pride, an attempt to lift the Lower West out of the Middle Ages. Horseshit."

"Oh?"

"It's about money. Nothing else. They'd slit the throat of every person here for a little spare change."

"Yes. Yes, I think they would."

The ball whizzed into a blur. It was hard to believe something so delicately constructed could move so fast. The gawkers stepped back—first a few inches, then as much as the crowd allowed—as Bourget's machine spun quicker and quicker, giving off only the faintest hum, like a fly flitting past your ear. Still, it did nothing. On the stage, Van Alen shook his head in disgust, Ida Greene inspected her cuticles, and Oliver Lee maintained a forced smile. Bourget dictated notes to an assistant, a baby-faced man in a white lab coat, her eyes unblinking as she stared, waiting for something that clearly was not going to come to pass.

"A bust," said the woman behind me. "Probably won't even get a column out of it. Damned waste of my—"

And then it happened.

An explosion of light as bright as a newborn star.

"Holy god," I said.

It was a silly thing to say, but when the impossible happens, it's never easy to choose one's words.

It had been twenty years since the lights went out on the Westside. I was just a child, and I remember the terror of light bulbs bursting in their sockets, of gas jets spitting uncontrollable fire. For most of my life, the nights had been lit by moonlight, candle, or nothing at all. Occasionally, scientists, hucksters, true believers, and outright lunatics had tried to bring electricity or something like it to our deadly streets. Their efforts had earned them nothing but humiliation, bankruptcy, and disfiguring burns.

But Professor Bourget had turned on the light.

The crowd screamed—a cry of the purest relief. They screamed because they had waited so long for light, they'd forgotten how badly they missed it. They screamed not because they were happy but from the sudden absence of pain. It is possible that I was screaming too.

The light grew brighter. The abandoned structures that ringed Spring Square—a sailor's hotel, a spice warehouse, a parochial school, a factory whose facade advertised "It Is Great! Pride of the Farm! Tomato Catsup!"—were so fiercely lit that I saw every missing brick, every nick in the iron. Look closely, and you could tell the light was flickering, but let your eyes rest, and it was the purest glow you'd ever seen. Bourget threw up her hands and, after quite some time, the crowd quieted enough for her to speak. She yelled now, loud enough that even over the wind, I could make out every word.

"How do you like it?" she cried. "How about more?"

A roar from the crowd. She clapped her hands and, up and down West Street, Peacekeepers tore away the wrapping on the other Devices. They jammed in the crystals and spun the cranks and stepped back sweating as the lights whirred to life and the crowd grew louder still. This time it took much longer for the roar to die.

"This is just the start, folks. I made this light at my factory, just a few blocks south of here, and I plan to make a whole lot more.

Lights big enough to tear a hole in the night sky, but small enough to put on your dinner table. You're never gonna eat in the dark again."

At that, her audience screamed so loud, nothing could have shut them up. People surged toward the Device, wanting to get a hand on it, forcing the Peacekeepers to fight them off with fist and boot and club. Eventually, the crowd dispersed to toast to the brilliance of Professor Bourget. Only a few stayed behind, entranced by the spinning machine, the light that had not been there before. I was among them. The tall woman who'd given me the champagne was as well.

"You got your column?" I asked her.

"And a whole lot more. This neighborhood has seized my interest. Anything left in that bottle?"

"A bit."

She snatched it back, drained it, and smashed it on the ground with a magnificent belch. She walked away and, to my surprise, I followed. As I would soon understand, she was even harder to ignore than Bourget's lights.

"What's your name?" she said.

"Gilda Carr."

"Marka Watson. You know my work?"

"No."

"Good. When it comes to serious drinking, there's no one worse than a fan. Let's find some oysters and more champagne. Light has come to the Westside, and we shall not sleep tonight."

I thought she was joking. I quickly learned Marka meant everything she said. I don't know where she got the oysters, but they were electric. I don't know how she found champagne, but it was as cold as the light outside. I ran out of conversation before the bottle was dry, but Marka had enough for both of us. She was a theater critic, a journalist, a poet, an essayist, a wit. Among the overeducated, she informed me, she was quite famous. I let her know I didn't care, and she was smitten. That night, at least, when her opinions seemed daring and her jokes were fresh, I didn't mind acting as her audience. She should have irritated me, but the light and champagne had me dizzy, and her charm was irresistible—like an artillery barrage.

We drank until dawn, stopping only because Marka's wallet was empty and the bartenders did not yet know her well enough to extend credit and I certainly wasn't buying. When we emerged onto Spring Square, Bourget's lights had been turned off. Marka tripped over a loose paving stone and fell into the dirt, which was littered with broken glass burned orange by the rising sun. She hadn't seemed drunk until now.

"Lord, this place is ugly in the morning," she said. "How do you stand it?"

"This time of day, I tend to be asleep."

"We'll break that habit. Do you mind if I use that line of yours, about the testicle, in this week's column?"

"So long as you promise not to use my name."

"Modesty! Amazing. I thought it was dead. My editor's a puritan, anyway, he won't print it, but it will be a pleasure to make him blush."

I helped her up. She slumped against my shoulder. We cut an uncertain path across Spring Square. When our weaving brought us to the base of the great lamp, we brushed our hands across its iron. It was too cold to touch.

"Gilda, darling," she said, "how on earth am I getting home?"

"I happen to know a man with a stolen boat."

And that is how the *Misery Queen* found her first passenger. There would be dozens more, but she was the one who mattered. Van Alen and Roebling had established the tenderloin, but Marka was the one who dubbed it the White Lights District, and she was the one who put it on the map, churning out column after column to tempt Eastsiders with holes in their souls and money to waste to walk overland from the fence or sail around the Battery for a taste of glorious squalor. Marka spent weeks at a time in the Huntington, a ramshackle old hotel not far from Spring Square, attended to by a clan of artists, critics, and hangers-on. On the nights they missed the comfort of their penthouses, Cherub and I sailed them home. The rest of the time, we drank at their side.

They were beautiful. They dressed well, spoke brilliantly, and spent money like they were allergic to it. To them, we were curiosities: real-life Westsiders kept around because we knew every bartender and because our presence kept them from feeling phony. They paid us in flattery and truly embarrassing amounts of cash, which was enough for Cherub but hardly satisfied me.

I don't know why I stuck around. At first they were amusing, but I can spend only so much time laughing at other people's jokes before my face gets sore. They were unapologetically happy, and I studied them to try to understand how I could be, too. When that failed, I found comfort being around people who didn't care if I was silent and whose gay squawking drowned out my private worry that happiness didn't fit me at all.

And so we vaulted from 1922 to '23. The roots of the District sank deeper. Bourget Devices proliferated along the waterfront, spinning out crystalline light that made all of us look paler, thinner, and more perfect than we could ever be in the day. A portable unit found a home on the deck of the *Misery Queen,* presented by Marka to light our way across the river in the predawn. Somewhere in there I turned twenty-nine, and realized I was probably as close to maturity as I would ever get. On our boat, Cherub and I were as perfect as a rhyming couplet. Onshore, everything was rotten, but not quite bad enough to flee. Everywhere I turned, I saw my grinning friends.

They seemed immortal.

Death was nearer than we knew.

TWO

Soon after the disappearance of Grover Hartley, Cherub and I were out with Marka and her clique, slurping warm ale in a furrier's warehouse that had been converted to a pool hall. Towering windows gave a view of the Hudson, which looked as clean and cold as the day it had been sliced into the earth, but the air in the bar was thick with sawdust and every surface gleamed with sweat. It was lunchtime. My head felt like I'd slept on a nail.

Cherub was playing pool with Lisbeth Frasier, a screeching heiress whose increasingly popular poetry was, Marka assured me, "strictly steerage." She'd given Cherub ten dollars to bet on their game and had spent all night winning it back. It wasn't hard to do. He played with the same frenzied enthusiasm with which he made love and had not yet realized that what works in the bedroom is death in the pool hall. Between shots, he wound his way through a story that had become legend among Marka and her friends: the tale of the night he stole the *Misery Queen*.

"It was well past midnight, that sweet spot in the evening when the drunks are dozing but the fish market hasn't woken up. There was no moon—I made sure of that—and it was so dark I could barely see my hands as I swam up to the pier. I slipped out of the water, quiet as you like, onto the deck of the ship that had stolen my heart. My breath caught as I heard movement in the cabin. I was not alone."

He went on through the epic fistfight that won him the boat, a battle with an East River giant who got more Bunyanesque with every telling. I happened to know the truth of the story—that he'd bribed a guard at a marina while the ship's owners were at Newport and simply sailed the trim little sloop away—but there was no sense ruining his fun. I was deep into a fantasy of my own. I had an audience of one: the playwright Stuyvesant Wells, one of Marka's nearest and dearest, whose high hairline, soft cheeks, and dead eyes made him look like a potato that had been left out in the rain. He was gin-sleepy and barely listening. I did not mind.

"It would be a hell of a case," I said, "finding a missing bird."

"Shame you can't fly."

"Flying's overrated. I could run the whole thing from the ground. I've been studying the birds on Spring Square, getting to know their habits. I haven't seen her. I need to go deeper."

"Oh?"

"I'll start by crashing an ornithology lecture at City College. Corner the professor and force him to tell me everything he knows about gulls. Once I have a handle on their diet and migratory patterns, I'll divide the District into zones, ten feet square, and chart out their nesting grounds, feeding grounds, spawning grounds—"

"Dying grounds?"

"Those too. And then I'll build a trap. Something clever, something that a two-legged bird can wriggle out of, but that would hold a one-legged gull fast."

"Sounds like a job for the esteemed Professor Bourget."

"I don't employ subcontractors. I'll find that bird myself."

"It'll be an awful lot of work."

"Yes. Yes indeed."

My fantasy dissolved like river foam. I rubbed my jaw, which had been hurting more and more lately. I looked down at the bar and found I'd been tracing a figure in the sawdust—a crude drawing of a lovely bird. The weight that had rested on my stomach since Grover's disappearance grew a little heavier. I swept the sawdust onto the floor and choked down another mouthful of warm beer. Across the room, Lisbeth and Marka roared with laughter as Cherub missed another shot.

"Why not take it to the authorities?" said Stuy, with his eyes fully shut.

"The police wouldn't care."

"Nor should they. But there must be someone in this strange place with power over the birds."

He smiled as his head rolled back. Perhaps, like Cherub, he dreamed of soaring through the sky. He was right, of course. There was one person in this city whose power over earth, surf, dirt, and sky was unmatched. His name was Glen-Richard Van Alen, and he was far away, secluded in his fortress at the far end of the Upper Westside. But here in the District, his power was held by Ida Greene. If my accounting was correct—and I will be honest, it very rarely was—she was in my debt. I had fought at her side; I had saved the Lower West on her behalf. It was the least she could do, I thought, to task a few lackeys with the recovery of my bird.

I plucked Stuy's drink from his hands before it spilled and sipped it as I swept toward the door. Marka glanced at me but did not get up. Cherub waved his cue, concern on his face. I raised my glass and smiled, as big as I could manage, and he returned to losing the game.

After the stale air of the pool hall, I was revived by the breeze blowing along the Boardwalk—an almost sturdy structure, built atop the remains of West Street, that ran the length of the District, from Morton Creek to Canal. I walked fast, putting warmth in my legs and purpose in my stride. The District's northern end was a little strip of hell. The buildings were hastily converted factories, like the pool room, or outright shanties built from whatever garbage the Hudson coughed up. In them you could purchase oily liquor at a nickel a shot, a fixed price that attracted thirsty Eastsiders by the hundreds. Behind the saloons were brothels, gambling halls, and drug dens that operated with the same brutal efficiency. For those who had nowhere else to go, it was a last shot at living. For Marka and her followers, it was the greatest show in town.

Closer to Houston, the District put on airs. Piers 34 through 38 had been rebuilt to receive yachts and improvised Eastside ferries, like the *Queen,* which brought wealthy slummers, bourgeois climbers, and anyone else with a few dollars to lose. To better part them from their money, the Roebling Company was experimenting with something unprecedented: quality. Here the liquor was aged—or at least dyed brown—and the bars had been sanded and stained. The hypodermic needles were clean and, if you believed the advertising, the women were too. Look closely and it was still hell, but much better dressed.

None of it interested me. Liquor is liquor, and I'd take mine however it made its way into my glass. But I wasn't bitter enough to refuse the breeze off the river, the creak of the Boardwalk, the stink of fried fish, the music that roared out of every window. Lose the people, I thought, and the District wouldn't be half bad.

The Boardwalk led me to Spring Square, the District's bloody heart, where men in wrinkled tuxedos slept off last night's drunk in the shade cast by Professor Bourget's unlit lamp. I passed the Casino, the Huntington, and a few boardinghouses whose fresh paint and luxe names couldn't conceal that eighteen months prior, they had been empty industrial shells.

On the far side of the square, I arrived at St. Abban's, Van Alen's local headquarters, an abandoned schoolhouse where the smack of rulers still echoed through the air. During the early days of the District, this jumble of Gothic arches and medieval turrets had been proposed as a site for the Casino, but Van Alen felt it inappropriate to profane what had once been a respectable Catholic school and instructed his people to make offices of it instead. Swilling booze in a parochial building was blasphemy, but using it to organize an empire of sin was simply good business. The rainbow guardsmen had their barracks here, and there were outposts of the various charitable enterprises that Ida Greene used to put a pretty face on Van Alen's empire, but my business was on the second floor, where the ledgers were kept and policy was made.

I climbed the sweeping stone steps and was reaching for the door when it swung open, nearly bashing me in the skull. Out bounded Oliver Lee, looking immaculate, like he'd never been tired in his entire life. If it weren't for a gray smudge on his left cuff, I might have mistaken him for a god.

"It must be nice," I said, "charging through life like there's never anyone on the other side of the door."

"A terrible habit. Are you okay?"

"Tolerable."

"Will you be out tonight with Marka and her crowd?"

"Probably."

"Where are they starting? I'd love to tag along."

Every time I saw Lee, which was more often than I cared to, he invited himself out for drinks. I had no idea why. I usually managed to dodge the request, but once I'd slipped up and told him where he'd find us that evening. Marka spent the entire night making cracks about my wardrobe—"You're so clever, Gilda, always wearing black. It very nearly hides the stains." Lee would not be welcome again. She loved it when criminals dropped by her table, but only when it was her idea.

"You're too good for them," I said. As the words came out of my mouth, I was surprised to find I actually thought they were true.

"Nonsense. I don't write, I don't dance, I don't—"

"But you work. It must be an immense effort, coordinating the Roeblings and Van Alen, keeping everyone happy, keeping the drugs flowing and the lights spinning and the party going on and on. You do it all, hours and hours a day, and your collar never loses its starch. Why waste time on Marka and her friends?"

He used a well-trimmed thumbnail to scratch his brow.

"They're like no one I've ever known," he said. "Life is so easy for them. I guess . . . I just want to understand."

I wanted to tell him to go home to his family, to forget the lights of the District and take solace in sleep, the greatest narcotic of all. But I could hardly give advice that I wouldn't follow myself.

"I don't know what Marka's plan is tonight," I said. "But if I see you, I suppose I could permit you to buy us a round."

Marka would crucify me for that. Perhaps I'd take the opportunity to tell her to go to hell. Perhaps, more likely, I would endure the humiliation in silence. After all, I was supposed to be retired.

Lee smiled. If I weren't so thoroughly hungover, I might have been charmed.

"It would be my pleasure," he said. "What brings you to St. Aban's?"

"I'm wanted in the principal's office."

"That's what you get for cutting class." A look of brotherly concern crossed his face. "Quite seriously though, Miss Carr, if you ever have any trouble with the Van Alen crowd, remember the Roebling Company is your friend."

Friends with the Roebling Company. It was not a comforting thought. And I wasn't quite sure I believed it.

He held the door open. I stepped into a musty hallway whose only light came from a pane of stained glass that showed a bearded man hip deep in a river, blessing the waters with his hands. I set my glass on the runner—no sense staining the wood—and proceeded up the creaking stairs.

My step slowed as it occurred to me that I had never handed a case over to the authorities before. Murder, arson, burglary, kidnapping—those I would toss aside at the first opportunity, but I had always kept the truly tiny mysteries to myself. The best of them, the ones intricate enough to hold my attention for weeks, so unimportant that no one would steal them—they were rare, and well worth hoarding. The disappearance of Grover Hartley had the makings of a classic, and I was about to throw it away.

"So I've never done it before," I said. "That's probably because it's a good idea."

I made my way down the hallway on a crimson carpet so thin I could feel every joint in the wood and stopped at the private office of Ida Greene. Neither of the voices that came from inside belonged to her.

"You've asked all the guardsmen?"

"Every one, once and twice and then a third time, just to make sure they all think I'm fully insane."

"And none of them have seen anything?"

"I'd have told you if they did."

"Ask them again. The cleaning people, too, and the office boys, and anyone else who might have been through here, and—"

"Cornelia."

There was real concern in the man's voice. It was a refreshing sound—I wasn't used to hearing people who gave a damn about each other. There was a pause, and then the *scritch* of a match erupting into flame.

"I know. It's ludicrous. It's one of those things that doesn't matter at all, except that if it doesn't matter, why is it keeping me up at night? We have staked everything on this place. Every penny counts. If Mrs. Greene knew . . ."

"She never will. I'll talk to the guards."

"Thank you."

Deep within my undertaxed brain, I felt the itch of curiosity. It was maddening and intoxicating all at once. I wondered what would happen if I gave it a scratch.

The door eased open. Out stalked a thick-necked man whose hair was smeared across his forehead in an unfortunate center part. His rimless spectacles showed red eyes sunk deep into his skull. He looked past me and then snapped his head back to look at me again. Disgust settled onto his face as he recognized me. His name was Marvin Howell.

I was thrilled to run into him, too.

I'd met him once before, at the end of a very long night, when Cherub and I were slumped against the Boardwalk railing, sharing a packet of greasy fries so hot they burned our throats. Howell spotted Cherub from across the street, shoved through the crowd, and smacked him across the face. The sound was a whip crack. The fries scattered across the ground.

"You know why," Howell snarled, and then he spun away.

I let Cherub breathe. His cheek was cherry red. Once he was standing upright, I asked: "And who was that charming man?"

"Howell. Marvin Howell, a friend from my One-Eyed days.

We called him Camembert, because whenever a fight started, he went all soft and tended to run. I wonder why he'd want to hit me."

"Doesn't everyone?"

"If they have sense. Watch this."

He tilted his head back then and let loose a sickening yowl, loud enough to make my ears ring. The screech took me right back to my childhood, to the days of the Westside's first wildness. It was the war cry of the One-Eyed Cats, a hideous, beautiful sound, and it cut through Howell like a straight razor. For a full minute he stood, shaking in terror, and then walked away.

"That's the hell of having a past," Cherub chuckled. "You can forget it, but it won't forget you."

That day at St. Abban's, Howell pried off his spectacles and made a great show of cleaning the glass.

"You seem an inoffensive young woman," he said. It was hard to tell if he meant this as a compliment, an insult, or some mixture of the two.

"I've been called many things, but never inoffensive. And I believe I'm older than you."

"Even so. Why you waste your time on that lout Cherub, I shall never understand."

"I'd explain it if I cared what you think. Do you mind getting out of the way? You're blocking the door."

He shook his head and walked away. I was about to knock when I remembered that knocking gets you nowhere, and so I opened the door.

In a classroom whose chalkboard was covered with the ghosts of diagrammed sentences, the woman who'd begged Howell for help sat behind a desk. Like Mrs. Greene, she was Black, precisely styled, and in no mood to waste time, but she was much younger—perhaps twenty-two. She wore a pale pink blouse whose scalloped frills curled around the lapels of a sharply tailored green suit. I had the strangest idea that her sleeves were hiding scars.

"I don't believe you're Ida Greene," I said.

"I'm not that lucky." She crossed her hands. "I'm Cornelia Prime, her assistant, overseeing things while she's away from St. Abban's. The office is shared. Perhaps you'd like a cup of tea?"

She rapped her pencil on her teapot, which was wreathed in a purple knitted cozy. It was the nicest greeting I'd received in some time, so nice that I wasn't sure how to respond. I sat in the only available place—a tiny chair with an attached desk—and before I could say anything, she poured me a cup.

"This isn't the same tea Van Alen drinks?" I asked, remembering the vile green muck I had once been served by the lord of light. Prime shook her head, smiling like we were sharing an embarrassing secret.

"That particular concoction is well out of my price range. This is an ordinary Assam. You can get it at the bazaar."

I took a cautious sip. The tea was bracing, almost bitter. It puckered my lips but did nothing to clear my head.

"I've come to report a missing . . ."

"Yes?"

Her head tilted to the side, exactly parallel with her pencil, which hovered over her notebook, ready to take down my report.

"I'm sorry, I just—I couldn't help overhearing. You've lost something?"

Her smile flicked off. She looked nothing but tired.

"Those doors are so horribly thin."

"No. I'm just very good at listening. What is it?"

"It's a minor matter, really. Certainly nothing to interest you."

"You may be surprised."

I pulled a card from my change purse and slid it across her desk. It was gray, creased, the ink starting to run. It was the last one I had.

G. CARR: TINY MYSTERIES SOLVED

"Ah. The detective. Mrs. Greene has mentioned you."

"Only good things, I'm sure."

"She said you're irritating, unpredictable, badly groomed, and occasionally useful."

"High praise, indeed. Now, what have you lost?"

"I really don't think—"

"Please. Tell me what you're missing. It may be hard to understand but, well, you'd be doing me a favor."

I'd always hated client interviews. Securing work forced me to switch seamlessly between so many contradictory roles—the compassionate young woman, the icy professional, the eccentric Westsider—but I put up with it because I enjoyed the cases and I was generally desperate for cash. I wasn't at the moment—the *Misery Queen* and mooching off Marka's friends took care of that—but the itch was growing. Watching Cornelia Prime lean back in her chair and unburden herself, I remembered how pleasant it could be to sink into someone else's problems. As long as she talked, I did not have to worry about me.

She held up her pencil like a nurse preparing a syringe.

"This is a Bishop's Blue Streak," she said. "Carved from Himalayan cedar, dyed with cobalt pulled from the Congo hills, and balanced like a rapier. In a stroke, it can fell an empire. Van Alen employees are permitted to use nothing else."

She offered it to me, with a look like she was reluctant to let it go. The pencil was sky blue, as round as a drum, and oddly heavy, with *C. P.* etched in gold beneath the eraser.

"It's blue all right," I said.

"Mr. Van Alen swears they're the finest pencil known to man."

"You don't agree?"

"The lead is soft. You have to sharpen them every twenty minutes, and even then it's like writing with a fistful of mud. But we're required to buy them, monogram and all, and told to guard them with our lives."

She took a cigarette from the case on the desk, lit it, and let the smoke settle deep into her lungs. She must be very close to Ida Greene, I thought, if she's allowed to smoke her tobacco.

"I am known for being careful with money. That's how I caught

Mrs. Greene's eye. When the District became a reality and Van Alen asked her to oversee the legitimate wing of the enterprise, she brought me along. We are understaffed, underpaid, and working ourselves to the bone."

"I didn't realize the District had a legitimate wing."

She laughed. It was deep, like her voice, and sounded like it belonged to someone who had lived a very long time.

"Food service, mostly," she said. "The pleasure boats. Soft jazz and swimming and perhaps, someday, a velodrome."

"Sober fun."

"What Van Alen prefers. The illicit side of the District will not last forever. Until now, the authorities have turned a blind eye, but at some point, the specter of sin on the Hudson will become too much for them to bear. Some congressman's wife will pick up a heroin addiction on Clarkson Street, or a muckraking journalist will begin asking questions about where the brothel girls go after they turn twenty-two. Mr. Van Alen has trusted St. Abban's to ensure that when the criminal side of this experiment collapses, there is enough honest money left to keep the District alive."

"And if you can't keep track of your pencils, what hope do you have?"

"Precisely."

I set the pencil on her desk. She opened the drawer, a scarred hulk that had probably been sitting in that room since before I was born. Two dozen pencils were lined up there, soldiers waiting to die.

"I keep mine here," she said. "Locked. Every few days, one has gone."

A locked drawer mystery. What fun it would be, I thought, to take this case, to spend a few weeks—or months!—staking out this office, collecting pencil shavings, tearing the masks off the polite people who worked for Van Alen to find the monsters that lurked beneath. I could earn a bit of money, a few favors with the powers at St. Abban's.

I could have some fun.

"Do you have any suspects?"

"Every person here, I trust with my life. Surely I can trust them with a pencil as well."

"What about Howell?"

Her eyebrows arched. She shook her head.

"I'd rather not. That boy's had a difficult time. He was one of Barbarossa's gangsters, a Dead Barrow Tough. Enlisted when he was seven years old. Given bad liquor and a sharp knife and taught to kill. Can you imagine what that would do to a young man?"

"I've seen it, yes."

His eyes had sparkled when he hit Cherub. He hadn't looked angry. It was as if he enjoyed it. I decided not to mention it—not to protect Howell, about whom I did not care, but because it would do Cherub no favors for those in power to know his name.

"He'd be dead if it weren't for Ida Greene," she said. "Van Alen prefers not to employ Barbarossa's people, but Mrs. Greene convinced him to make an exception for Marvin. She considers him a project. She once saw me the same way. But of course . . ."

Another wave. Another twist of smoke.

"Is this your sort of case?"

Electricity hummed in my chest. I'd come here to discard a case and was on the verge of taking on a second. It would be so easy to say yes, to lose myself in this utterly unimportant problem that just happened to be ruining a kind woman's life. I'd need to do nothing more complicated than betray Cherub and myself and the *Queen* and Grover Hartley and every piece of driftwood we'd lashed together to form our new lives. How tempting it was, in that moment, to throw it all away.

I picked the pencil up again and reached for Prime's notepad.

"May I?"

She nodded, and I tore the top sheet free. I drew a line across the page and saw that she was right. The lead was butter soft. As soon as it smeared across the paper, my spark went out.

"I'm sorry. I can't take this case."

Her brow creased. She was surprised, I think, at how disappointed that news made her feel.

"Why not?"

"For one thing, I'm not working cases at the moment. I made the decision to take the summer off, and I'm trying to stick to it."

"Trying to?"

"I've never quite known how to relax."

"It's the hardest thing in the world for a woman who likes to work. Take a moment to breathe, and you'll find Marvin Howell sitting in your chair. What's the other thing?"

"I already know who's taking them."

Her eyes went wide. It felt nice. It had been so long since I'd seen anyone so impressed.

I leaned across her desk and poised the pencil above the curling cuffs of her blouse.

"Do you mind?" I said.

"The Casino handles all our laundry—a rare perk of this job. Do your worst."

I smeared a line across her cuff. She inspected it, smiling, waiting for me to explain.

"Only Van Alen people have these pencils?"

"No one else could stand the expense."

"Then the person you're looking for is Oliver Lee. I saw a smudge on his cuff that looked just like that. I bet he's got a whole cupboard full of your Blue Streaks."

"That doesn't seem possible."

"And yet."

"Really, though. When Roebling men break protocol, they die. He wouldn't risk his life for a pencil."

"You've misunderstood the Gray Boys. They don't steal from each other, but they take from everyone else. He probably doesn't even know he's doing it. Men like that go through life unprepared, picking up whatever they need and assuming it's theirs."

She leaned back, eyeing the mark on her sleeve.

"Do you have any proof?"

"That's what I love about my work—I don't need it. Tiny mysteries rarely end up in front of a judge."

"If you're right, there's nothing I can do to stop it. Relations between St. Abban's and the Roeblings are never simple, and with the season ending, well . . . the fewer customers we have, the more tense things will be. I can hardly risk an incident over something like this."

"But you don't think I'm right."

"I just can't believe Oliver Lee would be so stupid. Even so, thank you for letting me talk about it. Perhaps now I can let this go."

She drained her tea. I looked down and saw, to my surprise, that I had emptied my cup. She raised the teapot, offering more. I shook my head.

"I almost forgot," she said. "You came in here to report a missing . . . what was it?"

"It's silly. A small thing. I think . . ."

"Yes?"

"I think I'd rather take care of it myself."

I extracted myself from the undersized desk and strolled out of the room, enjoying the warmth of the tea, the feeling of having solved a pointless problem, and the sensation that, deep inside me, old machinery was humming again. I wondered if Cherub would hear.

Each Friday, Marka gifted us ten crisp dollar bills—"a touch of spending money"—for use in the rare moments when she was not around. I broke a dollar buying a fried oyster sandwich and walked to the end of Pier 34 to eat. A line of yachts bobbed in the water, waiting to unload a herd of people in spotless whites whose skin was just beginning to scorch. Downriver, pairs of Peacekeepers patrolled the Long Pier, a ramshackle structure where men and women who had welshed on their tabs or gotten caught counting cards awaited deportation to the Eastside.

I dropped a hunk of bread into the water. Before it sank, a family of gulls tore it apart. None of them were missing a leg. For the millionth time, I wondered if the twisting in my stomach was really due to the absence of work. If it was something else—if it was Cherub, or the boat, or my friends, or this entire hideous place—

then fixing it would take courage I no longer had. If I dove head-first into a case, perhaps it would fix everything, and life would be easy again. If it didn't, well, then I would have harder questions to answer.

I had made a promise to Cherub, a promise to myself, but this was Labor Day weekend. My oath had only a few days left to run. There would be no harm in getting an early start on a little field research—following the gulls, getting to know their habits. A long weekend boozing with Marka and her gang would be tolerable if I knew I had a secret, a purpose, a life.

I shredded what remained of the sandwich. With each rip, the knot in my stomach loosened just a little bit. When I hurled the mess of food into the water, I felt suddenly so light, so unencumbered, that there was nothing to do but taunt them.

"Gorge, you flying rats, and enjoy it, because Gilda Carr is—"

Before I could finish my threat, a dignified old woman bashed an umbrella into my skull.

"That's a noble bird!" she barked. She hit me again. I took the blow on my wrists. It hurt. "You'd feed it filth?"

Her skin was as gray as charcoal; her hair was as white as the clouds above. She wore it twisted behind her head in a tight bun, beneath a hat weighed down with enough flowers to make two or three bouquets. She reared back for a third strike, but when I went to dodge it, she jabbed me in the belly instead. A fencer, I thought, as I sank to my knees, trying not to vomit on her shoes.

"A bully," she said, "that's you. Picking on the poor defenseless gulls, but when Lady Birdlady comes along, you fall down to nothing. Women these days are made out of cardboard. When I was a girl—"

"What should I feed them?"

"Huh?"

"I mean, what does a gull like to eat?"

She squatted, close enough that I could see the wisps of her moustache, and sprayed spittle into my face.

"Like to eat? Like to eat? Well, they like to eat almost anything, same way the human body likes getting stuffed with Irish whiskey and cocaine and cheap sex and fried food. A gull'll eat trash or French fries or human waste, given the chance, and it won't pay no mind to the way it rots from the inside out."

I was fully aware that if I said the wrong thing, she would start hitting me again. The yachting crowd was already staring. I did not need to give them any more reason to laugh.

"Then what should I give them?"

"Plain spaghetti. Bits of fish. The things a bird should have."

And then, as quickly as she had crashed down on me, Lady Birdlady left, striding down the Boardwalk, swinging her umbrella with all the ease of the cop on the beat.

I spent a few minutes breathing. When I tired of that, I slunk back to the vendor who'd sold me the sandwich. While she tended to her vat of spluttering clams, I snatched a bucket of fish guts from the back of the stand. I stashed them belowdecks on the *Misery Queen*. They stank like a plague victim. It had been months since I smelled anything so fine.

THREE

As the sun set on that long, strange afternoon, I found myself pressed against the bow of the *Misery Queen,* fending off a portrait painter. Aside from Cherub, Eva Distler was the sole Black person allowed access to Marka's inner circle. She wore a sleek yellow dress adorned with impractically long fringe and a ribbed white cap over tightly wrapped braids. Her hands were avian, every finger weighed down with gold, but they were stronger than they looked, and they had me in their grip.

"It's an absolute *sin* that you've never had your portrait painted," she said. "A girl with your coloring. I've seen white people and I've seen *white* people, but I've never met anyone quite as pale as you."

She scraped a calloused thumb across my cheek.

"Like an old sheet, bleached and bleached and left for a year in the sun. Please let me paint you, Gilda dear. The world deserves to see what a real Westsider *really* looks like."

"The world must do without. I've seen your portraits. Everyone you paint comes out looking like a corpse."

"Everyone *is* a corpse. Some of us just don't know it yet."

I chuckled, because Marka's people expected you to laugh at their epigrams. She did not let go. My cheeks grew sore.

Behind her on the flat stretch of boat we called the party deck, Marka and five immaculate Eastside wits huddled around a cabinet that held life vests, tin cups, dwindling bottles of liquor, and the portable Bourget Device. Although night was just upon us, the Device had been spinning for an hour or more, so that Marka could pour champagne precisely as she prepared her assault on the District. She drained her cup and sliced across the deck. When her flickering shadow fell across us, Eva backed away.

"Stop pestering the girl," Marka told Eva. "Hers is a beauty that cannot be imprisoned on a canvas. And she's right. You make everyone look like shit."

"If you're going to be nasty," said Eva, "at least pour me another drink."

"The good bottles are empty. It's time to go ashore."

Marka slid her arm into the crook of my elbow. Her skin was smooth and cold, like marble. Every time she touched me, I felt perfectly steady, as though the boat had stopped rocking and the world was still.

"And where shall we begin this evening's debauch?" said Eva.

"I feel like dancing," said Marka.

"The Casino?" suggested another of the gang, a hard-edged choreographer named Bess Barron whose only outfit, as far as I could tell, was a tuxedo she'd dyed crimson and recut to suit her long, slim frame.

"I want a band with a pulse," Marka said. "What about that barge, the red one? Their band plays so loud I can hear it in my nightmares."

"Screaming Minnie's," I said. "The one with the birds."

"I can't have them making a mess on my dress," said Eva, but her eyes were downcast. Marka had made up her mind, and no power on earth could change it.

Marka clapped her hands. The group shifted. I hung back, watching my last sip of champagne tilt with the rocking of the boat. Marka snapped her fingers in front of my face.

"Asleep on your feet?"

"Just tired. Staying in tonight."

"Speak English. 'Tired' is not a word I understand."

"It's a condition that occasionally afflicts mortal women. If it passes, I'll meet you at Minnie's. I want to make sure I have some fight left for the long weekend."

She bent down to kiss my forehead. Her lips, as always, were cold. In a voice lower and softer than the one she used for marching orders, she said, "Get some rest. Tomorrow waits."

Cherub popped his head up from below. His feet were bare and his chest was too, but he'd pulled out his old top hat and tried to hammer out the dents. No one at Minnie's would look more elegant.

"Don't tell me you're hanging back, too," said Marka.

"I don't know," said Cherub, looking at me. "Am I?"

"You got all dressed up," I said. "Shame to waste it. Go on. I'll catch up later."

Placated, Marka glided down the gangway, moving steadily in heels so high they made me dizzy.

Cherub pulled on his boots, kissed me on the cheek, and whispered in my ear: "Any idea why our cabin smells all corpsey?"

"We gave up bathing over a year ago."

"And? As far as I can tell, we smell better with every added layer of grime."

I kissed him. I put everything I had into it, but I must have left something out, because when I was finished he asked me, "Something wrong?"

There was quite a bit I could tell him. Too much, in fact, and I was impatient to start my investigation. So I just said, "Go out. Have fun. I'll see you soon."

He squeezed my thigh and scurried to join the waiting crowd. As they chortled down the dock, I tried to settle into the silence. It was so strange being alone, even though it had been for so long my natural state. I flipped off the light and slipped below. I opened a cabinet, tossed aside a wad of uncommonly filthy sheets, and withdrew the bucket of fish scraps and my long, shapeless bag. For the first time in quite a while, I tasted adrenaline in my mouth. What I was doing wasn't dangerous, but it was just a little bit wrong, and I found the fear of getting caught quite preferable to feeling nothing at all.

I brought the bucket up top, hitched it to a cleat, and let it dangle off the *Queen*'s prow. I slunk back to our airless cabin, stripped down to roughly nothing, and pressed up against the porthole, listening to the current's wet slap. I rooted through my bag for something to eat and found nothing but a stale brown roll that was as brittle as slate. Even I wasn't that desperate. I chucked it back in the bag and watched the bucket hang.

Gulls came, dozens of them. When one got close, I'd count its legs. Invariably, there were two. After swallowing my disappointment, I'd slam the porthole and yell, "That's not your dinner!" until the offending bird went away. I wasn't sure what I'd do if Grover Hartley appeared—grab her by the scruff and drag her into the boat?—but I needn't have worried. Of all the gulls drawn by my stinking bucket of fish, she was not among them.

This was no tragedy. Finding her would have ended the case before it started. Approached with the correct level of carelessness, the search for Grover Hartley could carry me through the onset of autumn, when the yachts vanished and all but the most desperate gamblers and drunks deserted the District, when our breath steamed the glass of the *Misery Queen* and Cherub finally agreed to come home for the winter. I wanted my bird, but there was no reason to hurry.

I was into my second pleasantly boring hour when I spotted a woman peering through tortoiseshell glasses at the boats, a notebook in one hand and a cigarette holder in the other. Cornelia Prime had said that Ida Greene was away from St. Abban's. I did not expect to find her here. She spent a long minute inspecting each ship, then clamped her holder between her teeth, scribbled something in her little book, and moved on. She wrote, naturally, with a Bishop's Blue Streak. Unless she'd done something to offend Van Alen, I doubted she'd been demoted to the post of harbormaster, but what she was doing there, I could not say. It was a tiny mystery, yes, but not one I cared about. She did not seem interested in the birds.

After she returned to shore, I continued my vigil. Staring at a bucket of maggoty fish bits was drowsy work, and my eyes were beginning to get heavy when I heard the cockpit hatch slide open. I pulled the blanket over my chest.

"Cherub?"

"Not quite," said Marka, chuckling as she ducked into the cabin. "Not used to seeing quite so much of Miss Gilda Carr."

Her laughter put me on edge. There had been something noble, I thought, about the search for my missing pet, but under Marka's cold gaze, my work felt pathetically small. I braced for some cutting remark. She sat on the edge of my bed, took my hand, and squeezed it tightly. The sudden intimacy was dizzying.

"Don't tell me you've decided to call it a night," I said, scrambling to remember how it was we spoke to each other. I must have gotten it right, because she took her hand away and put on her old bulletproof smile.

"Of course not. Screaming Minnie's is amazing. The band plays loud enough to drown out the screeching of the birds, and they have warm towels at every table to wipe off the droppings."

She brushed her shoulder, where her dress was marred by the faintest damp stain.

"So what could have possibly tempted you back here?" I said.

"Something had me tense."

"What?"

"The thought of Gilda Carr with a dry throat."

She nestled a nearly full bottle into the crook of my arm. It was faint pink, adorned with an image of a woman, straight-backed and naked, pulling the string of a golden bow.

"What is it?" I said.

"The good stuff. Something new. The boys are calling it Diana's Fire."

I cracked the seal and took a drink, scorching my throat and making my stomach lurch in a most pleasant way. It was like gin but, somehow, more so. I offered the bottle to Marka. She shook her head.

"I left a highball back at the bar. I can hear the ice melting—a sickening sound."

But she did not go. She just stared down at me, a big sister noticing her sibling for the first time. I don't think she'd ever been quiet that long.

"Are you well, girl?" she said.

"Well enough."

"You look like an overexposed picture. I shouldn't have interrupted you. You need the sleep. We all need the sleep. Let me fix your bed."

She shoved her hands under my thin mattress and tugged the sheet tight. It was the first time I'd ever seen her do something for another person besides light a cigarette or pour a drink, and it occurred to me that our friendship might mean more to her than she let on.

Her fingers drummed on the bunk. For a moment, it looked like she might say something meaningful, but she spared us both.

"Get some sleep," she said. "We sail an hour before dawn."

"I thought you'd be at the Huntington for the holiday weekend."

"I shall be—though I don't intend to sleep much while I'm here—but Bess and Stuy want to watch sunrise on the river, and Cherub, the darling, is sailing us out. Would you like me to wake you for it?"

"I've seen sunrise before."

"That's what I told them—it's just like sunset, only backward. Even so . . ."

She checked her face in her mirror. Once her smirk was firmly in place, she slouched out. I lay until the click of her heels faded. Then I kicked off the blanket and tried to fan the sweat off my chest before I resumed my watch. I took a deep drink, the first of many. Long before midnight, the bottle was mostly empty and I was fully asleep.

I dreamed of the subway. I was at Fourteenth Street, trying to go uptown, but every train I found was running the wrong way. The station corridors wound and dipped past platforms that had been walled off when the fence was built. I ran weightlessly. I was very late.

At last, a metal staircase led me to an unlit platform and a tunnel that carried me deep into the dark, at the end of which I found a woman's rotting corpse, her hands clawed down to the bone.

The dream meant nothing—I had endured it many times before—but that night it came with a coda: the ivory hands of Marka Watson, plunging from the dark like vengeful spirits. They squeezed the sheets around my chest, pulling them tighter and tighter until—

Thunk.

The sound woke me slowly. My eyes were weighed down by liquor, and it took a long time to wrench them open.

Thunk.

I squeezed my temples. The stink of fish was worse than ever. My stomach lurched with the ship.

I got onto my elbows. Out the porthole I saw the inky silhouette of the deep Westside. There was no wind. There was no rain. There were no human sounds.

But if I was alone, why the hell was the ship so far from shore?

"Baby?" I shouted. "Cherub?"

Thunk.

I lay for a minute or two, trying to find an excuse to close my eyes and go back to sleep. Whatever was happening, surely it could wait an hour or ten. But no matter how tightly I closed my eyes, sleep could not be recaptured. Curiosity would not let me rest.

I stepped out of the bunk and fell hard as the ship *thunked* viciously to port. I'd never felt the *Queen* so unsteady. It was as if no one were sailing her at all.

It was possible that I was alone on the boat. Cherub was an enthusiastic sailor, but he'd never been trained. His knots were improvised affairs, and it was easy to imagine that one had slipped loose and let the Hudson carry the *Queen* away.

I braced my hand against the cabin's cool, smooth wood. Any other night when I'd woken, drunk or hungover or caught between the two, the touch of that wood had put me back in my bedroom at Washington Square. Tonight, it was nothing but a dead tree, and I was a woman who was very far from home.

I pulled my dress off the floor and, as I struggled into it, I discovered my hands were shaking. Perhaps it was a side effect of Marka's new liquor. Perhaps it was simple fear.

I unlatched the galley door. It swung open and thudded against the wall. The galley was pitch dark, but that was not unusual. It should not have bothered me, but I had the feeling of being deep underwater, and every step felt like I was sinking a little more.

The floor was heaped with mess, just as it always was. I kept my feet flat on the wood, easing them forward, strangely afraid of the embarrassment that would come if I tripped and fell.

Again, I called Cherub's name. Again, no answer but—

Thunk.

The hatch to the cockpit was open. Through it I looked up to the black, blank sky. There had been a moon when I'd fallen asleep, but it had been swallowed by the clouds.

I tried to call out again, but Cherub's name stuck in my throat. Above my head, something skidded across the deck. It could have been footsteps. It could have been, well, I simply couldn't say.

I took hold of the rails and was about to climb when the ship pitched forward. An object clattered down the steps. Something so small that it took me a moment to find it among the debris, and even longer to work out what it was.

It was yellow, pointed, and slick with blood.

A tooth.

Thunk.

"Who's up there?" I called, fighting to contain the tremor in my voice. "There must be someone up there. Teeth don't just fall out on their own. There must be someone, and this is my goddamned boat, and . . ."

I trailed off, feeling foolish. Not even the wind replied.

I squeezed the tooth. It dug into my palm, hurting just enough to keep me from losing my head.

I was alone on the ship, I told myself, alone on the Hudson, and something had happened, something quite bad, but I was alone. Whatever it was, it was over now, and I was alone.

Thunk.

Or was I?

I dropped the tooth. It landed on the wood, the smallest possible sound.

There was nothing to do but go up the stairs.

I gripped the railings and hurled myself into the cockpit. I nearly slipped. In fact, I'm surprised I didn't. There was quite a lot of blood.

I must have said something. I'm sure it was quite clever—"Dear god," perhaps, or that old standby "No no no." Or maybe my mouth just hung open as my eyes took in the scene. It didn't really matter. There were certain sights for which no reaction was appropriate, for which there was nothing we could do but fight to keep our eyes from closing.

Gore streaked every inch of the cockpit. There was blood on the tiller, on the canopy, the seats, the wood, on every length of rope, on the sails that flapped uselessly in the wind. I tried to focus on the rare patches that had been spared, which showed so white they were almost blinding, but there were not enough to distract me from what had to be seen.

The bench beside the wheel. The little bench where Cherub used to stretch out, where I occasionally dozed, where Grover Hartley liked to defecate. There was something on the bench.

Two somethings, in fact.

Bodies.

They were wrapped so tightly around each other, it was impossible to tell where one ended and the other began. The things that used to be their faces were obscured by the things that used to be their arms. Most of their skin had been peeled away, leaving dripping muscle and spilled organs and cracked bones. Their clothes were gone, too, save for some shredded fabric that clung to their hips and legs. By the red trousers with the thin satin stripe, I recognized Bess Barron. By the fringe on the yellow dress, I knew I had found Eva Distler.

Their bodies. My friends.

Trying to steady myself, I took a deep breath. It was a mistake.

The smell jolted through me, twisting my stomach into a knot. A bucket of rotten fish I could abide, but this was simply too much.

The ship lurched again. My stomach did, too. I fell to my knees and emptied it across the cockpit. The sweet stench of liquor and hot bile cut through the funk of death but did not really improve matters. My hands splayed open against the wood and were instantly dyed red.

Such things are not possible, I thought. Such horror cannot be real.

But these things do happen. Moments of true, blistering horror that the polite newspapers bury on page twelve and the *Police Gazette* splashes across the cover. Families burn, babies fall, old men slip on the elevated platform and are thrashed to death. Sometimes there is a survivor—the boy sent out for milk before the start of the tragic fire, the mother of the dead child—and you cluck your tongue and think, That poor creature. Wouldn't they be better off dead?

I had been abducted into a cheap melodrama—*Blood on the* Misery Queen. I wanted to throw myself under the quilt and hide, but I had a part to play. I was the one who survived.

Perhaps.

The *Queen* rocked violently to one side, whipping the boom across the cockpit. It slammed into place.

Thunk.

Ah, so that's what that noise was. A mystery solved. What comfort.

I grabbed the nearest line and dragged myself to my feet. Fists tight on the railing, I breathed in the river, coating every hidden part of me with bitter air. Over the city, night was sliding from black to gray. The sky was clear. It was going to be a beautiful day.

"You are a detective," I told myself. "This is a crime scene. Do your work."

I tugged my dress over my nose and stopped myself from looking away from the bodies. I put one foot in front of the other until I was as close as I could bear.

The skin of their chests and faces was not cut—it was simply gone. Where their arms covered their faces, the muscles and bone were chipped, hanging loosely, savaged by whatever nightmarish tool their killer used.

"Who did this to you?" I asked them. "You were tiresome people. You repeated your jokes, you danced like fools, you talked without listening and laughed without joy. That's no reason to die."

The boat rolled. The boom swung above my head. I no longer flinched when it fell into place. I no longer felt anything at all.

Farther up the ship, something splashed into the water. It was becoming harder to believe I was alone on the boat. I should have crept back to the cabin and hid under my blankets, but I was quivering with something that may have been impatience and may have been fear. Whatever was going to happen to me, I wanted it to happen soon.

An empty champagne bottle was trapped between Bess Barron's ankles. I tugged it free and held it like a club. I had no hope against the person or persons who had massacred these women, but I would give it a try.

"Someone there?" I called.

There was no reply, save for the meaningless rhythm of clacking steel and flapping canvas, and the awful *thunk* of the boom. I hopped onto the deck, hand tight on the railing, and worked my way forward.

The ship rose with the current. A thick slop of blood and meat swept down the deck. My foot slipped on a chunk of viscera, but I stayed on my feet. I walked on, trying to hold my head high, intending to greet the monsters with a smile. But when I rounded the corner, the bottle slipped from my fingers and splashed into the river. There was nothing here that was even close to being alive.

The Bourget Device was out, but the faint glow of the rising sun was enough to show me the scene. Half a corpse was draped over the railing. There was no telling where the rest of it had gone. Everyone else was in pieces. Shards of bone, of leg, of arm, of torso, of foot, of skull rolled across the deck with every movement of the water. Broken bottles mixed with the mess, giving the stench of a cocktail party's last desperate hour, when the carpet had gone squishy with spilled booze.

I squeezed the line tighter, knowing that if my knees buckled I would not be able to get back up, and attempted to distract myself with a bit of cheerful mental math. That night there had been quite a crowd on the *Misery Queen*: myself and Cherub, plus seven guests. There were two dead in the back. That left six to find.

"You are a detective," I hissed. "Count the bodies. Find six and he's dead. Find less and he might be alive. Just count them. Count them, and you'll know what you have to do."

But there was nothing left to count.

I forced myself to wade through the carnage, nudging bits of flesh aside with my boot, trying to fit the pieces together to imagine what person they might have been. Gashes had been hacked into the wood of the deck, presumably from the weapon or weapons that had torn these people apart. It must have been something big—an ax, a saw—and whoever wielded it either had assistance or was fearsome enough that no help was required.

I looked for evidence of the people who died here. I found a bloody handkerchief that could have belonged to Stuyvesant Wells and the heel of a shoe that may have been Mercury Tyne's. I tried to keep track of what I found, to match each bit to one of the people who had passed through here, but this puzzle was missing too many pieces. Even at my best—and that morning I was far from my best—I could not have filled in the gaps.

A rare unbroken bottle rolled to my feet. More Diana's Fire. There was no liquor left inside. I flung it at the deck. Glass exploded across the wood, catching the light of the steadily rising sun. It was not the only thing that shone. In a tangle of sodden rope just before the bow, I found something hard, gleaming—perhaps the only thing on the ship untouched by blood.

A pearl. One of Marka's pearls.

I squeezed it, as I'd done with the tooth, then let it drop. It rolled across the deck and plinked into the river. I saw no other pearls.

I tried to hang on to the idea that I could think through this, that I could be a detective, that I could be steel. There was no telling what flesh had belonged to whom, or how much had already washed over the side. This was not six bodies, not necessarily, and that meant Cherub might have gotten away. Perhaps he saw the killers approaching and dove overboard, like any good coward would. Perhaps the boat had been stolen before he'd come aboard, and he was back on land, pacing and cursing and demanding someone take him out on the river to find his missing *Queen*.

Perhaps Cherub Stevens was alive.

And then the boom whipped across my head and I saw what was written on the mainsail, and I knew that he was dead.

Thunk.

A portrait of a one-legged seagull, red as the blood sloshing over my feet, ran the length of the long sail.

Beneath it, the words that ended me:

CHERUB GOT HIS

There was a roar so loud, it made me flinch. It sounded like an oncoming wave or water gushing into the hull, but it was just the blood thudding in my ears. I looked back at the sail. The letters did not move. They did not become any less true.

Cherub got his.

Well, that was that.

I glanced at the life preservers and found I had no life to preserve. I stood at the railing and leaned back until I toppled into the river. I let it take me away.

I sank fast. It was black under there and the current was strong. My dress was heavy as cement; water filled my shoes. I fought the urge to kick.

There had been times in my life when I wanted everything to end. When my mother died, when my father followed, when the city I loved turned on its citizens and so many of my friends and neighbors vanished, punching holes in Manhattan as neatly as a biscuit cutter through dough—these were sensible times to crave death. Through cowardice or inertia or animal stubbornness, I did not give in. But that night, the river was the first cool thing I'd felt since summer hit, and it felt like home.

My lungs ached. I tried to think beyond the pain. I seized on an autumn day in 1915, when the world was at war and the Westside, newly walled off from the city, had taken its true, insane form. Mammoth trees burst into every color fire has ever burned. Birds sang like lunatics. Unknown flowers grew, bloomed, and died in an hour. The entire spectacle seemed put there for the sake of two new lovers, Cherub and Gilda, who were certain they were the only people who mattered in the world.

I was dozing on the parlor couch, enjoying cold air and a heavy blanket, when I heard him on the sidewalk, cursing the wind.

"Still, goddamn it, be still!"

Propped on one elbow, I watched him dash across the mossy pavement, snatching at dancing leaves. His legs tangled. He went sprawling but did not drop the foliage clutched in his hands. I might have called to him, but his struggle was simply too much fun.

The wind died. He got to his feet and began laying a row of leaves across the sidewalk, choosing each as carefully as a mason assembling a wall. Every few seconds, he consulted a scrap of paper and adjusted what he had made. The work was slow, but he was smiling until the wind whipped up, scattering his masterpiece and starting him cursing again.

Oh, I thought, he's lost his mind. What a shame.

Wrapping the blanket tight, I abandoned my couch and opened the front door. He snapped around like he'd been caught.

"Not yet, not for hours!" he said. "You're not to see it till it's through."

"Until what's through? You haven't made anything but a mess."

"And that's just why I won't have you looking until it's ready. Your gaze is corrosive. You'll spoil it."

I shrugged the blanket off my shoulders and gave my arm a little wiggle. He blushed, flooded with the kind of foolish lust I'd never imagined I could inspire. But instead of following me up the steps, he squeezed his eyes and shook his head.

"I must see to my work."

I slammed the door. I threw on actual clothes and hunted through the storage closet until I found a jar of paste. I walked back outside and shoved it into his hand.

"Paste is cheating," he said.

"So cheat. Who cares?"

"Don't you?"

"I've based my entire professional life on the principle that corners were made to be cut. I'm going to go eat some ham. Find me when you're done."

I swallowed two plates of ham and was just finishing the previous day's coffee when Cherub strolled into the kitchen and said, "It's time to cover your eyes." I wiped my hands on the wallpaper and clapped them over my face. Despite myself, I was excited to see what nonsense he had put together. My heart beat quickly as he led me outside.

"Well?" he said, hopefully.

"My eyes are still covered."

"Oh! Oh right. You can look now. I hope you like it."

I did. Of course I did. The sidewalk was in shade by then, but the dipping sun lit up the trees of Washington Square like stained glass. By golden light I read a message written in leaves whose colors shifted from summer green to yellow, orange, flaming red, and petrified brown.

ALL THINGS DIE BUT MY LOVE FOR GILDA CARR

I blotted my eyes and kissed him until he fell off the stoop. Then, at last, I dragged him upstairs.

That was the first time he said he loved me. I told him I loved him too, and he said he was well aware, and we kept telling each other every chance we got. That was the first time around, before he proposed, before I broke his heart, when fun came easily. Years later, when he gave me my second chance and we took to the water, he still said it all the time, but I rarely answered. I didn't need those words tying me down. But I loved him relentlessly, and he knew it without ever being told.

Surely he knew.

My lungs wanted air. Suddenly, I did too. Cherub Stevens was the finest lover to ever grace the city of New York. Someone had killed him.

That someone deserved to die. And I did not—not yet.

A shard of light caught my eye. I kicked for it but only fell farther away. I wrenched off my shoes, dropping them as an offering to the river's dead. I could not escape my dress. I kicked and thrashed, eyes on that shimmering light, lungs howling. I got nowhere. And then, without warning, my head broke the surface. The breeze kissed my face and humid air poured into my lungs.

My relief did not last.

The river surged as a silver longboat bore down on me. It grew like a tumor, filling the sky, following no matter how hard I tried to swim out of the way.

"Look out!" I cried. "Look out, goddamn it, there's a woman down here!"

If they heard, they didn't care.

Right as it would have rammed me, I ducked under the water, twisting so that the keel caught my left shoulder instead of my head. It hurt. Dear god, it hurt, an explosion of pain so hot I was surprised it didn't make the water boil. I came up scrambling, reaching with my one good arm for an oar. Just before I touched it, it sprang out of reach.

"Stop!" I shouted, but those oars stopped for nothing. They split the water and the boat was halfway past. Again, and it was nearly gone. With my last bit of strength, I smashed a fist against the hull and screamed something vile.

The oars dropped again. Before they pushed away, an iron hook fell in front of my face. I threw my arm across it and held on as it jerked me out of the water and threw me across the deck of that beautiful ship, where I quivered like a dying fish.

The agony in my shoulder, the burning in my lungs and limbs, the liquor coursing through my blood swept over me. There really was no point being awake.

"Nice fishing," I said. Before my eyes sagged shut, I recognized the uniforms: Roebling Company flannel and the rainbow silks of Van Alen's guards. The only face that stood out had eyes the color of Cornelia Prime's pencils and jowls like hanging meat.

"Have I met you before?" I murmured. "Didn't I watch you die?"

If he answered, I didn't hear it. I slept, appropriately, like a corpse.

I woke in a cage.

FOUR

The sun climbed. It heated the metal of my little prison and scorched every bit of exposed flesh. The skin on my face started to peel. The bottom of my stomach had dropped out, and there was nothing in me but a sucking desire for griddled ham and fried potatoes and runny eggs. I wanted coffee and ice water and tomato juice spiked with raw liquor. I wanted to shovel food down my throat until there was none left on the island, and then I wanted revenge.

When I find the person who killed Cherub, I thought, I shall crush their skull.

When I find them, I shall force them to drink a bottle of Ida Greene's cheapest gin, flavored with a quarter cup of arsenic.

When I find them, I shall trap them thoroughly, and then I shall force them to peel their own skin and hack their body to bits.

But first, I supposed, I would need to get out of this goddamned cage.

The ceiling was high enough that I could almost kneel, if I didn't mind the metal digging into my knees. The gate was padlocked, and no matter how hard I kicked, it didn't come free. I might have picked the lock if I had my burglar's tools, but they were in my bag and my bag was on the boat, and the boat was, well, not someplace I wanted to return.

I was at the far end of the Long Pier, my back to the swift Hudson current. There was no one in the neighboring cells, no jailer making the rounds. Pressing my face against the cage, I could just make out the crowd on the Boardwalk: couples dressed in white, gangs of men drunk from breakfast and prowling for women, and Peacekeepers paired like lovebirds on every corner. I screamed for help. No one turned their heads.

The wind shifted and I smelled ketchup and powdered sugar, roasted meats and charred vegetables, riding on a current of sizzling batter. My stomach clenched and I hated all of them so much more.

I kicked and screamed and clawed, bloodying my fingertips and straining my voice. Finally I tried to sleep. The cage was not long enough for me to stretch out, so I curled into a ball and tried to imagine I was dozing in the shade of Washington Square on a cool spring day.

Instead I saw Cherub being torn apart.

I was no stranger to blood. I had survived the Battle of Eighth Avenue, when the cream of the city's teenage gangsters was slaughtered like a herd of sick cattle. I had stabbed men and beaten women. I had sustained beatings myself. But I had never seen anything, never heard of anything, so awful as the massacre on the *Misery Queen*. Those people hadn't just been killed. They had been pulped, and as I roasted in that little metal oven, I saw it happen again and again and again.

Cherub's skin peeled back from his skull.

His perfect smile shattered.

His hands, so coarse and so gentle, crushed into hamburger.

His heart torn from his chest.

I could have made him give up the river. If I'd had the courage or the sense to tell him how badly I wanted something else, he'd have followed me back to the town house. No matter how miserable it made him, he'd have returned to life on land. But it was easier to say nothing, and because I took the easy path, he was dead.

The sun beat down harder. I surrendered to the ache in my joints and stomach and skull. The Boardwalk filled and the smells continued to torture. As the sun burned my hands redder, I fancied the skin was stained with blood—of the children who died at Eighth Avenue, of a man I shot in the stomach, of a gentle printer crushed beneath the wheels of a tram. I rubbed my hands raw but, as expected, they did not come clean.

It was late afternoon when my captors came to call.

Oliver Lee's tuxedo was immaculate—no smudged cuffs today—and his shoes sparkled in the sun, but his eyes were red and his skin looked drained of blood. Trailing behind him was the blue-eyed man from the boat. I still couldn't place him, but I didn't care, because he had a hunk of bread in his hands that was as black and lush as Lee's tux. I'd never seen anything look so good.

"Miss Carr," said Lee. His voice was hoarse, so faint I could barely hear. "I never expected to see you in this position."

Twelve hours prior, I might have said something clever. Instead, I snapped: "Give me the bread."

"It won't fit through the bars," said the other man.

"An easy fix. Let me out."

Lee shook his head.

"Not until we've had a little chat."

"Then tear it into pieces and shove it through the slats."

The blue-eyed man tore off wads of bread and forced them through the gaps in the iron. I caught every crumb. Some of my pain backed away. When the bread was gone, he wandered to the far side of the pier to stare at the sky. Lee squatted beside me.

"I am having a very difficult day," he said.

"You're not the one who's trapped in a cage."

He smacked his hand against the slats. The metal rattled. My head throbbed.

"This is no time for wit," he said. "We are in the midst of a catastrophe."

"I take it you found my boat."

"The Peacekeepers boarded it after they fished you out of the river. They told me what they saw. What happened there?"

"I slept through it."

"Jesus, Gilda. This is no joke. This is . . . you have no idea what's going to happen next."

He looked over my shoulder. At first I thought he was simply trying to collect himself, but then I realized what he was staring at: a little white speck, some ways down the river but coming up fast. Now I understood why he looked so afraid.

"That's a police boat," I said.

"Yes."

For the first time since I dove into the river, I felt cold. I saw where this was going, as sure as that ship was sailing up the river, and I did not approve.

"But this is a Westside crime."

"And if it were a stolen purse or a broken window, they'd be happy to leave it to our Peacekeepers. But this is a massacre. Of rich Eastsiders. There was no keeping them away."

I pulled my shoulders as straight as the cage would allow.

"And what does that mean for me?"

"That's just what I'm here to discuss. As far as the NYPD is concerned, the District does not exist. If they can't see it, they can't police it, and we've all worked very hard to keep them from having to see. I spent all morning on the Eastside conferring with our contacts in the department, and the deal we worked out is this: their boat ties up, but they don't come ashore. We hand you to them. Life in the District goes on as it always has."

"That is a wonderful agreement for everyone besides Gilda Carr."

He squeezed his mouth tight. He looked to be in terrible pain. He tried to speak, but his voice broke. He collected himself and tried again.

"You're my friend, Gilda. I've always meant that, no matter what you think of me. I'm not going to let . . . I'll join you on the boat. I'll see to it that you get the full backing of the Roebling Company, and Cornelia Prime assures the same for the Van Alen team. Between us, we have the kind of lawyers that make policemen cry. At this point, what more could you ask?"

There was something appealing about being given over to the police. In the past, my dealings with the law had been with the ragged remains of the Westside NYPD—drunks and lunatics, mostly, with a few sadists thrown in for seasoning. The men cruising up here on their boat, which gleamed as brightly as the white suits on the Boardwalk, would not be like that. They would be clean, efficient, ready to tell me what to do and where to go and when to die. Only the image of Cherub gluing leaves to the sidewalk held me back.

"I'm afraid I'm too busy at the moment to take a vacation at the Tombs," I said. "Someone killed the man I loved. How can I let that go?"

He buried his face in his hands. When he came up for air, he said, "I know. I know. But there is no other way. This is too big for you. It's too big for me. Marka and her friends were famous, and they had powerful friends. Every paper in the city is screaming for justice. The police are under immense pressure. Lieutenant Koszler—"

The name went through me like a cleaver. I banged my fist on the cage. Lee shut up.

"What was that name?" I said. My voice was calm and still, but my heart was threatening to burst out of my chest.

"Emil Koszler. My contact at Centre Street. Used to be a Westside man. Do you know him?"

Oh yes. I absolutely did.

"Release me from this cage."

"Not until you agree to—"

"Open the goddamned lock!"

I thrust my fingers through the slats and got as close to Lee as my captivity allowed. He shook. It occurred to me that I had been approaching this from the wrong angle. He needed me as badly as I needed him. This was no time to beg.

"The moment those police step onto this dock," I said, "your business is under threat, and for a Roebling man, that's a matter of life and death. You want me to board their boat? I won't even consider it until you let me out of this cage."

Lee ran his hands across his hair. There was no point to the gesture—his mop was slicked down so tight, it would take a crowbar to loosen a strand—but perhaps it made him feel better. He stared down the river. The police were almost here.

"Conforto!" called Lee. The other man returned, pulling at

the ring of keys that dangled from his hip. After an interminable search, he found the one to my cage. As he popped the lock, I saw he had stumps where his pinkie fingers once had been. Interesting.

The door to the cage swung open. I ducked out of it. Things in my back cracked and fire shot through my joints, but I held myself straight. Even without my boots, I was nearly as tall as Oliver Lee.

"I've known Koszler since he walked a beat for the Fourth Precinct. His uniform was tattered and he rarely opened his mouth, because he was shy about the gaps in his teeth. He was known to celebrate the end of a shift by finding a drunk to beat senseless. At Eighth Avenue, I saw him put bullet after bullet into children's chests. Their bodies clogged the gutters."

The mention of Eighth Avenue put a jolt through Conforto. Perhaps that was where I last saw his face. I wondered whom he fought for, and how he was still alive.

Lee glanced down the river and saw the NYPD boat was nearly upon us. He got a little more pale. He tried to speak, but I shouted him down.

"The last time I encountered Emil Koszler, he was forcing a friend of mine to kneel in a heap of broken glass. I buried a broken bottle in his back and twisted until I hit bone."

I said it like I was proud of what I'd done, but I'd never gotten comfortable with it. I still had dreams of plunging bottles into Emil Koszler's back, and every time I woke up certain I could feel his blood.

"The lieutenant has spent two years on the Eastside," said Lee. "I'm sure he's put all that behind him."

I looked at him like he was an utter lunatic.

"A Westsider never forgets," grunted Conforto in agreement.

The NYPD boat pulled up to the dock. Police swarmed across its deck like eager cockroaches. A rope flew through the air. Conforto caught it and busied himself with tying it to the pier. From deep within the boat, there echoed the thud of wood.

Thump, thump, thump. Each impact sent a shock through me. I remembered the way Koszler had squirmed underneath me when I buried that glass against his spine. I had always counted it a blessing that I never saw him again. I did not want to see what I had done.

Another thump, and Koszler emerged. His skin was blotchy; his lips were swollen. When I'd known him he'd been skinny, ratlike. His face had plumped out in the last two years. On some men, that would have been an improvement. He just looked like a fat rat. He stood at the top of the gangway, breathing heavy, leaning on a gleaming black cane.

"You got her?" he said. His voice had not changed. I wanted to answer him, but my throat was painfully dry.

Lee put a gentle hand on my shoulder.

"It's time to go. As I said, we will do everything to make sure you're given fair treatment. If you say you didn't kill the people on the boat, I believe you. We are friends, after all."

Perhaps we were. But I was past the point where friends could help. I felt my hand curling into a fist.

Koszler tapped his cane on the deck of his ship. Lee tried to look stern. It didn't suit him. This man had always tried to be nice to me. He'd laughed at my jokes, bought me drinks, asked me to dance when Cherub was away. He really had been a friend.

He had also put me in a cage.

"Now, Miss Carr. Now—"

I punched him in the throat. Men hate that. He collapsed like his legs had been dynamited. The cops on the boat scrambled for the gangway, shouting curses. Conforto held his arms wide, blocking the path to shore. He smiled, waiting to see what mistake I would make next.

I planted a foot on the roof of my cage.

"There's a reason most prisons have walls," I said, and flung myself over the edge.

I was in the air for a long while before the Hudson took me back.

The current grabbed like a noose. By the time I spluttered to the surface, my little prison was very far away. I was closer to the middle of the river than the shore. A gull flicked its head at me, neck cocked, trying to figure out if I was food. I slipped back under the water, kicked, and surfaced again. The bird was gone.

Since we came to the river, Sundays had been for swimming lessons. Cherub insisted on it, not because he was particularly concerned about my safety, but because he was a passable diver and liked showing off. Between dives, he would stretch out across the deck of the *Queen,* letting the sun dry the water on his chest, and opine.

"You can't trust the Hudson," he'd say, as though he'd spent his life on the river and not a scant few months. "Let it grab you, and there's no telling where you'll end up. We're lucky to be where we are—on it but not in it, not quite onshore, not quite off. We see the way it bends, we know how quickly it can change its mind. We have to learn how to dip in and out."

I'd press myself against him until I felt the water on his body seep through my bathing costume and soak my skin. It was a lovely place to be.

"And should the river take me, Captain Stevens, whatever shall I do?"

"Kick and kick and don't stop kicking until the water's shallow enough to stand."

It wasn't clever advice, but that didn't make it wrong. I thrashed until I reached the rotted remains of the nearest pier. After a day in the cage, it almost felt good to move. I took one heaving breath and was about to collapse into the mud when I heard the far-off barks of the police. They'd seen me go into the river; they'd seen me surface. They would be here soon.

A plain of mud sloped into the darkness beneath the Boardwalk. I hobbled away from the water, ankle deep in muck, following the fragments of sun that peeked through the cracks in the wood. With the light came bits of conversation—the chatter of a world that felt hundreds of miles away.

"Cold beer!"

"I'll break your neck."

"Hot donuts!"

"Kiss me again."

"Hot donuts, cold beer!"

"You stupid bastard!"

"Cold beer!"

"Being with you is like making love to a sewing machine."

"Cold beer!"

"At least come back to the boat."

Their footsteps were like machine gun fire. Their conversation didn't matter at all.

The mud stopped at a wet stone wall that looked like it had been imported from the dungeon of some grisly French prison. I turned uptown, staying under the Boardwalk, praying for a break in the wall. Water splashed beneath my feet. The tide was coming in.

I walked faster. The wall continued, unbroken and impenetrable. At the edge of the Boardwalk, there were two heavy splashes as a pair of cops dropped into the water. They stared at me but did not advance. At first, I thought they were afraid of venturing beneath the Boardwalk, but they were simply blinded by the sun. It would not take long for that to change.

They took a step under the Boardwalk, their hands shielding their eyes, squinting into the gloom. God knows I should have stayed put, hidden, bargained, fought, but all of that would have meant trusting my luck, and my luck had been rancid.

I ran.

The water was knee deep and rising fast. The moment my foot hit it, they heard me. Perhaps they saw me, too. They shouted things—clever remarks like "Stop!" and "Get back here!" I did not oblige. I ran on aching legs, my bare feet slurping in the mud, the filthy water doing its best to drag me down. They closed the gap quickly.

The river bent and the wall bent with it. I followed the curve and, for a moment, I was out of their sight. I picked up my knees, begging my body for a little more speed. It was too much to ask. My foot came down hard on a jagged piece of rock. My legs went out from under me. I landed on all fours.

When I got my head above water, I heard them behind me,

breathing hard, very close. I stuck out my hand, looking for something to grab on to. For the first time since I entered that wet hell, I touched wood. It was a door, hip high, half buried in the muck. I kicked it hard, forcing it open an inch or two.

"I see her!" cried one of the cops, terribly pleased with himself. They were just a few feet away.

I rammed my shoulder against the little door. The surf spilled into it, pressing it open farther, enough for me to squeeze myself through. Splinters sank into my skin as I squirmed into a tunnel of soft, stinking mud.

A hand closed on my ankle, calloused and cold.

I jerked my leg into the passage and braced my feet against the little door. The darkness was complete.

The cops threw their full weight against the door. My shoulders sank into the mud. I straightened my legs. The door stayed closed.

"This is stupid," said one of the cops.

"Even so."

"Let's go up and tell him we saw her."

"Koszler will skin us."

"I know, I know. But I can't take another minute under here."

"She's right here, Frank. A girl. We can't get beat by a girl. Let's try the door one more time."

I scrambled up the lightless tunnel and kicked a heap of mud against the door. The cops heaved and wheezed and cursed and, finally, gave up.

"Forget it," said the one who was not Frank. "We'll tell 'em where we saw her. We'll grab her the second she comes up for air."

Their plan was not terribly sporting, but it would work. I would have to find another way out.

FIVE

The tunnel squeezed like a fist, tighter and tighter as I got farther from the door. In that absolute blackness, it was hard to judge distance, but I crawled for what seemed like a long time, twisting my hips and squirming my shoulders, fighting for every miserable inch. There was air, but not much, and it quickly grew stale.

And to think, just a few hours prior, I had been relaxing in the sun in my own personal riverfront cage. As I forced onward, continuing simply because I was certain I would suffocate if I tried to stay still, I wondered why I had bothered to run. It would have been so simple to surrender to the police and ask Emil Koszler to cut my throat and dump me in the river. Perhaps my corpse would have found Cherub's. Instead it seemed I would die here, choking on dirt in a muddy tomb, refused even the chance to rot alongside my beloved.

But surrender would have meant giving up whatever hope I had of finding the people who killed him and inflicting upon them some measure of pain. That vile hope was all I had, and it pushed me steadily on.

The mud was infinite. It caked my hair and fingernails, clogged my eyes and hung so heavy on my nose that every breath was a battle. I shut my eyes against it and kept crawling. It's not like there was anything to see. The tunnel grew more and more cramped, until there was not a part of me the mud did not touch, and still I fought on, inch by agonizing inch, another awful hour in what was proving to be a remarkably awful day.

And then came the stench. It started as a tickle in my nose, a pleasant distraction from the wet rank earth. It was sweet, with a playful tang, like the favorite candy of some hideous child. It quickly became suffocating, clogging my nose and filling my throat, making my eyes water through the mud.

As the stench grew stronger, a sickly gray light filtered into the tunnel. It was one of the most beautiful things I'd ever seen. The tunnel sloped up sharply and that smell dragged me along like fish-hooks in my nostrils. It took so much work not to gag that I hardly noticed when the tunnel reached its end.

Gray light filtered through a canvas flap. I pushed it open and tumbled onto a coarse woven rug. My body burned, inside and out, and I found myself divided between the need to breathe and the fear that another taste of that foul, sweet air would make me vomit. Before I could make up my mind, the tip of an umbrella jammed itself under my collarbone.

I sat up straight and saw the woman whose peace I had disturbed: Lady Birdlady. Her floral hat was gone, and her white hair floated like a halo around her head. She'd been angry when we met. Now her rage was volcanic.

I didn't have the time.

I smacked the umbrella away and got to my feet. My legs worked badly. I forced them across the room, a candlelit windowless box whose wooden walls were painted a sickly, peeling green. The floor was crowded with faded rugs and oversized furniture that had once been expensive. I reached for the door. A swift blow from the woman's umbrella knocked my hand away.

"What are you doing in my wall?" she said.

"Having a picnic."

I reached for the door again. She bashed her shoulder into me, knocking me across the floor, and leveled her umbrella at my throat.

"You're the girl, the human girl, the one doesn't know how to treat a gull. What happened to you?"

I tore the umbrella from her hand and tossed it over my shoulder. She lunged for it, and I slipped past her.

"You mustn't go in there," she screamed. I had no interest in listening to, well, anyone, and so I opened the door.

This was an error.

The doorway led not to a hallway, not to the street. It opened onto a closet—or perhaps it would be more accurate to call it a cavern—clawed into the mud as roughly as my tunnel had been. The space was low, rising just to my jaw, but cut so deep into the earth that I could not see a back wall. It was filled to hip height with feather mattresses that had been torn to shreds.

Except that feather mattresses do not stink like that, and feather mattresses do not ooze.

They were birds. Hundreds of rotting birds, the ones on top freshly dead, the ones on the bottom nothing but wads of feather and flesh dripping milky white. Their blank eyes stared at me, as hard as ball bearings. Their feet were wrinkled leather; their beaks a brittle point.

They all looked like Grover Hartley.

I slammed the door and spun on the balls of my feet. Lady Birdlady stood pointlessly in the center of the floor. Before I quite knew what I was doing, I had the lapels of her suit gripped in my fists. She let me do it. The fight had gone out of her. It had not gone out of me.

"What did you do to them?"

She only sobbed. I squeezed her jacket tighter. She seemed weightless, but perhaps I was just that mad. I spoke as slowly as I could, trying to make clear that answering me was not optional.

"What did you do?"

"I loved them."

I dropped her into a massive wingback chair. Dust bloomed, gritty and dry. She draped her arm over her eyes. Her chest shook. I couldn't tell if she was crying or laughing. As I waited for her episode to conclude, I spotted a ladder in the corner of the room that led to a hatch in the ceiling. I could have left, but something I did not yet understand had my feet stuck to the spot.

"I shall ask you one more time, and you will answer clearly and calmly. Do you understand?"

She nodded, her arm still clamped tight over her eyes. I sucked in as much breath as my lungs could hold and tried to keep the rage out of my voice.

"Good. That's very good. Now, my dear lady, did you kill those birds?"

"Kill 'em? Kill 'em? I would never, never, never . . ."

"Then what happened?"

She let her arm fall away from her face. Lumps of wet mascara were smeared across her eyes. Her face looked like one large bruise. She shuffled across the floor and pulled a purse off a hook. Inside was a small package wrapped in newspaper. She knelt on the floor and, with the greatest delicacy, peeled the paper away. Another dead gull.

"Poor creatures," she sniffed. "Noble creatures. Touched by god, is a gull. Given the power to fly, to rule land and sea, to live on filth and turn it into perfection. But they're tender as a cracker, and don't weigh more than one or two pounds."

She gave the bird's feathers a gentle tug. They came loose without resistance and scattered across the floor. Beneath, the skin was as smooth and pale as clean sheets.

"Rotting from the inside out. And its eyes, look at them, they've gone all rheumy. All of 'em in there are the same. Touch it."

"I'd rather not."

"Do it anyway. How can you expect to understand anything, won't touch a dead bird with your hands?"

I ran my finger across the dead bird's skin. It felt thin enough to puncture with my thumbnail. My anger seeped away, leaving pity behind.

"Where do they come from?" I said.

"Found this one at Clarkson and West, but they're all over the District. Anywhere there's people, I'm finding these dead birds. Pull 'em from the gutters, trash bins, drainpipes, or just kicked under piles of dirt. I've always seen to it to rescue the dead ones, give 'em a proper burial, return 'em to the water. That's why I have that chute you spilled out of. But since this sickness started, I didn't want to risk spreading it to the Hudson, so I kept 'em in my room."

She wrapped the newspaper tight and set it aside. The pain in my stomach and the pain in my head were back, stronger than ever before.

"What sickness?" I said.

She looked at me like I was the world's greatest fool.

"I thought that's why you was here."

I started to answer. Before I got anywhere, she threw up her hands and shuffled across the floor.

"Stupid woman," she said. "Dumb as the rest of them. Your average idiot, you know, they don't even know a gull unless it's snatching their frankfurter. Don't even see 'em, not even when the birds're suffering most. The other woman, she was the only one who understood."

She opened the door to her closet of horrors and hurled the paper-wrapped gull inside. She slammed the door quickly, as though the rot inside might attempt escape. She leaned on the door, watching me, waiting for me to leave. Once again, I wondered why I did not. There was a heap of corpses on my boat and an entire city police force on my heels. But in that moment, this seemed to matter more.

"What other woman?"

Above her little stove, an uneven shelf held desiccated onions, a few pouches of spices, a dried sausage, and a single thin book. She grabbed the book and placed it in my hands. It was forest green, with no dust jacket and nothing but an abstract brand embossed on the cover. I did not have to open it to know its name, to recognize what I had been told repeatedly was "one of the most important volumes of criticism published this century."

"*Paid in Kind.* This is Marka Watson's book."

"And she was quite proud of it, too. Gave it to me like she was doing me a favor. Pah. I've met authors before, real ones—men who could turn out a much thicker book than that."

I felt like I might fall off the floor. I squeezed the book, trying to steady myself. It did not help.

"Marka Watson came here? Marka Watson, who had champagne for blood, came *here*?"

Lady Birdlady snatched the book away.

"Why shouldn't she?"

"I'm sorry, I didn't mean anything, I simply . . . what brought her?"

"She was a woman of taste, wasn't she? Refinement? So naturally, she was interested in the birds."

She certainly was not. I'd listened to Marka talk for hours on every subject under the sun. She had opinions on food, fashion, real estate, high art, low art, decorum, her friends. She could spend thirty minutes lambasting a bartender for serving her a cocktail that was a slightly incorrect shade of green. She had never once mentioned birds.

"How did you meet her?"

"I spotted her on the District's edge a few weeks back, marching up and down after the birds, writing nonsense down in a little book, scaring the creatures something awful. She was a sharp one, though. Knew the birds were sick. Wanted to know why. I tempted her down here, told her I'd show her how bad it really was. She wrote down every word I said. I'm going to be in her article."

Lady Birdlady's spine stiffened with pride.

"Marka was writing an article about the birds." I said it aloud, mostly to myself. "But Marka didn't write articles."

"She certainly does. Told me herself. For the *Sentinel*, she said, and several of the prominent ladies' magazines."

"She was a critic. She wrote about plays, paintings, music, books. She would never sully her hands with actual reporting."

"That's not how she tells it. She says she's writing an exposé. Says it's going to be sensational. All about the birds."

"And the sickness."

"She doesn't call it that. She says they're being poisoned."

"By what?"

"By the District. By that filth you call food, or the vomit and oil and everything you dump into the river, or the booze. Gulls shouldn't have too much booze. She had all sorts of theories. Said she hadn't settled on a favorite. They all sounded good to me."

I twisted my hands together. It proved a very good way to stop myself from wringing the woman's neck.

"Marka didn't care about anything besides herself, her work, and the next glass of wine. Why did she want to know what's poisoning the birds?"

"Simple curiosity, I suppose. And she had an idea—she mentioned it in passing, but she seemed quite taken with it—that whatever's killing the birds was killing her too. Killing everyone fool enough to live up in the District, she said. Sounds a good bit of business, far as I'm concerned, if only the birds didn't have to die first."

I ran my hand across the chipped top of the dresser and thought of the deck of the *Misery Queen*. I inhaled the scent of freshly spilled blood, heard the bones clattering across the wood. Marka Watson had seized on a mystery, somewhere in that dangerous middle ground between tiny and huge. She had told no one, made no jokes about it, not even mined it for an anecdote. She had chased the story in secret and, soon after, she had died. It was a thread worth pulling, if only because I preferred asking questions to running for my life, and because it spared me having to wonder why Cherub had to die at her side. I did not know where to start, and so I began with the thing that mattered to no one but me.

"Have you found any birds with just one leg?"

"Why?"

"I've been living on the river for the last year. There was a one-legged gull, we called her Grover Hartley. We fed her sometimes. She disappeared a few weeks ago. I had a vague idea that she'd been kidnapped, but if what you say is true . . . it would mean something to know she is alive."

For the first time since I'd met her, Lady Birdlady stopped fidgeting. It was shocking, that sudden stillness, as if the river outside had simply decided to freeze.

"That's a very serious thing," she said. "Would you like something to eat?"

"More than you know."

She pointed at one of the chairs. I sat. I doubted I'd ever enjoyed sitting more. From a cabinet in the kitchen she pulled a plate of finger sandwiches. She set them on my lap. They were cucumber with a thick green mayonnaise. It was hard to tell how long they'd been in there, but I was in no state for concern. With all the daintiness I could muster, I crammed them into my mouth. They tasted like mud and death and the Hudson and they were absolutely delicious. When I'd finished swallowing, she asked me her questions.

"Which leg was it missing?" she said.

I thought hard, saw the bird landing on the rail of the *Misery Queen,* saw her namesake crouching behind home plate with a leg stretched out to the side.

"The left."

"What color were its wings? Slate or silver?"

"White, I think, with bits of gray."

"What *shade* of gray?"

"I didn't know there was more than one."

She scowled at the plate, wishing she could take the sandwiches back.

"Was its breast ivory or was it mottled, too?"

"I don't recall."

"The eyes?"

"Yellow."

"Of course they were yellow. Nearly all gulls have yellow eyes. But were they golden or watery?"

I shook my head, cucumber roiling in my stomach, feeling useless and ashamed that I could not tell her more.

"How many flecks of white were on its tail?"

"I'm sorry. I just . . . I can't say."

She took the plate off my lap and thrust it into the dresser. She smoothed the rugs with her feet, accomplishing nothing but moving the lumps around. Without looking at me, she asked, "Why do you want the bird back?"

"Marka Watson is dead."

She blinked. If this information made an impression on her, she did not show it. I pressed on.

"So are her friends, so is the man I loved. The police are after me. They think I killed them."

She raised an eyebrow. I shook my head.

"I'm not the murdering type." A white lie. "Whoever killed them left behind a painting of the one-legged gull. Now you tell me that Marka was chasing a story about the birds. If there's a connection there, if it has to do with Grover Hartley, maybe I'll understand."

She grunted, as close to satisfied as I expected she'd ever come.

"I've seen your bird. Don't think it's dead. Hangs around the east side of the Casino, pecking at the fire escape. I'll fetch it."

"I'll go myself."

Laughter rattled out of her.

"Aren't you trying to hide? Go up there like that, wet and muddy, you'll draw attention quick. Besides—what do you know about luring a gull?"

"Nothing but what you told me."

"And look what a mess you made of that!"

She smoothed her hair, stuffing as much of it under her hat as she could fit. She pulled on gloves and gripped the ladder.

"Stay here. We'll sort this out together, yes we will, and all our birds will be fine."

Before I could say anything, she launched herself up the ladder and was gone. I wanted to go after her, but I forced myself to stay put. I pulled a rag off a hook and scraped off as much of the mud as I could get. There was no mirror, which was just as well—I don't think my efforts made much difference. When the rag was too caked with mud to absorb any more, I slumped into the armchair and tried to be still. For the first time that day, I felt neither furious nor afraid. I was simply tired.

Music filtered through the ceiling. It was raucous, as if the whole orchestra were blowing at once, but everyone had chosen to play a different tune. It had to be Screaming Minnie's. Right now, wealthy bastards in skintight tuxedos and evening gowns were thumping their way around the barge, their blood hot from cheap liquor and cheaper lust, and I was here, scraping mud off my wrists. I was surprised to find the thought of those oblivious dancers a comfort. I had always hated them before.

I wrapped my finger around the hooked nail that protruded from Lady Birdlady's closet of rotting birds. They were still there, just as dead as before. It was pathetic. They really were so very small.

It occurred to me that for as wretched as my day had been, I had not yet cried.

I felt my cheeks.

I was crying now.

Above my head, the boards creaked. Lady Birdlady's voice filtered down through the cracks.

She was not alone.

"And of course it's so nice to have you here, so nice to have a gentleman with authority to look into the problems I've been telling you about. Poor creatures blind and miserable, can't even keep their food down, starving to death surrounded by everything in the world they could ever want to eat. It's a tragedy, no other word for it, a civic tragedy, and nobody has done a thing."

The hatch opened. I had no weapon, no way out but the tunnel, which I would rather die than enter again. The umbrella rested on Lady Birdlady's bed. I grabbed it, hurled myself into a corner, and watched as the man Oliver Lee called Conforto climbed down. He moved slowly, his eyes locked on his feet. When he finally reached the bottom, he just stared.

"This was not what I asked you to bring me," I called up to Lady Birdlady. I was answered with a sharp, ugly laugh.

"She don't even know her own bird," said the woman. "Why should I help a girl as stupid as that?"

"Is she alive? Is Grover Hartley really alive?"

She only laughed. I wanted to scale that ladder and teach her how unpleasant it was to get smacked with an umbrella, but Conforto blocked my path.

"Enough. You'll be coming with me."

"I'm not going back in that cage."

"Lee was telling the truth, you know. If you'd gone quietly, we'd have tried to help."

"'Tried' isn't enough. And I suspect it's too late for that now."

"Yeah. I guess it is."

The candlelight filled the deep wrinkles on his face with soft shadows. His eyes, which had shone blue by the water, looked black. He smiled. It did not comfort me.

"How do I know you?" I said.

"I used to work for Barbarossa. She called me her bodyguard. Mostly I held open doors. Name's Conforto, but folks call me Otto, on account of I'm two fingers short."

An image flashed across my mind of the bootlegging queen of the Lower West, her face red and chest heaving, swinging a curved knife over her head as she marched an army of children to the jaws of death. This man had been at her shoulder. He was thinner then, more alive. As were we all.

"You fought at Eighth Avenue," I said.

"Mostly, I ran."

"You're lucky to be alive."

"So are you. I was there the night you met her, down in the tunnels. Watched you press a pistol to her gut. You wanted to kill her. You didn't. I thought that was very kind."

"Why bring it up?"

"To remind you that you're not stupid. You know when you're beaten. And Gilda Carr, you are beaten today."

I peeled myself off the wall. The door to the bird room was still open. I nodded toward it.

"You seen what's in there?" I said.

"I smell it."

"There's something going on with those birds. Marka Watson

may have died over it. My Cherub died, too. If I go with you, is anybody going to bother with this?"

"I will."

"You're lying."

"Even when I killed for a living, I never liked to lie. It's not worth the headache. After Barbie died, I went to work for Van Alen because I think he feels the same way. His people aren't like the Roeblings. We tell the truth. If you come with me, and come nice, I'll take all this to Van Alen myself. Make sure he finds out exactly what happened to Marka, the birds, and your man. But none of that happens until you play along."

"And what if the thing that's killing the birds is coming from Van Alen's people? What if it's connected to Ida Greene?"

"I won't promise anything save that I'll try."

That word again. I twisted the umbrella in my hand. My palms had gone sweaty. Conforto stepped into a pool of candlelight. His expression was gentle, trustworthy. But I had to be certain.

"Prove it," I said.

"How?"

"Take a good look at what's behind that door. Once you see what this mess really looks like, well . . . it will stay with you."

With a shrug, he crossed the floor. He covered his mouth and nose with one thick hand, but the way his eyes watered, it wasn't enough to keep out the smell. He plucked a candle from the nearest holder and bent into the doorway. He was there for a long second before he spoke.

"Sweet god. Sweet merciful—"

I did not let him finish the thought. I smashed the tip of the umbrella into the base of his spine, sending him sprawling forward into the soft heap of dead birds. He thrashed, trying to get to his feet, but each movement sucked him deeper into the pile. His mouth filled with feathers and gore, choking away his screams.

"That's for the cage," I said.

He rolled onto his back and fixed his gaze on me. His eyes went wide as I slammed the door. I shoved my shoulder into Lady

Birdlady's dresser. It crashed to the floor, shaking every part of that strange little room.

"What on earth is going on down there?" called Lady Birdlady, irritation in her voice.

I pushed the dresser until it blocked most of the door. By the time Conforto escaped, I hoped to be very far away.

Assuming he got out at all.

Perhaps he hadn't deserved such wretched punishment. Perhaps Emil Koszler hadn't deserved a bottle in his kidneys. Perhaps, perhaps, perhaps. I would answer those questions another day. At that moment, I had to move.

I tore up the ladder and shoved open the hatch. I emerged into an empty mechanic's shop, where heaps of rusted machinery were pushed back against the wall. Through grimy windows, I saw the pink of the setting sun. All that misery, I thought, and night had not even come.

Lady Birdlady jolted out of a chair and stalked across the floor. I looked down and saw that, improbably, I was still holding on to her umbrella. I tossed it to her. She froze.

"Thanks for the sandwiches," I said, and headed for the setting sun.

SIX

As a girl, I had a terror of automobiles. The deadly contraptions were just becoming common, and the rich men who drove them believed they had a right to go as fast as internal combustion allowed. They tore down the alleys of the Village, their hands planted on their horns, screaming for the world to get out of their way.

One damp April morning, I was exiting Washington Square when a crimson automobile exploded down Fourth Street, driving the wrong way. By the time I saw it, it was nearly on top of me. I hurled myself backward, landing in a puddle of cold rainwater. Before I was collected enough to start screaming profanities, the driver was out of sight.

After that unpleasantness, I began to show an uncharacteristic hesitancy while crossing the street. This made my father mad.

On a walk a week or two after the incident with the red car, he felt me flinch as I stepped off the sidewalk. He jerked me backward, sat me on a stoop, and asked me to explain.

"I don't like the cars."

"Forget they're there."

"That seems a good way to get run over."

"For an ordinary person, maybe, but you're a New Yorker, and what's more, you're my girl. This is how you cross the street."

He clamped his fingers around my wrist, hauled me up, and dragged me into the street. All traffic stopped. He stared straight ahead as we marched to the other side. Once we were safe, he squatted before me and ran his hands through my hair.

"Look before you cross, sure," he said. "But once you step into that street, do not make eye contact. Show no fear. Never break stride."

I never hesitated at a crosswalk again.

The mechanic's shop atop Lady Birdlady's palace of avian death let out onto the Boardwalk, where the crowd was thick and the sun was almost gone. I paused in the doorway and fixed my eyes on Screaming Minnie's barge, where a dozen tourists waited at the door. It was not far. All I had to do was cut through the crowd.

There were hundreds of revelers on the Boardwalk. The wealthy moved in packs, their white clothes gleaming, their crisp voices cutting through the thick night air. They were outnumbered, but not outshone, by the common herd of Eastsiders, most of whom had trekked overland through the Lower West, and who were celebrating their ordeal by getting stinking drunk. Sprinkled throughout were Peacekeepers and cops, more cops than I'd seen since the destruction of the Fourth Precinct. They circulated lazily, glancing at every face, looking for the woman who'd broken free of the Long Pier.

I cut through the herd like a bullet, my eyes locked on Screaming Minnie's door. Everyone saw me. There was no way for them to miss a barefoot woman in a damp black dress whose every inch was caked in Westside mud. But like a true New Yorker, I did not meet their eyes, and I did not break stride. It was only when my foot landed on Minnie's gangway that I realized I had been holding my breath.

"You!" cried someone behind me, sending Lady Birdlady's cucumber sandwiches rising to my throat. "You there!"

If I were lucky, he wasn't shouting at me, but I hadn't been lucky in weeks. I shuffled down the gangway, pushing around the people waiting in line, ignoring their protests, just trying to get to the door.

I didn't make it.

A hand closed on my elbow. The grip was not the meaty clasp of a New York cop, but something gentle, fragile, old.

Brass Aiken had my arm.

He was floating in an oversized checked suit. A panama hat perched on top of hair as soft as a baby's, and a ghoulish grin spread across his pale white face. I hadn't seen the old jazz addict in two years—not since the last time I visited his suite at the Hyperion Hotel to ask him what he knew about the night my father died—but he started talking like no time had passed at all.

"Minnie hasn't got the best band in the District, but they're unquestionably the loudest, and that's worth my dime. Did you know you're covered in mud?"

"I'd picked up on it."

"Let's get you inside."

Brass led me to the front of the line. The doorman's eyes bulged at the sight of me, but a smile from Brass was enough to open the door.

The music rattled my ribs and crushed the breath from my chest. The room was long and broad, with a bar on the shore side, tables scattered around the edges, and a bank of windows cranked open to let in the Hudson breeze—in theory, at least. Bourget Devices at either end provided just enough light to keep it from being pitch black. Red shrouds had been hung around them, and everyone's skin looked wet with blood, calling back unwanted memories of the *Misery Queen*. To distract myself from those unhappy thoughts, I tried to focus on the velvet décor, which might have looked stylish when first installed. Now, however, every flat surface—including the floor, ceiling, walls, and tabletops—had been stained white by the birds.

It was hard to count them, because they never stayed still for long, but there must have been at least twenty-five. Most were small—pigeons and sparrows and bright, delicate things I could not name—but there were a few gulls and, at the far corner of the room, just below the opened skylight that gave them access to the roof, a lone hawk perched on a silver rail, eyeing the scene with disdain. The rest of the birds circulated between the network of crisscrossing mesh suspended from the ceiling and tables whose patrons had made the mistake of looking away from their drinks, their cigarettes, their food. When a bird swooped down to snatch something a customer had left behind, the people laughed and the birds screamed, but none of them could be heard above the band.

Screaming Minnie and her Mignonettes occupied a low stage at the far end of the room. They were all women, mostly Black, with a few white faces scattered about for seasoning. All wore yellow. They attacked their instruments like they were trying to kill them, and none of them seemed to be playing the same song. By the look of glee on Brass Aiken's face, I could see that didn't matter. The music was too loud to think, to talk, to feel pain, and that was all the crowd desired. Minnie herself was at the piano, hammering at it like she was trying to break her fingers. She wore a long silver dress and a platinum wig that looked as solid as a football helmet.

"I need to talk to her," I screamed in his ear.

"But she's busy."

"I don't care."

He smiled—perhaps at the music, perhaps at the discovery that I was just as stubborn as he remembered—and guided me across the floor, so that the music might be properly earsplitting. Shuffling couples parted for the quaking old man. He plucked a pair of highballs off the tray of a passing waiter and pressed one into my hand. I drained it as we walked. It tasted like nothing at all. The band paused for breath. The birds plunged down from the ceiling. Everyone was having a marvelous time.

"So good to see young people taking an interest in culture," said Brass. "Not that rot they peddle at the Philharmonic, no, but good honest gutter jazz, strong enough to scrape the enamel off your teeth."

"Can you get me backstage?"

"This set will finish in an hour or two. I'll introduce you then."

"I can't wait that long."

"So impatient! Just like your father. I remember one night at this hideous saloon in the old Tenderloin, he pulled a razor on a fellow just for—"

"Brass!"

"So sorry. It's the most inconvenient thing. The older you get, the more time you have to remember. Can't we at least wait for this number to end?"

I looked around. Once I was reasonably satisfied that the room was ignoring me, I nodded my head. The band roared on through something that was perhaps technically music, and I really did feel like my teeth were starting to peel. Brass's head bobbed like his neck was a spring.

"Were you here last night?" I shouted.

"From dusk to dawn."

"Did you see Marka Watson?"

Brass's light dimmed. He took a small sip of his drink and set it on the bar.

"That poor woman. She was dull, no interest in music, death to talk to, but that's no reason to get chopped into fish food."

"Did you talk to her?"

"As soon as she got here, Marka dragged Minnie backstage. They were cloistered for an hour or more. I spent the whole time chatting with Bess Barron—absolutely adore her, the things she makes her dancers do are simply insane. She was nipping the whole time from a bottle in her purse. Something pink. She and Marka had a bit of a row when Marka returned from backstage and snatched the bottle out of Bess's hands. Bess was still screaming when Marka left."

"I think she was coming to see me."

"That's certainly possible. She wasn't gone long. Three numbers, maybe five. When she came back, she snapped her fingers and the group departed. It was hellishly rude—the first set wasn't even done—but that's the sort of woman she is. I mean, was."

"Was Cherub with them?"

"That's that man of yours? The one who's allergic to shirts?"

I nodded, trying to smile, surely failing terribly.

"He was with them but not *with* them, if you understand me."

"I rarely do."

"I mean he spent the whole night staring moodily into a single cocktail. I tried to draw him into the conversation, but it was like he couldn't hear me over the noise."

"And he followed when they left?"

"He did."

"Do you know where they were going?"

"No. Somewhere less interesting than here, I'm sure."

The song droned on. After a few more bars, Brass's forehead smoothed out and his smile returned. He was almost his carefree old self when he saw something at the front door that made his eyes go wide.

"Remind me, dearest," he bellowed at me, "but aren't the police after you?"

"A bit. Why?"

"They're here."

I resisted the urge to turn around. I felt like someone had set my spine on fire.

"How many?"

"Two in uniform, one in a gray suit, badge on his breast, walking with a cane. Are you all right? Your face has gone all green."

I scanned the back of the room. There were no windows, no doors, nothing but the curtain that blocked off the area behind the stage.

"Get me back there."

"It's impossible. Let's go."

He took a final minute sip of his drink, set the glass precisely in the middle of his coaster, and took my hand. As my feet sank into that thick damp velvet, my shoulders tingled, expecting Koszler's hand. As we passed the bandstand, we caught the attention of the trombonist, who had arms like a longshoreman's and hair nearly as matted as mine. She looked puzzled but continued to play.

Brass lifted the curtain and waved me backstage, where empty instrument cases were heaped in a corner and a dozen stools crowded around a small mirror on the back wall. The music was slightly quieter here—one could almost speak without shouting—and I did not feel so exposed. But no velvet curtain would keep Koszler out. A door opened onto a small platform. Beyond it was the river, which burned like lava in the light of the plummeting sun. I did not want to go that way again.

"Get Minnie," I said.

"She's going to hate this."

"Even so."

Brass poked his head through the curtain and waved frantically until he caught Minnie's eye. The piano stopped but the band roared on. The curtain snapped open and Screaming Minnie stepped down from the stage. She looked me over. I did not impress.

"What is *that*?" she said.

"I want to join the band."

"The band is full."

She turned back to the stage. I got in her way. She was as small as me, and some years older, but her muscles were coiled steel. If she chose, I was certain, she could rip me apart.

"Put an instrument in my hand and stash me in the back of the orchestra. Please."

"Why?"

"There are violent men out there looking for me. I'd rather not be found."

"What do you play?"

"Nothing."

"Good god."

The number ended. In the stark, cold silence, I heard Koszler talking to the bartender, his voice a throaty rasp.

"I'm looking for a girl," he said. Minnie and Brass stared at me, taking in his words. "Quite dangerous, a confirmed lunatic, in a black dress. Shoeless. Wet, perhaps muddy. Have you seen her here?"

The band erupted, drowning out the bartender's reply. What he said didn't matter. Koszler was close enough for me to recall the heat of his blood under my hands. I did not want to find out how he'd planned his revenge.

"I can do you a favor," I said.

"Oh?" said Minnie.

Brass lit up.

"She solves mysteries," he said. "Little ones. It's the darndest trick. She helped me get a song out of my head that had been stuck there for years. It went like 'dah-dah-dah-dum-dum.' Or, no, it, it was more like 'dum-dum-dee-dee-dee.' Or maybe—"

"Tiny mysteries," I said. "The little things that keep you up at night. Have you got one of those?"

Minnie thought for a few seconds that seemed to take most of my life. Finally, she nodded.

"The bandleader at the Casino is named Roy B. Sharp," she said.

"I've heard him. He's mediocre."

"'Mediocre' is putting it nice. I want to know what the *B* stands for."

"Why?"

"Because it's the corniest joke in the world. Roy swears it's his given name, but I know he's a goddamned liar and I want to prove it."

"I'll get you the answer by dawn."

"Okay."

With two hands, Minnie grabbed the collar of my dress and tore it down the middle. It shredded like wet newspaper. Blushing like a Jersey tomato, Brass slipped back into the main room. Suddenly a blur, Minnie snatched a yellow frock off the vanity and jammed it over my head. After I'd struggled into it, she was holding a pair of scissors.

"Fix the hair."

I bent over the dressing table and stared at myself in the mirror. My eyes were mostly red. My skin was as gray as boiled chicken. On the other side of the curtain, I heard Brass say, "Just the dressing room, officers. Some ladies changing in there. I'm sure they'll be done soon."

I hacked off fistfuls of mud-caked hair, shaping what remained into a truly tragic bob. Minnie opened the back door and tossed my shorn locks into the current. She smacked a tambourine against my chest and a beret on my head. Her fingers clamped onto my wrist. Before I knew it, I was onstage.

I saw nothing but red. The Bourget Device was so close, it was like staring into a bloody sun. The headache I'd fought off that afternoon resettled in my forehead, and I stumbled clumsily behind

Minnie, who sat me in a folding chair behind her piano bench, where my ineptitude might be at least partially obscured.

"'Knickerbocker Blues,'" grumbled Minnie, and the band roared to life. It was a number I knew, but whatever I remembered of its rhythm was blasted out of my brain by the noise, so I simply rattled my tambourine and tried to look like I wasn't afraid. I saw no sign of Koszler, but I couldn't see anyone else either, and with every shake of the instrument I sensed him about to grab me by the ankles and drag me away.

The song bled into another. The smoke from a hundred pipes and cigars stung my eyes. Sweat poured across my face like toxic runoff. I tried to remember a time when I had loved this music. Now, on top of all my other troubles, I found myself worrying I might never enjoy jazz again. Without warning, the horns went silent so the banjo player could take her turn in the spotlight. Minnie whispered something to me. Over the ringing in my ears, I could not make out a word.

"What?" I said, not sure if I was whispering or screaming.

That's when my ankle got grabbed.

I had no weapon but the tambourine, and so I lashed out. It caught the top of my assailant's head, knocking his hat to the floor.

"Hey!" cried Brass, and I saw him through the lights, and I knew I must be safe. He smoothed down what hair he had left, smiling proudly.

"They've gone."

Minnie tore the tambourine out of my grip and hissed, "So get off my stage."

On shaking legs, I picked my way through the band and slipped backstage. It took a while for my eyes to adjust to the light, and even longer for my hands to still. I leaned out the back door of the barge. The evening air was like ice water. In the light from the District, the Hudson's current looked like fluttering silk. I let the borrowed dress fall to the floor, tossed the beret aside, and dove.

"Chin tucked, arms on the ears, hands together."

When he taught me to dive, that had been Cherub's mantra. I'd never quite mastered it, but as I launched into the river, I thought he might have been proud of my form.

The water shook me until all the smoke and blood and mud and filth I'd accumulated over the course of the day fell off, until nothing but my exhausted body remained. I stayed close to the lip of the barge, not trusting the current, trying to work out where the hell I might go next.

Grover Hartley was missing.

Cherub was dead.

Marka, too.

The District's birds were dying.

And Marka wanted to know why.

Unraveling this mystery might save me from the hangman, but that was not why I wanted to do it. Death was nothing but an ending, and I did not fear it as I once had. It was the time in the cell that had me worried, because time in a cell was time to think, and being alone with my thoughts was the terror that had driven me onto the river in the first place. As long as I was searching for a killer, grief could wait, and that was the most I could ask.

Back on the barge, the curtain parted, and Minnie's voice called out, "Get back in before somebody sees."

I crawled onto the deck. The wind caught me, and my teeth began to chatter. A towel thudded into my chest.

"Get dry."

I followed the instructions. When I stepped into the dim light of the dressing room, Minnie handed me the yellow dress. I guess that made it mine. She lit a cigarette and let her eyes close for a moment. It seemed the closest she would ever get to letting herself relax.

"You did good up there."

"With the tambourine?"

"God no. You're the worst I've ever seen. But you know how to vanish. That's a skill."

"Thank you for the chance. You probably saved my life."

She shrugged. This was her little moment of peace. Sadly, spoiling such moments is my life's work.

"Marka came to you last night. About the birds."

"She said they're dying."

"Was she right?"

"I think so. I've been seeing it too. They don't fly straight. Their feathers are loose, their beaks brittle. I've been keeping my birds out of it, but the wild ones look worse every day. For a while I was thinking it's just my imagination but no, it's real, and it's awful."

"How have you kept your birds safe?"

She drummed her fingers on the table, thumping it as hard as she had the piano keys. A starling dove from the ceiling and marched back and forth in front of the vanity, its feathers glistening purple and black.

Minnie reached out her finger and let the starling peck at her nail. Once it was satisfied, she went on.

"It's the booze. Two years ago, there were no people on this stretch of the waterfront, and the birds were fine. Then people came here to drink, and the birds drank too, and now they're falling from the sky."

My chest tightened. I'd pushed so much of that liquor through my system. It had never left me feeling healthy, but the idea that it was poison gave me a chill. I could not afford to believe it was true.

"I've been drinking Ida Greene's red gin for some time," I said, fighting to keep the fear out of my voice. "It's treated me to some hellish hangovers, but nothing worse than that."

"Oh, that slop is harmless. It'll put holes in your liver and rot in your brain, but that's the end of it. That gin isn't what concerns me."

She rooted through a trunk until she found an empty pint bottle. Diana's Fire.

"I've seen this before."

"I hope you haven't been drinking it. You probably can't afford to. I caught a table of Newport types topping up their drinks with it, acting all secret, as if the whole bar couldn't see their little trick. I threw them in the river and kept the bottle. Was going to drink it, but it smelled so rancid that I dumped it out. Those bastards looked as sick as the gulls. Since then, anytime I've seen someone drinking this stuff, they've looked just as bad."

"What is it? Gin? Rye?"

"Nothing. Just raw liquor cut with god knows what, worse than anything Barbarossa ever spewed out, but it's expensive and that means it must be good."

I gripped the bottle in my hands, twisting it until it caught the light and the glass turned the color of blood. If it was the best, Marka would want to drink it. If it made her sick, she would want to know why. What better test subject than her dear friend Gilda Carr?

"You told Marka this?"

"All of it."

"Did she believe you?"

"I think so."

"Where's this stuff coming from?"

She took a drag on her cigarette and found it had gone out some time ago. Smiling at herself, she ground it into the ashtray.

"Everybody I ask says they get it at the Casino," she said. "I believe that's where Marka and her people went after they finished here. The man who runs it is—"

"Ugly La Rocca."

"He must adore you if he lets you call him Ugly."

"I don't think he likes me at all."

Furio La Rocca. A very strange, possibly handsome man. The first time I met him, he'd trapped me in a coffin and driven me uptown in a hearse for a private meeting with his patron, Glen-Richard Van Alen. I'd thanked him for the ride by breaking his nose. His nose had mended. Our relationship had not. When the District was built, he'd found himself in charge of the Casino, acting as a bridge between the unabashed criminals of the Roebling Company and the preening St. Abban's crowd. Whenever Marka had dragged me to the Casino, I'd noticed La Rocca watching me from his balcony. He never said hello.

"Onward to the Casino," I said, trying to summon some of the enthusiasm Marka would have shown.

Minnie considered lighting another cigarette. Instead, she closed her case.

"You could do that," she said. "Or you could stay here. I have friends on the river. Before dawn, I could have a boat at that door that could take you to Hoboken."

"I'd rather die in Manhattan than live in Jersey."

"A girl after my own heart. Still, the offer remains."

"And give up on the mystery of Roy B. Sharp?"

"I could let that slide."

"I can't. Besides, why risk anything for me?"

"Brass is my best customer, and Marka was, well . . . a familiar face. Or maybe I just have a soft spot for barefoot girls."

"About that . . ."

She flipped open the lid of a chest beneath the window, full of loafers and boots in various stages of disrepair, none of which quite matched. I found two that roughly approximated the size of my feet. Pulling them on felt like sliding into a suit of armor.

"Thank you. For the dress and the boots and . . ."

I looked over my shoulder. There was no point finishing the thought. The piano was screaming. Minnie had gone back to her girls. I straightened my shoulders and headed for the front door. I passed Brass at the bar, but he was lost in the music and did not notice me go. As I walked through the room of deafened revelers, I allowed myself the faintest feeling of pride. I was the only one there whose clothes had not been soiled by the birds.

SEVEN

I stepped off the gangway. No one screamed my name. I slipped into the throng and followed the traffic south. I had worn nothing but black for most of my adult life, and in that pale yellow dress I felt like I was under a spotlight. There were Peacekeepers or uniformed cops—honest-to-god cops, here on the Lower West!—every ten feet, but the crowd was thick enough that I simply drifted by. I rounded the corner onto Spring Square, where the great light pierced the sky. I picked my way around it, stepping over groaning men in stained tuxedos and couples rutting in the grime. I was a hunted fox driven into the open, but I strode like my father taught me and the world got out of my way.

As I walked, I watched the drunks. They were laughing, sobbing, dancing, fighting, staring at the stars, or smiling private smiles with their chins tucked against their chests. One was vomiting; many more were fighting the urge. There was nothing unusual in any of this, but that did not mean they looked well.

The Casino's lights burned brightly. A flight of sagging steps led to the front door, where gigantic doormen in white overalls leered at the crowd, daring them to make trouble. No one took the bait. I walked around the back and passed through the staff entrance. I looked miserable enough that no one could mistake me for a customer, and no one questioned me when I walked inside.

The kitchen had been a chemical storeroom when the Casino was a factory. The rusted vats that once filled the floor had been replaced with a few lopsided tables and an ankle-deep carpet of molding food scraps. The air stank of old poison. Mosquitos swarmed. There was no light but a half dozen candles, and no conversation but a ceaseless stream of some of the vilest profanity I'd ever heard.

I was about to pass through the double doors that led to the Casino floor when I heard a grunting that could have been a pig but was, improbably, a man. A playwright had parked himself by a rack of hors d'oeuvres. There was a streak of mayonnaise on his shoulder and flakes of parsley in his moustache. He picked up a cone of puff pastry, slurped out the filling, and put the remains back on the tray. I'd never thought I'd be so happy to see Stuyvesant Wells.

"Hullo, Gilda," he said without removing his eyes from the tray. "Want one of these? They may be crab."

"I thought you were dead."

"I'm not. Lucky me."

The double doors swung open. A busboy spun to avoid smashing into me. To get out of the line of fire, I stepped close to Stuy, almost choking on the stench of raw liquor and poached fish.

"Why didn't you die on the *Misery Queen*?" I said.

"I've been asking that question in between every bite. I started the evening with them. I should have been there until the end. I should have been—"

He choked. At first I thought it was emotion, but it turned out to be shrimp. After a bit of gagging and chest-pounding, he went on.

"The only reason I wasn't there was because I got rather caught up in this blackjack game, up in La Rocca's private room. It turns out one should always split aces and eights. Or never split aces and eights. Someday I'll have to learn how that game works. Incidentally, might I borrow some cash?"

"Do I look like I have any to spare?"

"That's a new dress, isn't it? And a haircut too, if you can call it that."

"Both free."

"You overpaid."

A waiter tried to scoot around us. Stuy blocked him, snatched a fistful of finger sandwiches, and waved him on.

"But who needs money? The food here is free as long as they don't catch you eating it. I keep meaning to stop, but whenever my mouth is empty I remember Marka and the others, and then . . ."

"Me too."

"You loved him, didn't you?"

I nodded. He lunged at me. I thought he was going for my throat, but it turned out to be a hug. The mess on his suit squished into my chest.

"Let go," I said, "or I'll bite your ear."

He released me. He noticed the filth on my dress and dabbed at it helplessly with a cocktail napkin. I began to fear he might cry.

"Have you ever tasted liquor from a pink bottle," I asked him, "with a picture of Diana on the label?"

"I rarely look at things before I put them in my mouth. Spoils the surprise."

"Marka would have given it to you."

"I really couldn't say. I don't want to talk about her. Murder, you know . . . it's upsetting."

"Then get me to La Rocca. I think he'll know."

He drained a glass of something bubbly and offered his arm. I shoved open the swinging doors and we swept into the main room.

The light was obscene. Miniature Bourget Devices hung from every flat surface, their dancing shadows clashing horribly with the massive chandelier that hung from the old factory ceiling. Nightclubs are not meant to be so bright, but on the Westside light was the greatest luxury, and La Rocca wanted his patrons to gorge on it. The Casino was the Roebling Company's first attempt at something high class, but they had done it—as they did everything—with their eyes glued to the bottom line. Soft white curtains dangled from the roof, not quite covering the creaking old walls, and stolen carpet hid a floor so warped that none of the roulette tables had a hope of spinning true. As long as the booze flowed and the band played, no one cared. The rough edges only added to the charm.

We were at the end of the long bar, facing a sea of gaming tables—blackjack and roulette, mostly, with some games I didn't recognize sprinkled in. Down three steps were the dance floor and a crowded bandstand, where the Roy B. Sharp Orchestra was murdering the "Baby Bear Stomp." The glare was dizzying. I leaned on the wall and fought to catch my breath.

"Where's La Rocca?" I said.

Stuy pointed a cucumber sandwich at the ceiling, where a catwalk ringed the room. La Rocca leaned on the railing, his suit as white as fresh snow. He lit a cigar and disappeared into his office. A switchbacking staircase looked to be the only way up. Reaching it would mean crossing the entire room. I squeezed Stuy's arm tight and dragged him toward the floor.

"Are we dancing?" he said. "It's one of my few skills."

"Another time. I just need you to get me to the stairs."

"Playing cards with La Rocca is one thing, but a conversation? I can't imagine anything more tedious. I told Marka the same thing."

"She went to see Ugly?"

"As soon as we arrived."

"Do you know what they talked about?"

"What could a critic possibly have to discuss with that lout?"

"Something she was writing, perhaps."

"As far as I know, the only thing she was working on was her review of my new play. I do hope she finished it before she died. A good notice in the *Sentinel* is so important, even for a name playwright, and—"

"Stuy. Shut up."

We approached the band. I got a good look at Roy B. Sharp, a puffy white man whose hair was slicked into artful curls. Like Screaming Minnie, he led the band from his piano, but where she pounded the keys, he caressed them, draping himself across the instrument like he was trying to talk it into bed. His orchestra followed his lead, drawing every last bit of sap out of music that didn't have the right to be called jazz.

"Do you know what the *B* stands for?" I asked Stuy.

"Barnacle."

"That's impossible."

"Yes, but wouldn't it be fun?"

Sharp launched the band into "Sharp's Serenade." It was his trademark number—the one the crowd had been waiting for. Dancers filled the floor, cutting off our path. Fear surged through me, and I was on the verge of doing something rash when Stuy seized my hand and threw his arm around my waist. Before I quite understood what was happening, we were spinning with the crowd. I had never considered that such a hopeless mess of a human being could dance with such effortless grace.

"My parents broke themselves to give me a good education," he said. "Tragically, dancing was the only thing that stuck."

"Can you get us to the staircase?"

"Just follow my lead. Why do you ask about Mr. Sharp's middle name?"

"A friend wants to know."

"Then we'll have to find out."

We swirled around the edge of the floor, orbiting beneath the spinning chandelier. By the time we swung up to the bandstand, my head was spinning as well.

"Sharp!" cried Stuy.

"It can wait," I hissed.

"You'll probably be dead tomorrow. You'd hate to expire with something like this on your mind."

He pounded on the stage. Roy B. Sharp shot Stuy a look of absolute hatred. Stuy laughed and pounded harder.

"Come now, Roy," he said, sickeningly amused with himself. "Your public wants to know your middle name!"

A boy scurried across the stage and whispered something in Roy B. Sharp's ear. Sharp stopped playing. The band did, too. The dancers stopped, surrounding us as firmly as a brick wall. Only Stuy did not notice that something had changed.

"I say—" he shouted.

I cuffed his ear. At last, he shut up. I grabbed him by the wrist and dragged him into the crowd, whose eyes were locked on something I was too short to see. We had only gone a few feet when a shout snapped across the room.

"Ladies and gentlemen, we have a killer in our midst."

The voice was cold, almost mechanical, and incredibly calm. Emil Koszler was here, and he had the floor.

I caught a glimpse through the break in the crowd. He leaned heavily on his cane, his other hand held high. At his elbows were Oliver Lee and Otto Conforto, whose suit was filthy with the remains of dead birds. Cornelia Prime and Marvin Howell were there, too, keeping their distance, as though these beacons of law and order were simply too dirty to touch.

"She's a woman of twenty-nine," he said, "just over five feet tall. She has matted black curls, and when last seen she was barefoot, wearing a muddy black dress. That was several hours ago, however, and it's likely she has since adopted a disguise. Her name is Gilda Carr."

There was no frenzy in his voice, no cruelty. He chose his words carefully and spoke as softly as the venue allowed. The gamblers and dancers scooted closer to hear, trapping us tighter.

"You've heard stories of the murder boat, which now floats adrift, farther up the Hudson. I've seen it, and I can tell you, it's worse than anything you can imagine. Some of the brightest people in New York hacked to pieces, their limbs scattered across the deck, their flesh hanging in strips, all because they made the mistake of offending Gilda Carr. Among the riffraff that crewed the ship, there were Bess Barron, Lisbeth Frasier, Yoshi Miyazaki, Eva Distler, Stuyvesant Wells, Mercury Tyne, and, of course, Marka Watson. I had not the privilege to meet that brilliant woman, but I read every word she wrote, and I know that without her, this District will be dimmer, and winter will be far more cold. The person who killed her deserves to hang."

Once again, it felt like a spotlight had fallen on me. I considered hauling myself onto the stage and trying to slip out the back, or pushing through the crowd and making for the kitchen. It was impossible. Any movement would mean more eyes on me, and so I did the hardest possible thing: I stood still.

"Most of you sailed here," Koszler continued. "Most of you are planning, on Tuesday morning, to sail home. Those shattered corpses on the *Misery Queen* could have been any one of you. If you encounter Gilda Carr, give her no shelter. Do not try to apprehend. Inform the nearest Peacekeeper or policeman, and we will deal with her ourselves. Thanks to you all."

Koszler released the crowd's attention. The band stayed quiet. The dancers looked at each other. Their brows were sweaty. Their eyes were alert. Many of them looked at me.

"Distract them," I whispered to Stuy.

"How?"

"Shout something. Throw something. Get up onstage and play the piano. I don't care—just get their attention so I can get up those stairs."

For an interminable moment, the wheels turned inside his head. Then he got an idea. In a voice trained for the cheap seats, he bellowed: "I am alive!"

Every eye turned to him. I pressed my back against the stage. He shouted again, louder this time.

"I am alive!"

The crowd stepped back to gawk as he barged his way to the front of the room, stomping heels and spilling cocktails, and shouting all the while. For the first time all day, I did not feel seen.

"Think you know Marka Watson?" Stuy said. He lurched up onstage and bellowed in Koszler's face, bathing the cop in his spit. Koszler smiled blandly and let him proceed. "You don't know the first damn thing about her! She was the greatest writer to grace Manhattan since Washington Irving, but she only put a tenth of her talent down on the page. Marka's true art was the put-down, the comeback, the smirk—she was the finest smirker that ever lived."

I headed for the stairs. I had to fight to keep from running.

"And she was a friend. Supported my work from the beginning. I'm the artist I am today—the man I am today—because of her."

There was an unsteady pause as the crowd tried to decide if what they'd just seen was funny or pathetic or simply insane. Koszler answered for them. The man I'd known on the Lower West would have smashed his forehead into Stuy's leering mouth. The 1923 vintage did something I thought cops weren't capable of: he made it a joke.

"And just who are you?"

Laughter rippled through the crowd. Stuy wheeled around to face them, grinning like it had all been a practiced bit.

"Stuyvesant Wells," he said. "And while I'm here, I'd like to remind the assemblage that my new show, *Ready, Willing, & Mable,* opens at the Belasco next week and, my my, I just happen to have a pair of passes right here. Would you do us the honor, lieutenant?"

Koszler took the tickets with a flourish. Stuy bowed. The people applauded. Those two should have gone on tour—they could certainly work a crowd.

I padded up the steps. They'd been carpeted, thank god, so my feet didn't echo, but the ancient metal whined under my weight. At the second landing I saw Koszler with his arm around Stuy, leading him to the bar. Marvin Howell was staring at me. He touched the wrist of Cornelia Prime and pointed my way. I pressed on.

The carpet stopped at the top of the stairs. I thundered across the iron platform and shoved open the office door. Ugly was at his desk, working by the light of a small Device, counting cash. In the bright white light, the long scar that ran down the side of his face looked freshly cut. I swept my arm across the desk and sent the money fluttering to the floor. He threw up his hands, not angry so much as extremely annoyed.

"And who's cleaning that up?" he said.

"Marka was here last night, asking about Diana's Fire—"

"She asked nothing, she was yelling—"

"And what did you tell her?"

"Same thing I'll tell you. There's nothing off about that liquor. I swear by it. It's all I drink."

He pulled a pint of the stuff from his desk drawer and drank a long sip. He covered his mouth to obscure a burp. He looked like he'd been left to rot in the sun.

"You don't look good," I said.

"You look worse. Drink?"

I shook my head. My forehead throbbed. I'd have done anything for a glass of cold water, but I doubted I'd find something so exotic here.

"Where's it come from?" I said.

"The Roeblings."

"They make it?"

"They don't make anything. They buy it from a gang called the Mudfoots. River pirates. You'd like them. They're the kind of lunatics the Westside doesn't make anymore."

"I'm sure they're charming. If their liquor were toxic—"

"It's not."

"But if it were, and Marka were planning to write about it, would the Mudfoots kill her for that?"

"The way Oliver Lee tells it, the Mudfoots would kill for a lot less."

"Delightful. Where can I find them?"

"I don't know. Lee's the one who works with them. I just pour the drinks."

This was taking too long. I kept thinking I heard steps outside, but no matter how many times I flinched, the door stayed shut.

"You're in a hell of a fix," he said.

"Don't. Don't try to sympathize, warn me, help me."

"If you won't take help from your friends—"

I smacked my hands together. The skin stung.

"You're my friend? Lucky me. So's Oliver Lee. So's Ida Greene. I've got so many friends I'm choking on them, but none bothered to help this morning when I was trapped in a cage."

"I'm sorry."

"Good for you."

I paced, trying to find the question whose answer would tell me where to go next. Heavy carpet muffled my footsteps. Ugly leaned back in his chair.

"Why drink Roebling booze? Doesn't Ida Greene give you red gin for free?"

"That woman doesn't give anything away. I used to get a discount, but not anymore."

"Why not?"

"We no longer see eye to eye. That woman used to be fun, you know? When I met her, she was an arson specialist. Had this black gunk she cooked up, burned like the devil, started fires no one could snuff out. Now, pah. Acts like she's too good for a little greed, a little violence, a little crime. Treats me like a stain. She hates the Casino, hates me running it. She's poisoned Van Alen against me—I can't even get in to see him anymore. I think she'd kill me if she could."

"I saw her last night at the docks, checking ships and taking notes. What was she doing there?"

"Nobody tells me anything. But she's not your friend, Gilda."

"She's always done right by me."

Laughing gently, he shoved a thin scrap of paper across his desk: a note written in the soft lead of a Bishop's Blue Streak, signed by Ida Greene.

"G. Carr escaped Long Pier. NYPD coming ashore. They will ask unpleasant questions. Cooperate fully. The girl must be found."

I was used to people wanting me dead. It surprised me how sharply I was stung by Mrs. Greene's betrayal.

"Well," I said, "perhaps I'm not burdened with as many friends as I thought."

"If I could help you, I would, but Greene is looking for an excuse to crucify me and—"

"Please. I wouldn't dream of asking you to inconvenience yourself on my behalf. Just tell me where I can find the Mudfoots and—"

I stopped speaking. I stopped breathing, too. There were footsteps on the catwalk. This time, there was no doubt they were real.

"Is there another way out?"

"A fire escape, but it's mostly rust."

Rust I did not fear. I darted around his desk and got my hand on the lever that opened the bank of grimy windows. The door opened. I pulled on the window. It groaned open, almost far enough to squeeze through. I was trying to climb out when a hand fell on my shoulder. It was Oliver Lee, with Cornelia Prime and Marvin Howell in the doorway. Koszler was not there.

"Please, Miss Carr," said Lee. "If you go out there, we'll only have to drag you back. Neither of us need abide any further indignity."

I scrambled into the corner, pressing myself between the wall and a filing cabinet. Something glinted on the top of it—a letter opener. I grabbed it and held it out straight.

"This thing isn't sharp," I said, "but I'm very angry. Another step and you'll get it in the eye."

Lee threw up his hands and turned to Cornelia Prime.

"This is what I've been telling you," he said. "She is impossible."

"Be human," she said. "She's scared."

"Shall I fetch the cop?" said Howell.

"Those were Mrs. Greene's instructions," said Prime. She looked like she hated to say it. I hated it, too.

With a disappointed shake of his head, Howell left to find justice. La Rocca perched his cigar in his mouth and reached for a book. Only Prime looked at me with any feeling, and so I spoke to her.

"Do you really believe I killed them? That I hacked my friends and lover to pieces with, what? An ax? A sword? Do I look like I have the strength for such a crime?"

"My opinion isn't what matters. The police want to speak to you, and Mrs. Greene insists we cooperate."

"That cop wants me dead."

"He didn't mention anything along those lines."

"Please." I was begging now. Perhaps I should have been embarrassed, but I simply didn't care. I would have done anything to get out of that room. "Give me a chance. Let me run."

Prime looked to La Rocca, to Lee. They shook their heads. I set the letter opener down.

"Then let me confess."

For the first time in too long, my enemies looked surprised.

"Excuse me?" said Lee.

"Were you at Eighth Avenue?"

"I didn't have the pleasure, no."

"Koszler and the Fourth Precinct stood in a line, rifles braced against their shoulders, firing indiscriminately into a pack of guardsmen and young soldiers. Children, really. Their bodies clogged the gutters. He will do worse to me. Let me surrender to you or I'll hurl myself out that window. The NYPD will be without their suspect. The cops will tear Spring Square apart looking for another scapegoat. The District will die."

Their smiles wilted. Prime nodded, looking relieved to have an opportunity to be merciful.

"It's a reasonable request." No one disagreed.

I snatched a sheet of stationery off La Rocca's desk and snapped my fingers.

"Come on! Someone give me something to write with!"

With a theatrical sigh, Oliver Lee reached inside his jacket pocket and withdrew a pencil that was sky blue and as sharp as death. I plucked it from his grasp. I kept my eyes on Cornelia Prime, whose cheeks were reddening, and who was very carefully twisting a ring so that its stone faced the inside of her hand.

"Bishop's Blue Streak," I said. "I hear they're the best."

"Shut up and write. If you're not done before—"

Prime smacked her open hand across his cheek. The stone sliced a perfect gash down Lee's cheek. He clapped his hand over it, his mouth gaping, his eyes wide.

"Bitch!" he shouted, rather predictably.

"Where did you get it?"

"Get what?"

"If I step out of the room during our morning meetings, do you take the chance to rummage through my desk drawer? Or do you sneak into St. Abban's after we lock up and steal at your leisure?"

"Are you talking about the pencil?"

He looked to La Rocca, to me, waiting for one of us to acknowledge how ridiculous this situation had become. Neither of us gave him anything.

"I thought we were in the middle of apprehending a murderer, but if we're really stopping to talk about office supplies, I'll state this plainly: I did not steal that damn thing off your desk."

"Then where did you get it? Don't try to pretend you have taste enough to order your own."

"I don't know. Where do pencils come from? You need one, you pick it up. What could be simpler?"

I twisted the object in question until the light caught on its monogram.

"It says *C. P.*," I said.

Prime's neck flexed. A fine trickle of blood ran down Lee's cheek, staining his collar beyond repair. When he spoke, he no longer sounded like he thought this was funny.

"That could stand for anything."

"Only it doesn't," I said. "It stands for Cornelia Prime. A woman who's worked her whole life for a half-decent job. A woman for whom a little piece of wood with her initials on it means absolutely everything."

If I'd been trying to calm them down, it would have been a terribly unhelpful thing to say. But that was not my goal.

Lee started to respond. Prime slammed her hand down on La Rocca's desk.

"You Roebling bastards, you Eastside bastards, you men are all the same. Cross the fence like conquering heroes, ready to make your own little empire, only you forget that we were already here. So you take and you take and you take and you have no idea that someday we will start to take back."

Her breath came in dry, heaving gasps. I took a step toward the door. Only La Rocca noticed what I was doing. He said nothing, and I took another step.

"It's just a pencil," said Lee.

"Maybe for you."

I reached the far side of the room. Lee and Prime were still snarling at each other. Neither looked my way. My little ruse had worked. I could have smiled if I weren't so shocked.

And then I reached for the door. Just before my hand touched the knob, it swung away. My escape had come a moment too late. Koszler filled the door. The look of genial authority he'd put on for the crowd downstairs was gone. In its place was pure, acid hate.

I'd expected him to have something to say to me, some little speech he'd been rehearsing, or even a simple hello. Instead, he swung his cane. It caught me on the side of the head, sending a shock wave through my skull that rattled every part of my body. Red bled across my vision; all I could see was pain.

Back in the office, someone muttered, "Holy hell." I couldn't tell if it was Prime or Lee.

If I'd fallen, I think he'd have killed me, but I stayed on my feet. Swinging the cane left him off balance, so when I threw myself into his chest, he fell hard. His head slapped into the wood; a horrid groan escaped his lips. I landed on hands and knees, and planted a foot on his face as I scrambled away.

I was nearly clear when he got the crook of his cane around my ankle. He pulled hard, and my hands went out from under me. Now it was my turn to smack my face on the ground. I rolled onto my back and found him standing above me, his hand so tight on the cane that his knuckles looked like bare bone.

"You stabbed me in the back," he said.

"You earned it."

"Eight months in the hospital before I could even sit up. Doc said I'd never walk again. He didn't know how badly I wanted a piece of you."

"Those were children you killed, Emil. Honest to god—"

The sentence would go unfinished, I'm sorry to say, for that was when my beating began.

He focused on my back. Shoulders, spine, waist, hips, then back up to the top. Parts of me splintered. Parts of me broke. The individual blows melted together, until it was hard to tell when he was hitting me and when he wasn't. It was an unbroken high note of pain.

After the second blow, my vision narrowed. I drifted away from myself. It seemed to be someone else who struggled, kicked, crawled, screamed. None of it mattered. The band played louder, and no one in the office came to help.

At last, Koszler paused for breath, and I snapped back into myself. I tasted blood. I felt like I had a knife in my spine. I rolled over and got a look at him. His fat seemed to have melted away, and he was the same devil I'd known in '21.

"That's just the start. Wait'll I have you at the station. Wait'll you're in a cell."

He was still stupid, too. He'd been so focused on my beating that he didn't notice the weapon in my hand.

I put everything I had behind it. It sank deep into his thigh. A cheaper pencil would have broken, but despite the soft lead, Bishop made their Blue Streaks to last. I was aiming for his manhood. I'd have settled for a vein. I'm not really sure what part of him I caught, but it bit deep into his leg. He crumpled like gold leaf.

I hurtled down the catwalk, limping wildly. I did not even glance at the stairs. Koszler would be on his feet in a second or two, and he'd be faster than me, and he'd beat my head next time, and he wouldn't stop until my skull was crushed and blood oozed thick from my mouth. I was running for the hatch at the catwalk's end.

It bore no warning labels, no threatening red *X*s, no skull and crossbones. It was labeled "Incinerator," and that spelled danger enough. But Koszler had gotten up and he was calling to me—"Nowhere to hide, detective, nowhere to hide!"—and anything was better than him.

I yanked open the chute. The corner of the opening cut my side as I slipped in. My feet dangled, feeling nothing, and I began to wonder if I was making a huge mistake. Then I saw Koszler tear the pencil out of his thigh and I let go.

EIGHT

For a long time, I fell.

That's not to say that I was plummeting through some ceaseless void. I was clattering down a rusted old chute that was scarcely wider than my shoulders, whose every bent edge seemed to be reaching out for its chunk of Gilda Carr.

If it had been a straight shot down, I'd have fallen to a well-earned death. Thankfully, after what felt like a mile but which was probably more like twenty feet, there was a kink in the line.

My feet slammed into it, sending spikes of pain straight up my tortured spine. I had a mind to catch my breath, but before I could inhale, I felt the chute slipping out beneath me. The metal groaned, and I felt myself sliding into the vast space between the factory walls.

I said something along the lines of "Oh hell oh hell oh hell" and shot out my hands to hold myself against the tube. Now instead of falling I was simply sliding, but the next section of the line continued drifting away. My legs pumped senselessly, touching nothing, and all the blood left my head and charged into my pulsing, overworked hands. If that weren't inconvenient enough, I still had to contend with Koszler, who chose that moment to whisper down the chute.

"You do not escape this, Miss Carr. Tunnels end. We will be waiting. Slip past us and we'll be at your house, on every corner, in every doorway. We are the NYPD. We do not lose."

His voice snaked down as thin and sharp as a piece of copper wire. He was trying to frighten me and he was not ineffective, but his words also gave me a sliver of hope. If he was at the top of the chute he could not be at the bottom. I still had a chance to beat him to the ground.

I slashed my legs out and hooked the lip of the disconnected ducting. Twisting insanely, I was able to hold it steady long enough to slip inside feetfirst.

It swayed like a drunk, threatening to tip me out backward into the innards of the wall. I pulled my knees up and pressed them against my chest, allowing me to brace myself against the metal and continue my descent at something less than maximum speed. At first, the weight of my legs against my ribs hurt immensely, but then the pressure helped to dull the pain.

And then, after another breath, it began to hurt so much more.

And so I continued in a vaguely controlled fall, as fast as I could go without losing my grip. Sweat sluiced down my forehead, and I found myself asking an uncomfortable question.

Could there be any chance, on summer's last weekend, that the incinerator was turned on?

Impossible, I thought. Yes, it was a cool night. Yes, the air sweeping off the river carried the scent of heavy sweaters and pennant race baseball. Yes, women who gamble in shear silk gowns prefer the air warm. But there was no way the fire was lit.

And yet it was beginning to get hot. And as I eased myself around another bend in the ducting, I saw an unmistakable orange glow.

I shut my eyes and crawled on. Breathing hurt more and more. All I could think, as I inched toward the inferno, was that this was such a stupid way to die.

"Cherub would laugh."

I saw him, his arms resting on the lines of the *Misery Queen*, laughter coursing through him—that full-body cackle that soothed me like rain on dry dirt.

I couldn't stand to let him see me looking such a fool, even if it was just in my mind. I forced my eyes open and took advantage of the brightening glow to have a look around. Above me, I saw another hatch—one I'd slid right past while my eyes were closed.

"Damn it."

Going up was harder than going down. My muscles locked, and the pain in my side felt more and more like a twisting knife. The rough edges of the chute tore at my back, dripping rivulets of blood down to the fire. But I dragged myself up to the door, and I kicked until it sagged open, and with one last agonized shove, I launched myself free.

I found myself surrounded by waiters. They stared like I was a corpse risen from the dead. Actually, I thought, a risen corpse probably wouldn't look so tired. The kitchen air was hot, the stink of garbage mingling with rancid oil and burned spices. All work had stopped. Even the steam held still, until the alley door burst open and the police poured inside.

There were three of them, young and eager, looking terribly proud. Their jaws were square and their clubs were raised high. The one in the front, an enterprising lad, spotted me first.

"There she is, boys," he said. He stepped forward, one hand open, like a man preparing to grab a snake.

I rose onto shaking legs. I slipped and caught myself on the incinerator door. That's when the kitchen came to life. Cooks shouted orders; waiters piled plates on trays; busboys dumped cocktail glasses into the sink. The room was as dense as jungle vegetation. The police could not find a path, but the staff just happened to get out of my way.

"Clear the room!" shouted the first of the cops.

"Like hell!" shouted back one of the dishwashers.

I sprinted past the ovens, scanning desperately for another way out. I turned a corner and found myself surrounded by patched trousers, stained work shirts, overalls and moth-eaten sweaters, and raincoats heaped on a few overloaded hooks. Footsteps sounded. I spun and saw a thick-limbed old waiter with a neatly clipped moustache and the sort of downturned mouth that looked as if it had never attempted a smile. He said nothing, did nothing, but his eyes flicked at the wall to his left. Beneath the street clothes I saw the thin outline of a door.

From the kitchen came the wet sound of a club striking skull. There was an explosion of profanity in a half dozen languages. I thrust my arm through the heaped clothes, found the knob, and stepped into the bowels of the factory this building had once been. The door slammed behind me, and I was alone in a lightless passageway where the air was pregnant with growth. I took a careful step. My foot smashed into a pile of empty metal cans. They clattered to the floor, making enough noise that everyone in the world surely knew I was here.

After that, I ran.

As I charged down that darkened hall, the wet air wrapped tight around me. Each breath pulled it deeper into my chest. I swore I could taste the mold.

The hallway terminated at a heavy steel door. It would have been prudent to ease it open and take a look around before stepping outside, but I was finished with prudence and sick of the dark. I hurled the door open. It swung on its hinges and slammed into the wall. The night air poured in like a waterfall. I was at the back of the building, which was so matted with ivy that you couldn't see the brick. The darkness was thick, just like it was supposed to be.

Down the alleyway, the lights of Spring Square glittered. Silhouettes drifted back and forth—the police trying to work out where the hell I'd gone. There was no going back to the District—not while I was this slow or this hurt, not in this yellow dress. But as Koszler had made so perfectly clear, I had nowhere else to run.

A whistle cut through the night.

Ugly La Rocca leaned out his office window, his cigar smoldering in the corner of his mouth. He raised a bottle, then moved his hand like he was about to toss it down. I shook my head. He threw it anyway.

The bottle spun, red glass glinting in the moonlight. It arced over my head, toward the far side of the street. I ran after it like

Fred Snodgrass chasing a fly ball. At my best, I could have gotten just close enough to miss it. That night I was far from my best.

The bottle smashed on the sidewalk. My feet crunched on the shards. I looked up to see La Rocca give a helpless shrug. A crumpled note lay in the center of the shattered glass. La Rocca could have tied it to a handkerchief, but a message in a bottle had poetry, and that was something no Westside tough could resist. I snatched it and, with every part of me bruised or broken or simply screaming in pain, I darted across the alleyway. In the light from Spring Square, my dress shone like a firefly's tail—shockingly bright, gone in an instant. Perhaps I'll get lucky, I thought. Perhaps they were looking the other way.

Not today.

Every cop in the alley saw me. They shouted for their brothers to join them. Their voices were confused, helpless, until Koszler reminded them why they were here.

"Kill on sight!"

They would have, I'm sure, if their guns were working. But these gentlemen had nothing but clubs and rage. If they wanted to kill me, they would have to do it with their hands.

The shadows of two policemen rose on the face of a ruined warehouse, monstrous and twisted and three stories high. I ran, sort of, along a wall of abandoned warehouses and factories sunk halfway beneath the earth. The block was a long one, perhaps a quarter mile, and there was no way I could run its length before the police caught up with me. My only hope was to disappear.

The shadows shrank as the men drew closer, their steps as heavy as everything a cop has ever done. I stopped before a grimy brick building whose ground floor was half underground. One window was roughly level with the street. I kicked the glass from its warped frame and hoisted myself inside. I lowered myself carefully, feet straining for the floor, but the floor was gone.

The warehouse was nothing but a shell, one massive room dropping farther into the earth than I cared to contemplate. I dangled from the windowsill, feet scrambling for a foothold, finding nothing.

I squeezed tight, tighter, waiting for the policemen to pass. But the farther they got from Spring Square, the slower they walked, until they stopped altogether. They were inches away.

A match flared. A cigarette burned.

"I hate it here."

"Upper West's not so bad. My sister-in-law lives there. Sometimes we take the kids."

"At night?"

"No. Not at night."

There was an endless pause. Pain surged in every one of my fingers. I kept them locked on the wood.

"You think she did it? One girl killing all those people. I know what the lieutenant says about her, but I don't know."

"Doesn't matter to me. Sooner we catch her, sooner we go home."

He flicked his cigarette through the window. The butt burned brightly as it fell. I followed it with my eyes, trying to get a sense of how far down the void went. The light vanished before it hit bottom. My fingers began to give.

"Forget it. There's nothing."

"Lieutenant won't like hearing that."

"Like I give a damn. Creepy son of a bitch. I think he likes it over here. Can we go?"

"You scared?"

"Shut up."

"We'll go as soon as you admit you're scared to death."

My right hand slipped. I tried to force it back up, but it was too weak. My left began to give way.

"Okay. Okay. I'm scared."

As his partner laughed, they walked away. I tried to pull myself up but couldn't find the strength. I kicked as hard as I could—once, twice, three times. Finally, a chunk of brick fell away, giving me a toehold. By wedging my feet into the wall, I was able to heave myself back over the sill. I crashed awkwardly into the pavement. I did not mind at all—with all my various aches, the pain hardly registered.

For a few minutes, I just breathed, waiting for the pain to ebb. It didn't. I dropped La Rocca's note on the sidewalk and smoothed it out. The paper was golden, and the words on it were golden as well.

"Had a word with Oliver Lee. The Mudfoots—where gin flows like water."

A bit of Westside code. Any cop would have taken it for gibberish, but its meaning was clear. I got to my feet and continued north. My feet were on Washington Street, but my head was far away, drifting back to an easy April afternoon when Cherub and I visited Hellida for breakfast—nothing in the District rivaled her crepes—and took our time returning to paradise. That day had been lovely until we crossed Eighth Avenue, where a list of names had been scrawled in lime on the face of an old clam bar. It was a memorial to those who had died there, a testament to the vanished Westside gangs.

Cherub insisted on stopping. His smile did not dim as he read the names of his dead rivals and friends, but it became very sad.

"The West Fourth Particulars," he read, "the Claw-Boys, Bart's Heroes. Oh, they were bastards, do you remember them? Brass knuckles on each hand. The Sheridan Sappers—they liked setting fires—the Kneecappers, the Mourning Doves. God, I hated the Mourning Doves."

I let him go on. It was so rare that either of us found the time to mourn, and I did not want to get in his way. He had nearly reached the end of the list when he saw one name, written just a bit bigger than the others, which filled him with unaccustomed rage.

"The One-Eyed Cats?" he said. "The One-Eyed Cats!"

"They died at Eighth Avenue."

"Most of us, yes. Briscoe and Big Anna and Luddy and sweet little Roach, of course, most of us died. But not me!"

"Is that so?"

"The Cats live, damn it! The Cats live! As long as Cherub Stevens pollutes the earth, the One-Eyed Cats will never die."

To prove his point, he let loose the old war cry. Barely managing not to laugh, I took his hand and led him back to the river, as he insisted over and over that the One-Eyed Cats would not perish from the earth.

They were gone now, and so were all the others, broken by civil war and frostbite and hunger and the organized muscle of the Eastside. The last true Westside warrior had been hacked to death on a boat and left to drift in the Hudson. I shook my head—I couldn't dwell on that. I had to focus on the Mudfoots. They sounded like a true relic. That pleased me, for I was a relic too.

The moon shone like a spotlight, but the darkness of the Lower West swallowed it. After a year in the District, I'd lost my night vision. I'd forgotten how quiet footsteps sounded when moss blanketed the street.

Far down an alley, a few dozen Westsiders gathered around a modest fire. Once they would have been singing, but there was little to sing about anymore. The smell of roasted meat and gutter produce drifted on the air, and for a moment, the pain in my stomach outpaced everything else. A woman with long white braids and a silver coat slouched against a wall, gnawing on a nearly bare bone. Her eyes locked on mine and for a moment, I thought she was about to offer a seat by her fire. Instead she sneered.

"Keep walking, tourist. You're a long way from home."

The back of my neck went hot. I wanted to spit at her, to scream my address, to thrash her until she understood that I was Lower West down to the calloused soles of my feet. I walked on, not only because this was no time to pick a fight but because, far down, I understood she was right. I did not belong here. I'd been on the river too long.

Every step seemed to shake a new part of me loose. I was fairly certain I had at least one broken rib, maybe two. The deeper I breathed, the harder they hurt. The less air I got, the slower I walked. By the time I neared Morton Creek, it was all I could do to stay upright. No matter how hard I tried not to think of Cherub, his face was all I saw.

"At least I never have to go back to that goddamned boat."

The words came unbidden. I didn't even realize I was saying them until they were out. And yet, I felt like I had been saying them, over and over, since I dove off the *Misery Queen* into the chill, dark Hudson. Even though it hurt to talk, I decided to voice some other unspoken truths.

"I hated that boat."

Step.

"I hate all boats, I think."

Step.

"Sleeping under the waterline is like being buried alive."

Step.

"Can't move an inch without cracking your head."

Step.

"Can't take a real bath."

Step.

"Can't take a proper shit."

Step.

"Never feel rested, never feel clean."

Step.

"God damn to hell the *Misery Queen*."

The rhyme made me laugh, which sent a new burst of pain coursing along my side, and that made me laugh even harder. I bent double and coughed and laughed and cried until my face was a mess of snot and tears.

I *did* hate that boat. I hated him for dragging me out there. I hated myself for never saying no. I'd never admitted it to myself because doing so would have meant telling Cherub, too, and I'd never been brave enough for that. There was solace in the thought that now, at least, that was one horror I'd be spared.

In the moonlight, Morton Creek looked clear and cool, its current gentle, its depths nothing to fear. It was hard to believe that in a few hundred yards, this water would pour into my Hudson and be remade into something infinite and deadly, but Westside girls get used to watching happy little boys grow up to be killers. This was nothing new.

Ida Greene's distillery towered over the little creek. The women of her distillery worked night and day to quench the District's thirst for raw liquor. Even now, its lights blazed brightly enough to see the *MCD* slashed in white paint across its side. Here gin flowed like water.

I turned into the shadow of the distillery, savoring its fumes. I could almost feel the liquor condensing on my lips. A figure stood in the window on the factory's top floor, its posture sharp enough that it could have been Ida Greene. Once, that woman had protected me. I wondered where that protection had gone.

A year before, it had been easy to tell the Roebling men from Van Alen's people. The Roebling boys were gray, merciless, content to kill ten people if it meant saving a dime. Van Alen's Westsiders were equally savage, of course, but they had a sense of pageantry. They were sentimental about things like life and death, and when they killed, they did it with style. But now Ugly La Rocca had a safe full of cash and a pocket flask; Cornelia Prime and Marvin Howell were as coldly savage as any Roebling goon; and the most stylish man in the District, Oliver Lee, was from the wrong side of the fence. Ida Greene had always cared for the bottom line, but I'd never thought she'd let me die for it. I'd have liked to go in and ask her what had changed. The Roeblings, perhaps, or Diana's Fire—or maybe mercy had simply gone out of style. But I doubted a confrontation with her was something I could survive.

I followed the creek toward the Hudson, seeing no sign of a still. That was not surprising. If the Mudfoots' operation were clearly visible, Ida Greene would have eradicated it. That they were able to operate in the shadow of her distillery was shocking and suggested that they possessed some of the suicidal flair that made the old Westside gangs so special—or they weren't really here at all.

To the south, the lights of the District beckoned, lighting the sky up white. After an hour away, it was hard to believe I'd ever felt at home someplace so bright, crowded, fun.

The sidewalk bent away from the creek. I walked the slippery path between the waterway and a strip of ruined one-story brick buildings whose purpose, if they'd ever had one, was unclear. Before I knew it, I was at the river, which looked a mile wide, and devoured Morton Creek as ravenously as it took everything else.

I'd found nothing, and I was close to accepting that the Mudfoots were elsewhere, or that they'd never existed in the first place.

I worked my way back along the river's lip. This time, I refused to let myself be distracted by the water. I inspected the bankside buildings instead. Just before I reached the street, something turned my head.

It was a mural, seven feet tall and painted so crudely that at first I'd mistaken it for streaks of grime. It was profoundly pornographic, a rendering of a couple making love—as loose an application of that phrase as there had ever been—standing up. Their anatomy was, to put it politely, inexact. Nipples pointed every which way, and none of the relevant organs were quite where nature intended them. There were only two elements of the painting that had been rendered with care: the couple's feet, ankle deep in brown muck, and the bird that hovered above their shoulders.

It was a one-legged seagull, painted in blood red—a precise match for the one that marred the sail of the *Misery Queen*.

"Hell."

There was no question, then, that the Mudfoots had been on the boat. Marka had come after their liquor and so they had come for her. They had killed for the only reason anyone seemed to do anything around here: to protect their profits. Marka's friends had been unwitting casualties.

Cherub, too.

A pipe burst inside my gut, flooding my system with bile. Cherub Stevens, the gentlest gangster the Westside ever spat forth, had been butchered because Marka Watson decided to play journalist. Just for that, I'd have killed her myself. I'd have to be satisfied with killing the Mudfoots instead.

NINE

A mat of grass and reeds lay piled at the base of the wall. I kicked it aside and found a wooden hatch. I wrapped my fingers around the metal ring and pulled. It was locked from the other side.

"Who cares?" I said.

I stomped on the soft wood door. I was prepared to take out an entire evening's frustration on it, giving it a kick for every person who'd tortured me, plus six or seven for Emil Koszler, but the wood caved on the first try. I would have to find some other opportunity to vent my rage.

A ladder stretched into the dark, far below the bottom of the creek. I took a last look at the moon, hoping to soak up some of its light, and began my descent. I made no effort to soften my step. My feet clanged on metal. The echoes traveled far.

Perhaps the Mudfoots would hear me coming.

Perhaps, if they had sense, they would run.

As I climbed, I remembered Barbarossa. The bootlegging queen of the Lower West, she'd ruled her empire from an abandoned subway platform underneath Seventh Avenue, where rusty old pot stills bubbled up liquor that made Ida Greene's red gin look like water from the purest spring. Two years prior, I had slipped into that tunnel with a pistol in my hand and murder on my mind. When I finally saw her, I could not pull the trigger. Because I was soft, hundreds of children died.

That night by Morton Creek, there was no doubt, save a lilting voice that was irritatingly similar to Cherub's and grew louder the farther I got below ground.

"Murder is an ugly thing," it said.

"That's precisely why I'm here."

"Even bootleggers deserve a trial. Even killers."

"Not these."

I spat out my words through clenched teeth. They echoed dully down the crawl space. I hadn't meant to speak out loud, but I couldn't quite stop.

The voice laughed Cherub's laugh, and I hated it even more.

"I love you," it said, "but let's be honest. You're in no shape to play executioner. You can barely grip that ladder."

"I'll find a way."

"In the dark, on their territory, without a weapon, without a plan?"

"That's how I work best."

"Please, Gilda—"

"Don't say my name—"

"You're a detective, not a killer. If you ever get to the bottom of this ladder, lie down and sleep awhile. Find the Mudfoots and talk to them. If you learn they were really on the *Queen,* well, proceed from there."

I grunted. I don't know what I meant by it, but the voice shut up, and that was good enough for me.

The ladder ended. I dropped the last few feet, landing on hard-packed dirt. Twin rails gleamed silver. I was in a tunnel cut for some forgotten train. It should have been absolutely dark. And yet, I could see.

The light was as green as swamp water, and it came from all around. As my eyes adjusted, I saw it was not one unbroken field, but pulsing streaks that wound their way across every surface in the tunnel. I went as close to the glow as I dared. They were plants, as hard and crinkled as coral but with a dusting of glowing moss on top. I brushed my knuckle against one of them. It shuddered, curling in on itself, and its light died. I knew that feeling well. After that, I kept my hands to myself.

Far down the tunnel, halfway to New Jersey, I heard the frail echo of a human voice. I walked that way. The rails sloped sharply. The ground grew damp. I was under the Hudson now.

Intellectually, I understood that rivers have bottoms. I knew the towers of the Brooklyn Bridge rested on caissons buried beneath the East River, where poor men died in darkness that two boroughs might be joined. I understood that tunnels had been cut under the Hudson to link Manhattan and Jersey, but I'd never believed it in my soul. Drifting across the river on the *Misery Queen,* I felt a spike of fear anytime I sank part of myself into the water, for I felt I was touching something infinite and dead. I'd seen the bottom of the Hudson when it crawled with hungry shadows. If there were anything below that, it could only be hell.

The tunnel bent. I came around the corner and discovered a shelter built from driftwood and trash. Beyond it, people sang—a Westside brawler's anthem whose words I'd forgotten but whose tune I loved to hum. Canoes dangled from the ceiling, along with nets filled with boating junk. Wax held stinking candles to the wall. Their light blended with the green of the glowing flowers to turn everything a sickly gray. The walls were decorated with drawings more technically accomplished than the mural on the surface, but far more lewd. In the center of the tunnel, a single figure stood watch. He wore a heavy black coat and a white bowler hat. His hand clutched a sword.

I held still in the shadows. I was certain I had been seen, but he neither advanced nor raised the alarm. He just stood there, candlelight flickering across him, swaying gently in the fetid breeze.

Minutes passed. The singing did not stop. Finally, I stepped into the light. The watchman stared. I approached him, my feet silent on the packed dirt between the railroad ties. Candlelight glinted off his frozen eyes. His mouth hung open and his teeth shone white. His skin was like jerky, and the nails that held him to the wooden frame were black with rust. He had been dead for a long time.

"Who were you?"

He did not reply.

His fingers cracked horribly as I prized them off the sword. It was dull with rust, but it was the best weapon I had.

Within the shelter, the singers pitched their voices higher. There were quite a lot of them, and I was one woman who had no strength and no ideas and a rusty blade. I would have to do better than a frontal assault.

I paced the tunnel, prodding my sword into the sacks that dangled from the ceiling, looking for an idea. Explosives would have been appreciated, or a canister of mustard gas. I found stained rags and rotten fruit. A few crates were stacked carelessly by the door to the shelter. I walked toward them, moving as slowly as I could, trying not to breathe. The singing fizzled into unintelligible conversation. Whoever was beyond that barricade, I hated them for being here, so close to the District and yet so fully hidden. I hated them for having fun. I slid my sword beneath a crate's lid and pressed until it opened. I eased the lid to the floor. I paused for a long, foolish moment, the sword held uselessly in front of me. No one came to investigate the sound.

I nudged aside the shredded paper at the top of the crate to find bottle after bottle of Diana's Fire. I pulled one out and slipped down the tunnel. Once I was out of sight of the Mudfoot bunker, I leaned on the wall, pulled the cork from the bottle, and tried to remember how to think.

The liquor smelled vile, but I'd woken hungover and done little to improve that condition, so this was no surprise. I tipped some of it into my mouth but did not swallow. It burned like, well, fire. I spat it onto the tracks and considered the taste. It was not so different from the gutter liquor I'd been drinking my whole life, but there was something else there. The flavor of nuts, perhaps almonds. I didn't particularly care. One book of matches and I could have burned the whole place to the ground, but the dress I'd borrowed had no pockets and no matches and, even if it had, I'd probably have just gotten them wet.

I was nearly resigned to kicking down the door and fighting until they decapitated me when I noticed a valve. It was mounted on the wall at hip height, perfect for Gilda Carr. It was labeled "Flood Control System," which suggested it was the only thing holding back the Hudson. I wondered what would happen if I twisted it.

I set the liquor bottle on the ledge, gripped the valve with both hands, and turned hard. It did not budge. I braced my hip and pulled as hard as I could. Every place where Koszler's cane had met my skin screamed, but the wheel did not turn.

Down the tunnel, the Mudfoots were singing again. This was a song I knew, "Sweet Mary's Mistake." My father used to sing it when he was working and he thought I couldn't hear, an endless loop of profanity and violence, whispered just under his breath.

Cherub was dead, and they were singing.

I slid the sword into the wheel. I wrapped my hands around the hilt and leaned backward, pulling until I was dizzy with pain. Rust fell like red snow. I let loose an awful scream. The sword snapped in half.

The wheel turned.

Water gushed in fast. I gave it a final twist and, with a horrid shriek, it spun all the way around. Around my calves, the current picked up. The water was ice cold and stank wonderfully of the Hudson.

The Mudfoots were not singing anymore.

I should have run, but I'd been running all night, from people and shadows and a past I was increasingly ashamed of. Before I fled, I felt I deserved to see the fear in their eyes.

The sagging mattress that served as the bunker's door flopped open. The Mudfoots spilled out of their ramshackle hideout as quickly as the water spilled in. The first was as dapper as Cherub always pretended to be, in a shirt open to the navel and a bowler hat that gleamed in the dark. The second had a drooping moustache and sleepy eyes and tattoos from hairline to waist. The rest were cast from the same mold—the sort of picturesque gangsters for whom the Lower West no longer had room.

The pack parted, and the chief waded to the fore. There was no question that she was in charge. She was tall and redheaded, tan as old leather and as strong as bronze. Unlike her crew, she dressed without flair, in a men's checked work shirt and a pair of heavy black trousers. Her hair was slicked back against her head, and her smile was black. Her eyes fixed on me, and I knew it was too late to run.

The water poured down the tunnel, up to her knees, to her hips. It slammed into the dead watchman, knocking him to the floor. Some of the Mudfoots tried to safeguard the crates of liquor; some looked for a way to stop the flood. The chief came for me.

I brandished the broken sword. It was lighter now, its shorn edge sharper than the blade had been when I found it, but it did not worry her. She was laughing when she reached me and did not stop when I swung my blade. Before the blow connected, she had my wrist in her hand, and she squeezed my fingers until I let the sword slip.

"The hell are you?" she snarled.

"Gilda Carr. Survivor of the *Misery Queen*."

I wrenched my arm free and swung a fist at her face. My blow bounced off her cheek. She threw herself at me, her teeth bared, and wrapped her hands around my throat. Her eyes, black and deep, stared through me. Her face remained locked in that same half smile. I thrust my hands at her face, trying to get my thumbs at her eyes, but she shook them off.

She squeezed tighter.

I kicked out with both legs, tumbling backward into the water. For a moment, she let me go. Beneath the water, everything was murky green. I thrashed to the surface, scrabbling my hand across the ledge, looking for the sword.

I found a hunk of concrete.

She grabbed me by the collar, tearing another rent in my much-abused dress. I stumbled backward, crashing into her chest. Her arm closed around my neck. She was about to choke me some more when I bashed the concrete into her cheek. She fell away from me, spitting and smiling, having a wonderful time. The water cleared my collarbone. The parts of me that weren't hurting were perfectly numb.

I held my concrete high. Shouts came from the entrance to the bunker. I wondered why her boys weren't coming to help her and realized it was because she didn't need the help.

She took a swing.

I tried to crack her across the brow with the concrete, but she was faster and her arms were longer and I'd run out of fight about three hours prior. She must have seen me favoring my ribs, because that's where she put her fist.

My side filled with shattered glass. The breath went out of me. The concrete fell away from my hand, and I sank beneath the water. I'd have drowned if she weren't set on killing me herself. She dug her fingers into my curls and pulled hard. My spine cracked like old leaves. She slammed her fist into my temple, and just like that, I wasn't awake anymore.

What followed had no shape, no color, merely shifting lines that swirled and twisted and stubbornly refused to cohere.

They danced to the song of Cherub's death.

He screamed pitifully—"Please! Please!"—until a wet *thunk* stopped his voice. And then it was only choking and gurgling as the city's one good man died.

I woke in a place that did not quite qualify as a room. It was nearly pitch dark. Hammocks and foot lockers surrounded unidentifiable boating mess, metal drums, and ruined food. There was no ceiling, save for the curved stone of the tunnel roof, whose weight seemed at odds with the flimsy structure below.

The water had gone down to just six inches, perhaps a foot. It would have been negligible if I had been right side up, but I was bound to the shelter wall with heavy chains, my feet in the air, my head dangling barely above the flood.

I screamed. It was a banal reaction, but when one is hanging upside down in the pitch dark nowhere, wit runs short. I screamed and thrashed, trying to tear the chains loose and succeeding only in making the boards they were lashed to creak. I kept up my racket until a head poked through the doorway—the man in the bowler hat. He smiled like he'd been offered a lobster dinner.

"Hello, sweetness," he said.

"Get me down, you ass."

"After I went to all that trouble tying you up?"

He cried over his shoulder: "It's awake!" The chief strode into the room, looking even bigger than she had before. Her trousers were soaked and there was a nasty bruise on her cheek, but our little battle had left no other mark. I had not been so fortunate. Every part of me hurt terribly, and there was so much blood in my head that I thought my eyes might burst. The water had me cold, fighting not to shiver, but she smiled like she loved it, like she'd been born in the water and had never lived a minute onshore.

But as I looked at her, I realized that was not true. I saw her younger, skinnier but still quite strong, scurrying up Washington Square's tallest trees, the ones that touched the sky. She was a few years younger than me—young enough that when the change came to the Westside, she had still been a child—and she climbed those trees fearlessly. She'd been one of Cherub's One-Eyed Cats. Her name was Amelia Slaybeck, but Cherub called her Gilly. She hated that. She fought relentlessly, and when there was no one to fight she worked, hacking at the brush around the square, building forts for the younger Cats. She moved constantly, as though she'd be struck dead if she ever stood still. The only time I ever saw her at peace, in those long years when I spent most of my hours watching the world outside my window, was on the first days of spring, when she would climb those high trees and admire her new green world.

Any hope of a cheerful reunion was dashed when she bent low and grabbed a fistful of my hair.

"Filthy girl. Needs a bath."

Whatever I was going to say was drowned out by another shout from the man in the bowler hat—"Turn it back on! Nice and easy!"—and the sound of liquid trickling into the room. The water below my head began to rise.

"This is insane," I said.

"Ain't it? You should know, dearie, you're on trial for your life. You don't try to drown my gang and live."

"Then why aren't I dead yet?"

"I'm one of those funny creatures. When there's something puzzling me, I just have to know why." I could respect that feeling. "I'd like to know what brings you here. Answer wrong and you'll die."

I could respect that, too. "And if I answer right?"

"I can't imagine a reason good enough for me to let you live, but hey—I'm always willing to be surprised."

She let go of my hair. It floated on the water, which was high enough to wet my scalp. It would be worth it, I felt, to speak quickly.

"You attacked my boat."

"That'd be the *Misery Queen*?"

"You killed my lover. You killed my friends. You—"

"It was never your boat."

"What?"

Slaybeck got closer, smiled bigger. Her breath smelled of mint. I could not imagine why.

"You're Cherub's girl, then? He used to talk about you all the time. 'The flower of the Lower West. The sweetest maniac in the world.' He wanted to make a life with you—those were his words, 'make a life.' Pathetic, middle-class delusion, but who am I to deny a man his dream?"

"Get to the point before I drown."

She leered.

"A year back, Cherub Stevens needed a boat. He wanted to steal it, but he didn't know how. So he came to me. We plucked the *Queen* off the Eastside docks. He owed us seven hundred fifty dollars for the trouble. We asked him nice. We asked him rough. He didn't respond. So we got serious. First we took your bird, that fat little seagull with the absent leg. It was supposed to scare Cherub into doing right and paying his debt. We thought about taking you, but took a vote on it and decided the bird would make better eating."

"You ate her."

"Meant to. Scrappy little thing got away. Cherub wasn't so quick. Oh, you should have heard him when we came aboard. Begging for his life, for his friends."

If she'd been three inches closer, I'd have bitten her nose. Instead, I contented myself with spitting a fat glob of phlegm. It landed in her eye. She acted like she didn't care, but I know from experience that nobody enjoys spit in their eye.

She snapped her fingers. The man in the bowler hat shouted another message up the corridor: "Quicker now!" The water rose faster. It was nearly at my eyes.

"What about Marka?"

"The tall woman, the one who'd been so interested in our booze? She made quite a fuss over Cherub. Got haughty, very 'Don't you know who I am?' I told her I didn't know and didn't care. When I knocked Cherub out, she threw a bottle at me. I cracked her across the jaw."

"And the rest of them?"

"They weren't just drunk. They were weak, like children or invalids. I told the boys to take their wallets and jewels while I climbed the mast to mark the sail."

"What next?"

"I was up there for a while. I always liked a view, you understand, and I had to make sure the gull looked nice. Then I came back down and we got underway."

"You killed Marka because she was writing about your liquor. Why did the others have to die?"

The water was over my eyebrows. I had to tilt my head to keep it out of my eyes. It was terrifying, I suspect, but I was too focused on Slaybeck to care. She ran her tongue across her lips, thinking for longer than I could afford before she said, "Dearie, I never killed anyone at all."

"Bullshit. Cherub and the rest of them—they were killed, skinned, and minced."

She cackled. Her laugh was dry, dead. Like Marka's.

"Gowdy!"

He pushed his hat back until it was barely on his head. My neck was in agony, but I couldn't let it dip without getting water in my nose.

"Aye?" he said, finally.

"Did we kill a boat full of people last night?"

"We did not."

"You certain? Don't think you might have—what was it?—*minced* anyone, and it just slipped your mind?"

"That's the kind of thing I'd recall."

Slaybeck cupped her hands under my head. I relaxed my neck, and she held me above the water. I didn't want her help, but there was nothing to do but accept it.

"So that's what you're here for?" she said. "To avenge Cherub and Marka and all those other wastes of space?"

"That was the idea."

"Barely even scratched me."

"I'll do better next time, I'm sure."

It wasn't a very funny thing to say. It certainly didn't merit the response it got from the next room. Through the loose collection of driftwood that made up the Mudfoots' wall, there came a chuckle that bloomed into full, roaring laughter.

Slaybeck removed her hands. My head tipped backward, and water shot straight up my nose. I pulled my head up, coughing and spluttering, and found that no matter how I strained, the water was nearly at my mouth. I was about to let my head drop, to give in to the river, when it occurred to me that I had heard that lunatic laughter before.

A heavenly day on Washington Square. A boy in stolen clothes, reclining in a battered armchair, swilling stolen liquor, and laughing at the sight of other people hard at work—that laugh as sweet and gentle as the world is cruel, that full-body cackle, a laugh like rain on dry dirt.

My pain was gone, my fear with it. The water rose higher and higher but it could not touch me—nothing could touch me—because Cherub Stevens was alive.

TEN

I don't know where I found the strength. I kicked my legs forward– once, twice, maybe more—and felt the world slide away. The chains around my ankles tore through the wall. Slaybeck's eyes went wide as she got out of the way. There was horror in her expression and, if I may flatter myself, a bit of awe. My legs tipped over my head, and I crashed face-first into the rising flood. It was not a graceful landing, but I was free.

Free, but drowning. I swallowed half the Hudson as I struggled to my knees. When I got above water, Slaybeck was reaching for me. I clasped my hands and swung wildly, clattering the chains that dangled from my wrists against her chest. I don't think I hurt her, but I got her out of my way.

The doorway was empty. Chains dragging behind me, I lurched into a kind of hallway, which sagged to its side like a blanket fort on the verge of collapse. Gowdy was down the corridor in what might have been the kitchen, banging two iron pots together.

"She got loose! Tore the whole damn wall off—you gotta see!"

Soon the entire gang would be on top of me. I did not care.

The next room was secured with a door made of flattened barrel staves. It was locked, in a way, by a piece of rope tied to a nail. I was fumbling with the rope when I heard Slaybeck splashing out of the storeroom. She reached out with wet hands.

"Don't be stupid, detective."

The only stupid thing would be to waste time responding. I

slammed my shoulder into the door. The staves came loose, and the door opened enough for me to slip inside. The drying fish that hung from the ceiling made the little room stink like the belly of a whale. There was no light here, but the candles in the hallway shone brightly enough for me to see the figure huddled in the corner with his hands over his eyes.

It was him.

I wrapped my hands around his face, feeling the stubble, the swelling, the bruises, the cuts. They'd given him clothes—it was so strange to see him in a shirt—but had not bothered chaining him because he could hardly stand. He wasn't going anywhere. I inhaled his breath and was surprised my chest did not burst. His head slumped against my shoulder. I dug my fingers into his hair and pressed him tight. He kissed my neck softly, the way that only he could, and every blow I'd taken on the way here was worth the pain.

"Darling," I whispered.

He did not reply.

Slaybeck's hands clamped down on my shoulders. Before I could speak, she hurled me into the hallway. I slammed into the wall, shaking the entire establishment, and then she had me in the crook of her arm, dragging me to the galley, which was stained black and dripping wet. Everything below waist height had been soaked and flipped on end. Nets hung from the ceiling, bulging with hooks, tackle, rope, dried meat, bottled liquor, and bits of metal that I was not seaworthy enough to identify. The lanterns were out; the only light came from a candelabra that dangled from the ceiling, where six stubby candles gave off greasy smoke. The whole place had the damp, ashy smell of an extinguished campfire. The water was around knee high and still trickling in through the gash that served as a front door.

Gowdy watched Slaybeck sit me down on a metal drum. With him were a pair of women with shaved heads and grim, bony faces who stared at me like they were waiting for permission to disembowel. The rest of the crew was trying to find somewhere to bail the water. They paid no attention to me. I glanced around, looking for a weakness. I saw nothing, but that did not trouble me. Cherub Stevens lived, and that meant there was nothing I could not do.

Slaybeck smacked me across the face. I barely felt it. She'd been hitting much harder before. She considered slapping me a second time, but instead leaned back, her hands on her hips. I wondered what brand of grease she used to keep her hair slicked back. After all our brawling, not a strand was out of place. She was flushed, fighting to control her anger, to be as unflappable as a captain is meant to be.

"Do you know," she said, "I try very hard not to kill people?"

"A true humanitarian."

"I give chances and second chances. I hear them out. And how do they thank me?"

"Tear a hole in the goddamned wall," said Gowdy. The bald women laughed until Slaybeck's scowl told them to stop.

"So it was pure human kindness that caused you to keep him alive?" I said.

Slaybeck tapped her fist against her palm.

"He's alive because we were friends once, and he was the only man in New York who could make me smile. He's alive because he swore he'd come up with the money if we gave him a day to think, even though I already gave him more than a year and he didn't produce a dime. But mostly, he's alive because I'm a pirate, not a killer. There's enough death on this river without me adding to the toll."

"You beat him until his eyes swelled shut."

"Well, yes. The crew must have their fun."

"Let him go."

"Happily. For seven hundred fifty dollars."

As perfectly impotent rage simmered in my chest, two of that celebrated crew, stripped to the waist and gleaming with water and sweat, trudged through the door, carrying a crate of Diana's Fire. They dropped it at Slaybeck's feet. Glass and water sloshed around.

"A bit of care!" she said.

"No point. These flipped on end when the water hit. Every bottle's shattered."

"The rest?"

"The same."

I admit that I took some satisfaction from this news. My little flood hadn't managed to kill any Mudfoots, but at least I spoiled their operation. Smiling to keep herself from screaming, Slaybeck pointed to the back of the bunker. The crew filtered out, and we were alone in that ruined room.

"You are a pestilence," she said. Her voice was lower now, all swagger drained, and I saw her for the first time as a woman who was simply overworked and overtired.

"I do try."

"In the space of an hour, you have ruined my home, disrupted my crew, and destroyed our stock."

"Credit, please! It was more like fifteen minutes."

"And you still think we slaughtered the people on your boat?"

I took a long look at her, slouching lazily against the wall, her hands like meat hooks at her hips. Somewhere in there was the girl I knew a decade prior, who worked until her palms were raw and still had strength to climb the trees to gaze at the clouds. But no one could spend so long on the river and remain the same.

"Why do you care what I think?" I said.

"Don't think I didn't recognize you. The girl in the window on Washington Square, too proper to play with the street kids. Cherub's favorite. I could never decide if I wanted to impress you or break your spine. I wish I could have done both."

"I was always jealous of you and the Cats."

"Then you were a stupid, spoiled fool."

Almost laughing, she sat on the nearest drum. Her thumbs tapped out a gentle rhythm. The container was empty and so was she.

"That crew . . . Some of them have been with me ten years. I promised freedom from work, from hunger, from boredom. I promised the river, and we live in a cave."

"A well-appointed cave."

"Even so. You know what we did at Eighth Avenue?"

"I don't recall seeing you there."

"Damn right. The kids wanted to go. Strapped knives to their wrists, painted their faces river green. I blocked the door."

"You saved their lives."

"Worst mistake of my life. They could have died like legends, had their names up on the wall. Instead . . . lord. Now there's nothing left. The NYPD has come to the Hudson; there are Peacekeepers on every dock. There's everything to steal and no way to get it."

"There must be other rivers."

"They wouldn't be ours. We laid in the liquor as a nest egg. Now that's gone, too."

"Was Marka right? Is the liquor toxic?"

"You tell me."

She flipped her barrel on its end. In the dim light, I could just make out the brand painted on the lid.

MCD.

"You're stealing your booze from Ida Greene."

"The woman's a great head for business, but not so sharp when it comes to locking doors. Last month we jumped a couple of her workers, stole a copy of the schedule. Right when a batch is done, before they stain it with the beets, we row up and help ourselves to a couple drums. Cut it with creek water, pour it in those lovely pink bottles, which we nicked from a glass factory on Long Island Sound, and we've got high-class booze. If folks think it's different from the run-of-the-mill red gin, well, that's just marketing."

A pirate, indeed. She should have been in finance. No banker on Wall Street would have been safe.

"Wouldn't it be easier to make your own?"

"If you like honest work. We don't. So if our product's killing people, it's the fault of Ida Greene."

"I've lived two years on MCD gin. It's vile, but not poison."

"Formulas change. She could put anything she wants in that and no one would question it as long as it got them high. How can you be sure?"

Because in the entire firmament of Westside villainy, no star was fixed as tightly as Ida Greene. She ran clinics; she saw that children had clothes to wear and books to read and fresh rolls to eat. When she killed, she did it thoughtfully. She was ruthless, certainly, but not devious. With Ida Greene, you always knew where you stood.

Or so I'd always wanted to believe. But a woman who'd ask Ugly to turn me over to the NYPD was capable of anything. I had trusted her too much for too long.

"I'll have to speak to her," I said.

"And what makes you think I'm going to let you leave?"

"You stopped hitting me."

"That doesn't make us friends. My crew watched you destroy our home, and over what? Because you thought I'd killed a man who's alive in the next room, and a bunch of rich bastards I'd never even met. If I let you leave, they'll mutiny."

"What if I can get your money?"

She cocked her head and drummed her fingers on her cheek. I wondered if she'd been working me around to this the entire time.

"Here's the offer," she said. "Get me the seven hundred fifty dollars by dawn and Cherub walks free."

"Why dawn?"

"My gang's got no future here. We've been faking it for a while, and we were not quite hanging on, and then a demon in a yellow dress came and blew up what little we had. When morning comes, we sail."

"For where?"

"A half-wise woman once told me that there must be other rivers."

"She sounds like a fool. If I'm not back by then, you'll take Cherub with you?"

"Do I look like I can support a freeloader? If you're not back by dawn, we tie him to a chair and throw open that valve of yours. Figure we'll just make it to the surface before he drowns."

"I see."

"Where you getting the cash?"

I shrugged, trying to look mysterious. I think both of us knew I had no idea. I'd been improvising ever since I jumped off the *Misery Queen*. It had been working terribly, but I would have to keep on.

"Why not let Cherub come with me?"

"If I let you out of here with him, I'd never see either of you again."

"You have my honor as a detective, as a Westsider, as—"

"Shut up."

She grabbed my chains. They cut my skin. I did not let her see the pain. She slipped a key from her shirt and opened the lock. The chains sank into the black water around my feet.

"I'll need a favor," I said.

"You just got one."

"The police are combing the District for a woman in a yellow dress. You'll never see a dime unless I get something else to wear."

"Jesus."

She spat in the water, then leapt onto a ladder. She pulled a fistful of rags from one of the hanging nets—a man's shirt and trousers, gray from too much washing and too much wear. She did not turn away while I changed.

"Ribs hurt?" she asked.

"Like they're packed with nails."

She nodded, pleased by that bit of good news. I finished buttoning the shirt.

"If all it takes to get rid of you is an old suit of clothes," she said, "it's good business."

"Much appreciated. One last request—"

"Go to hell."

"Before I leave, can I see him once more?"

She shook her head. Fury rose in my chest. It was hard to believe anyone could be so callous, but she was a pirate, and I *had* tried to drown her. She saw how angry I looked, and that made her smile.

"You're wasting minutes, detective. Dawn comes soon."

She flopped into a sodden, moldy armchair. She enjoyed watching me leave.

The space outside the bunker looked like it had survived a hurricane. Smashed crates and split nets had scattered their contents across the train tracks. Shards of glass littered the ground. The few candles that had survived cast nearly no light, and my mind filled the dark by conjuring up images of Cherub, broken and speechless and ready for death but not yet dead. They were little comfort. I should have been running. I should have been filled with fire, with inspiration, but every step that took me away from him became harder to take.

The tunnel bent. I stopped walking. I let my hand rest on the flood control valve. The last bottle of Diana's Fire rested unbroken on the wall. In the candlelight, the pink glass glowed darker than blood.

A miracle had come to pass. This was the Lower West, so it was an ugly miracle, a violent one. But it was magnificent nonetheless.

Cherub Stevens lived.

I could not turn that miracle away.

My hand closed around the ruby bottle. The glass was heavy. It fit nicely in my hand. Before, I had trudged. Now I ran, skipping lightly across the water, and swept into the Mudfoot lair like a second flood. Slaybeck was where I'd left her—sitting in the old chair, her knees spread wide. She started to stand. She started to speak. She finished neither before I smashed the bottle against her skull.

The bottle did not break. That surprised me. There was no rain of glass, no pouring blood. It took one hard thump, and the fight left Amelia Slaybeck. Her head snapped to the side. Her eyes sagged. She slumped across the chair. My chest heaved as I waited for her crew to storm the room, but they had not heard a thing.

I slipped down the hallway, easing my feet in and out of the water, trying not to splash. I found Cherub where I'd left him: a helpless lump in a stinking room. His mouth was open; his gaze was flat.

"On your feet," I hissed.

When he did not stand, I wrapped my arm around his chest and pulled until his legs remembered what to do. I was in agony, but he was not much bigger than me, and my body did what I needed until his came through.

The candles in the hallway showed every bruise, every streak of clotted blood that marred his perfect skin. His lip was split. One eye was swollen shut; the other was streaked with red. Even so, he was the most handsome thing I'd ever seen.

I marched him to the front room, where Slaybeck remained slumped in her chair. As we passed her, Cherub's eye went wide. He brushed her with his hand. She stirred—was she reaching for him?—and the chair toppled. She splashed into the water and, at last, the Mudfoots were roused.

A voice cried from the back—"The hell was that?"—and one of the bald girls stepped into the doorway. At the sight of the sinking chief, her mouth twisted into a sneer that showed off a very unusual set of teeth—some blackened, some missing, some covered with pointed steel.

"By god."

"Stop us," I said, "or save her. Choose quick."

Her eyes flicked to Slaybeck, facedown in the water on the floor. The chief was writhing—slowly, thoughtlessly, like an eel. She would be dead soon, and the bald girl knew it. She dropped to Slaybeck's side and let out a guttural cry for help. Deep in the bunker, her companions stirred.

I did not have to tell Cherub to flee. In the entire sordid history of the Lower West, no one had ever run quicker from a fight. He bolted out of the bunker's front door and I did the same. It's hard to say which of us was in more pain.

Before we reached the bend in the tunnel, the Mudfoots were in pursuit. It was nearly all of them: Gowdy in his bowler and the second bald girl looking magnificent in her rags. There was the one with the tattoos, and another with a glistening naked chest, and a third wearing an eye patch that simply had to be an affectation. Some of them looked truly fearsome; the others simply wet and sad. But it didn't really matter who was who or how they looked because they all had knives in their hands.

We ran, blood pounding in our ears, fear hot in our mouths, Mudfoots a few lengths behind. The rails sloped up and the earth dried out. The streaks of glowing creatures gave just enough light to show the ladder bolted onto the tunnel wall. Normally, Cherub would have insisted that I go first, forcing us into a tedious argument about the oppressive nature of chivalry. That night, decorum was out the window. He threw his foot onto the first rung and hurled himself up. I followed as quickly as I could. I was halfway to freedom when the Mudfoots caught up.

They attached like leeches. The first one to grab me was the woman with the eye patch. I slammed my heel down on her face. She crumpled. Another pair of hands gripped my ankles. It was Gowdy this time, and he was stronger than he looked. I could not kick; I could not shake him free.

"Come on, girlie. Come on back down."

He pulled, laughing obscenely. One of my hands slipped off the ladder. The other strained. I hooked my elbow around the rung and squeezed. If he wanted me, he'd have to break my arm. I didn't think he'd mind.

Cherub tried to help, the dear. He was far above, almost at the exit. He dropped down a rung or two and extended an arm, trying to grab hold of some part of me, but it was useless. He was too far away, he was too weak, and there was no way he could get back before I fell.

What a waste the day had been. Aside from one stabbed cop and one bludgeoned pirate, I'd accomplished nothing but survival, and it was getting harder and harder to see the point. If a person can only survive through violence, through hiding, through absorbing punishment and acting like she doesn't mind, life stops looking so attractive.

Except that Cherub was alive, and that was reason enough to hurt a little more.

I squeezed tighter. The pain was remarkable, but nothing I hadn't encountered before. Gowdy loosened his hold, trying to climb alongside me to get a better grip. I punished him for it, stomping on his fingers until my boot cut through to bone. He didn't fall, but by the way he screamed, he didn't like it. More hands wrapped around my ankles, my calves—too many to count, too many to resist.

My arm slipped.

I was about to let go when the hatch above us opened, and light poured in.

It was white and glittering, so cold you could almost see your breath. The Mudfoots were blinded. So was I. Their grip eased. I kicked once more, enough to free myself, and scurried up the ladder with my eyes squeezed shut. Remarkably, I managed not to fall. I was nearly at the top when Cherub grabbed me by the wrists and dragged. It was a little bit like flying, but it hurt to holy hell. I crashed onto the wet earth, right beside the Bourget Device whose blinding light had saved us both. I didn't know what it was doing there and I certainly didn't care. I slammed the hatch down so hard it splintered—hopefully on a Mudfoot's head—and together we dragged the Device on top of it. Its weight would hold them for a minute, maybe more.

"You pulled me out," I gasped. "You should have run."

"Don't be a fool."

His voice was flat, and even forcing out those few words seemed to hurt. I wrapped my hand around his—light, dark, light, dark—and led him down the mossy creek bank toward an alley. I wanted to run, but I could hardly lift my legs. Somewhere, I hoped, we would find a quiet corner to sit, to rest, to whisper all the things I had neither the courage nor the breath to say.

"Where did you get the light?" I said.

"Just sitting there. Whole bank lit up, clear as day. No sign why."

We'd nearly reached the alley when that particular mystery was solved. A cop rounded the corner. When he saw us, he broke into a run. He was young. His face was as soft as a baby's, and his eyes and shield shone brightly. This would be his first ever Westside patrol, probably his first trip beyond the fence.

He looked terrified. Smart boy.

"Stop!" he barked. We stopped. Cherub pulled his hand away

from mine, a quiet gesture that filled me with a new kind of dread. The cop approached us, his hand resting lightly on his club.

"Were you interfering with that light?"

We did not answer. This did not make the policeman any happier.

"That is city property, NYPD property, put there to flush out a killer, and if I find you disturbed its operation . . ."

He trailed off. He was looking past us now, staring at the light. It was shaking violently as the Mudfoots attacked the hatch below. They thumped on it once, twice. It did not quite fall.

I risked a glance at Cherub. He had a look on his face like he was about to do something brave. Before he enacted whatever piece of foolishness he had in mind, I threw myself at the policeman's feet. I'd spent all night swallowing my fear. Now, I let it loose.

"She's after us," I said. "Please, god, help. Please!"

"What the hell are you talking about?"

"The detective! The killer with the yellow dress and ragged curls! We was sleeping in the tunnels and she attacked us and we ran and we got up through that hatch and she's going to tear us apart."

"Whoa, girl. It's all right. I'm here to help."

I glanced up at him. He was smiling now, warm and friendly, so happy to have a maiden to rescue. I clasped his hand.

"You don't know what it's like over here for an honest woman, how much it means to have real police on our side."

Another thump on the hatch. The Device tilted farther this time, almost toppling before it slammed back into place. The next one would get it. I squeezed the policeman's hand. He wiped the back of his other hand across his wet mouth, clasped the handle of his club, and drew it like he was pulling a broad sword.

"There's more cops on the next block," he said. "Find 'em. Tell 'em Jenkins has cornered Gilda Carr."

I got to my feet, grabbed Cherub by the wrist, and ran. We bolted toward the alley where rusted metal littered dead grass. Beside us, the walls of a factory had been shorn off as if by a bomb blast. Inside, the ruins of massive sewing machines lay broken on the floor, like the corpse of some unknown beast.

The Mudfoots gave the Device one more thump. The hatch tore open. The light slammed to the ground, sending an insane swirl of shadows dancing down the alleyway.

“Stop,” shouted Jenkins. “This is the—”

That’s as far as he got. There was a thud, a crack. By the time we reached the sidewalk, he wasn’t even screaming anymore.

Poor Jenkins.

We kept running.

ELEVEN

"Your attention, please! The New York Police Department is offering a thousand dollars for information leading to the capture of the fugitive Gilda Carr. When last seen, she wore a yellow dress and short black curls, but her disguise may change. She is ruthless, cunning, and dangerous. Do not attempt to apprehend her. Notify the nearest policeman and this most generous reward will be yours."

The policeman stood on a barrel at the north end of the Boardwalk, where the District's pleasure palaces gave way to shanties and open pits of sin. His chest was broad and his belly strained his uniform. After a deep breath, he began his message again. His voice was loud enough to carry all the way to Long Island, but he would be hoarse by morning—assuming I were still alive then.

"Are you all right?" I said.

Cherub didn't answer, and I didn't blame him. It was a stupid question. We were leaning on the rail where the Boardwalk died, watching people in various states of intoxication stagger from saloon to saloon. No one paid any attention to us here. Cherub chewed on his split lip. I didn't know if I'd ever seen him be quiet for so long.

"This is a nightmare, yes, but we will not survive it without each other," I said.

"You're right."

"So tell me what you need."

"Water. To drink, to clean off the blood. And I'm so hungry, Gilda, my god—"

"Say no more."

Just down the Boardwalk, a thick-chested man with a bulbous nose and a cartoonish moustache was selling sausages. The smell was intoxicating, and I'd noticed Cherub darting his eyes toward it even before he mentioned that he was hungry. I had no money, of course, but such a thing was no object for a daughter of the Lower West. I simply waited until the vendor turned to deal with a pair of customers who were both drunk and indecisive, and snatched as many sausages as I could carry. Cherub looked at me like I was a god.

"For water," I said, "right this way."

At the Boardwalk's end, a flight of untrustworthy steps led to the riverbank. Cherub and I sat in the mud, water lapping at our ankles, watching the moon shimmer on the Hudson. We drank from the river and ate until our stomachs hurt, and then I washed the blood off his face. By the time I was done, he looked nearly at peace. And so, naturally, it was time to spoil his fun.

"You said *you* stole that boat," I said. "Why did you lie?"

"Take a guess."

He said it like it was funny. I tried not to let my anger show, but I didn't try that hard.

"Let me see. You spent a week marching up and down the waterfront looking for likely candidates. You saw a sloop, fell in love, tried to steal it, bungled it terribly. You were out of practice, afraid to get caught. You were too proud to admit that you failed."

His skin burned red. I'd hit the mark.

"When it comes to something as technical as boat theft," I went on, "there's no shame in going to the professionals. I wouldn't have thought any less of you."

"It wasn't just you. It was every crook on the waterfront, every refugee from the old gangs. I've lived outside the law my entire life. The idea that I couldn't steal a simple boat . . ."

He sighed. I waited for him to finish his thought. He didn't.

"What bothers me," I said, "what I would call indefensible—is that when the Mudfoots began threatening you, when they kidnapped our pet, you didn't see fit to tell me what was going on."

"I know."

"I could have helped."

"That's precisely what I didn't want."

I took a deep breath, resisting the urge to smack the mud. I was afraid that once I started hitting things, I wouldn't be able to stop.

"Don't tell me this was some absurd masculine fantasy about 'handling it all yourself.'"

"No, god no. I just . . . didn't want to spoil what we had. When we came here, you were so desperate to get away from, well, everything. You deserved to rest as long as you could. Our time here, the boat—it was a dream that I wanted very badly to be real. I'd have done anything to . . ."

He sucked in air, and I realized he was trying not to cry. I placed my hand on his, and my anger washed away.

"Anyway, it was one of the stupidest mistakes I've made in a long career of stupid mistakes, and I'm sorry."

"It's fine. Totally fine."

He smiled. Perhaps it was the lights from the Boardwalk, but some of the old twinkle had come back into his eyes.

"You sound like you really mean that."

"I do. I don't care about the boat or the lies, darling. I don't care at all."

I kissed him then, because it seemed the thing to do. He melted under my touch, all tension gone. I had told the truth, and that terrified me. I truly didn't care.

"I heard what you told Gilly," he said. "Marka and the others. All of them dead?"

"All but Stuy. God protects drunks and fools, and he's both."

"But the rest of them, lord. It's an idea I can't really catch hold of."

"Spend a few minutes crawling through their blood, and it will become quite clear. Did the Mudfoots kill them?"

"Not that I saw. I was busy being bludgeoned, of course, but as far as I could tell, when we left the *Queen* everyone else was still alive." His eyes closed for a few breaths. "Once this is done and we're tolerably safe, I'm going to need to spend a few days crying."

"Until then?"

"We'll just have to keep having fun."

He chuckled. It sounded forced, but I was grateful for the effort. I had so missed his laugh.

"I want to get the hell out of here," he said.

"Squatting in the Hudson mud isn't romantic enough for you?"

"I mean, I want to run as fast and as far as we can."

"It's impossible."

"If we could get to the boat—"

"The boat is gone."

"Then the town house. There's money there. Hellida will give us shelter, food, and—"

"The police are watching it. They are watching everywhere. Emil Koszler assured me that they will kill on sight." Some people couldn't get over being stabbed.

"That bastard? I thought he was dead."

"If only."

He squeezed his hands so hard that his fingers paled. His terror was real, and it was all consuming.

"When the Mudfoots stormed the boat, I didn't yell. I knew you were sleeping, and I was afraid of waking you up."

"Why?"

"Because you'd have fought them, and they'd have killed you, and that would be worse to me than anything they could do. I want you safe, Gilda. It's the only thing in the world I want."

"Say we run. By some miracle, we escape the police. We sneak across the fence. We find money enough to get out of New York. Where do we go?"

"Hoboken? Philadelphia? Albany or Rochester or Buffalo, Boston even, or Canada. They must have cities in Canada."

"Wonderful. So we make our way to Hoboken or Albany or any of those other glittering metropolises. We look for work. I'm barred for being a woman, you for being Black. We seek an apartment but find no one daring enough to tolerate a Black man and a white woman living under the same roof. Perhaps we make the cosmic mistake of having children, and—"

"Stop, will you?"

"There's nowhere else in the country that you and I can live openly. Anywhere else, in this state or any other, they would kill you for loving me. We only have the Westside."

His mouth was tight, the way it got when he was trying not to scream. I stepped closer to him. Sweat collected on the lip of his collarbone. I ran my thumb along it, wiping his chest dry.

"You'd rather live apart than die together," I said.

"Yes."

"That's terribly sensible."

Above our heads, the crowd swept on: hundreds of miserable, giddy bastards, out for fun, ignoring us the way only New Yorkers can. The music was earsplitting and the lights were too bright. The Hudson slapped against the Boardwalk's supports, insistent, a child refusing to be ignored. Words came to my lips—words I had been thinking for a very long time.

"I belong to New York. New York belongs to me. Dig me up and plant me elsewhere and I'd die in a week. For me to stay, the police must be satisfied that I didn't kill those people. I need satisfaction, too. People died on our boat. They were innocents, more or less. They deserve . . . something. If you can't help, go to Screaming Minnie's. Tell her I sent you. At dawn she'll have you on a boat to wherever you'd rather be."

He wrapped his arms around me and squeezed hard. I wondered if I was crying again. I could not tell what was more frightening—that he might actually go or that some part of me did not want him to stay.

For a long time, there was no sound but his ragged breath. Then he gave his answer.

"I lost you once. I've no interest in making that mistake again."

I stepped back from him. We looked at the water long enough for both of us to dry our eyes.

"Then it starts with the birds," I said, grateful to fix my mind on a concrete horror. "They're dying by the hundreds. An awful death, feathers falling out, skin bleached and wrinkled. Why?"

"Who cares?"

"Marka did. At first she thought it was the liquor. But if the Mudfoots aren't poisoning it, Ida Greene might be."

"Should we go to her? If she's behind this, we could end it there. If she's not, she may help us."

I shook my head. I was far from ready to confront Ida Greene. I wasn't sure that would ever change.

"What happened last night?" I said. "You left the boat, you went to Screaming Minnie's. After that, the Casino?"

"That's right. It felt like an ordinary evening. Marka bought drinks, insulted her friends, and laughed like she was being paid for it. Yoshi and Merc were bickering about which of them owed the other money; Stuy was trying to get La Rocca to let him join his private blackjack game; the others were . . . I don't know. Doing whatever it was they did."

"Ugly was downstairs?"

"When we got there, he was behind the bar pouring some new cocktail he'd invented. A Bitter End. Smelled like vomit, but no one seemed to mind."

"That's when Stuy started pestering him?"

"No, that was later. Marka got to him first—she went straight up to him. They traded a couple of words and then she followed him upstairs."

"Was she up there long?"

"Perhaps fifteen minutes."

I went to rub my jaw and found to my surprise that it did not ache at all. All the tension I'd been storing there had disappeared. For the truly miserable, work is the greatest cure.

"What time was this?"

"Around eight thirty, nine o'clock."

"And when did you return to the boat?"

"Three A.M."

"Were you with Marka the whole time?"

He shook his head. His curls bounced gently. I put my hand around the back of his head, and he closed his eyes.

"When Marka came back from La Rocca, she looked drained. Said she needed to recharge if she was going to be of any use the rest of the evening. Merc and Yoshi convinced her to go back to the Huntington for a nap. She didn't want to—you know how much she hated sleep—but they talked her into it. They walked her home."

"Why didn't you go with them?"

"Bess had killed one of those bottles of Mudfoot liquor and was screaming at the croupier, threatening to take her head off if the ball kept landing on black. I stuck around in case I was needed to break up the fight."

I withdrew my hand, rubbing my fingers together, savoring the way they felt when they'd been in his hair.

"Do you think Marka slept?" I said.

"I don't think that woman slept more than an hour in her life."

"To the Huntington, then. Let's fill in the gap."

"It's a bad idea. I don't care how many birds die or how many columnists follow them. None of this is worth risking our necks."

He was right, but that didn't mean I could stop. I had no way to explain why, and so I took his hand. We walked along the river, our shoes squelching in the mud, until we reached a ladder that brought us back to the Boardwalk. We slipped into the rush of people like Morton Creek losing itself in the Hudson. The crowd was thick, though not as thick as I'd have liked. The people looked ravenous, wolves starved for music, sex, liquor, grease, and everything else the District could provide. At any moment, I felt, one of them would leap on me and start tearing at my throat. For a thousand dollars, I'm not sure I could blame them. I kept my head down. At every corner, another cop barked out the message about the reward for the head of Gilda Carr.

Even through the noise, I could hear the river. It pulsed in my ears as strong as my own heartbeat. If I were dead, if we were all dead, that river would flow on. It wouldn't miss us. It would never even know we'd been there. The thought was terrifying but offered a kind of certainty. That night, there was nothing I needed more.

The Huntington loomed over the Boardwalk like a great mossy rock. Once a boardinghouse, it had been hastily converted to a cramped six-floor luxury hotel the summer the District opened. When the Roeblings cleaned it out, they assumed they could simply strip away the climbing plants that covered every surface in the building and be done with it. They did not understand that on the Westside, plants fight back.

The vines grew with visible speed, exploding out of the brick, swallowing doorways and windows and any furniture left in the same spot for more than a few days. To keep the place inhabitable, the Roeblings hired a dozen gardeners to patrol the halls day and night, snipping back the plants as they spawned. The guests were rich enough to find all of this amusing. They laughed every day when housekeeping came to rearrange their furniture, and they walked barefoot across the soft green down that lined the floor, as happy as children in spring.

The main entrance was flanked by Peacekeepers, and so Cherub and I went around the back. Even when the Roeblings made pretenses of luxury, they could be counted on to cut corners. The back of the building had not been trimmed in months. The vines were Westside thick: a green carpet running right to the roof.

"Think we can climb it?" said Cherub.

"I'll bet you can. With my ribs . . ."

"Don't fret. Cherub will provide."

He kissed my cheek and skipped toward the building. For a moment, it was easy to believe the last ten years had fallen away, that he was truly carefree. Then I remembered that whatever cheer he was showing was an imitation of his old self. Whether that was for his benefit or mine, I was not sure. He leapt up the vines, hopped onto the fire escape, and lowered the stairs for me to climb. He bowed deeply as I ascended, and I responded with a forced smile.

"Faster than a squirrel, aren't I?" he said.

"And nearly as handsome."

The stairs were more rust than steel, but the vines that bound them to the hotel brick were stronger than anything in the District. It was a comfortable ascent. We were two floors from the top when we heard the music and smelled the smoke, which poured from the windows of the sixth floor like the tendrils of some vengeful ghost. It wasn't a fire. It was a party, and it was time for us to crash.

At the top of the fire escape, Cherub tumbled through the window, then helped me over the bare vines that clung to the lip. The hallway ran the length of the building. Every door was open wide. The smoke was thick and the drinks were strong. Several people watched us enter through the window, but no one said a thing. They were distracted by a chipper blonde with a thick green choker and bulging eyes, who was standing in a doorway screaming at her date.

"Gimme the glass, Jerome!"

"Now now."

Jerome had the wiry build of a man who, not long ago, had been dodging tackles on the Ivy League gridiron. His hair was arranged in nifty little curls, and his smile looked like it had been fixed with varnish. He had about three years left of being handsome. "Now now" was all he had to say.

She prodded him in the sternum. He looked around, waiting for someone else to step in. No one did.

"The glass, damn it, or I drink from the bottle."

With a mighty sigh, Jerome produced a heavy rocks glass. The blonde bent for the bottle of liquor that sat protected between her feet. Diana's Fire. With two shaking hands, she emptied it into the glass and drank as much as she could before she started to gag. She coughed for a while—neither Jerome nor anyone else tried to help her—and when she was done, her eyes shone with triumph.

"I told you I could keep another one down," she said. She slumped against the doorway, enjoying her win.

As that little scene played out, Cherub and I slipped down the hall. Women in silver gowns slouched against doorframes, enduring the attentions of men whose tuxedos made them look as slender as skeletons. All of them had the same hair, the same eyes, the same friends, the same opinions, the same life. We had never fit with this crowd, but we were tolerated as long as Marka was at our side. She would protect us no more. I wonder if she really ever had.

We fought our way down the crowded hall, whose carpets were powdered green by leaves trampled into dust. I drew some stares, but after a moment of panic I realized that for the first time all night, people were gawking not because I was suspected of murder but because I was wearing trousers. As long as no one looked at my face, I didn't mind.

Down the hall, the blonde fought to bring her glass to her lips. She succeeded in taking another swig and began to convulse. It could have been a heart attack, but no. She was only dancing.

"Did Marka ever bring you here?" said Cherub.

"No. You?"

"These are not my people."

"They're mine?"

"More than me. They're white. Excruciatingly so. And, I don't know, you always fit so well with Marka and her friends."

"I never felt that way."

"Then why go out boozing with them every night?"

"You did the same thing."

"They were my customers. They were paying me."

"In drinks and cigars, mostly."

"It was something. I never made the mistake of believing we were friends."

"Why else would they keep us around?"

"To make fun? To use as props? Authentic Westside toughs, rented by the evening for the cost of champagne?"

"If that's the case, it was us taking advantage of them, not the other way around."

He wasn't convinced and neither was I, but it hardly mattered now. Marka was dead, and we were outside her room. I nudged the door with my toe. It swung wide.

"My rooms at the Huntington," she would tell anyone who asked and many who didn't, "are a perfect bohemian fantasy. Just the sort of thing we dreamed of at boarding school. Cramped, of course, so cramped you can hardly breathe, and simply impossible to keep clean. Shrubs grow from the ceiling, I swear to god, and there's moss on the floor and the whole place smells of damp, but throw open those curtains and, my god, you get a view of the Hudson squeezing Manhattan like a bicep on some poor wrestler's neck. Oh, it's so awful, how could you not fall in love?"

The rooms were one long space, with a sitting area divided from the bedroom by steamer trunks laid on end. Either the gardening staff had forsaken her or she just wasn't letting them in, because the foliage had not been trimmed in weeks. Tangled grapevine blocked the celebrated vista. Weeds three feet high sprouted from the carpet, their mossy tops bowing like penitents. In places, they were weighed down by refuse, empty champagne bottles, wadded newspaper, and books with cracked spines. Cigarettes spilled out of at least ten full ashtrays, and their butts cluttered every other surface. Moss as soft as a newborn's hair blanketed the bed, and every gorgeous garment Marka owned lay in a heap on the floor. As I approached the clothes, they seemed to twitch. Whether it was rodents living in them or a quick-growing plant, I had no desire to find out.

Secrets were my profession. If I'd decided someone's life had bearing on my work, I was not shy about digging as deep as I needed to go. But Marka was less a person than a work of living art, and the wreckage of her hotel room felt like something I should not have witnessed. It was like seeing an acquaintance naked, or dead. I tried to remember the last time I'd felt so uneasy being in someone else's space, and I saw myself as a girl, tiptoeing around my father's passed-out bulk, picking up his empty bottles and trying to pretend I hadn't seen.

At the desk, Cherub nudged the papers back and forth. He picked up one sheet, read a few lines, and whistled. It was a grating sound.

"What is it?" I said.

"An assassination."

He handed it over. It began:

"For the last decade, Stuyvesant Wells has clung to Broadway with the stubbornness of a venereal disease. We regret to report that there has been another outbreak. His latest attempt at stage comedy, *Ready, Willing, & Mable,* is currently polluting the Belasco Theatre. If these doors actually open, it could infect the rest of the city. Having been subjected to a preview of this supposed farce, your faithful critic can confirm the rumors: *Mable* may be the worst tragedy to strike New York since the *General Slocum*."

That was the nice part. From there it got personal. The review called Stuy's nasal accent "as affected as a monocle," criticized his personal style as "looking like he'd been bludgeoned with a charity shop," and spent a full paragraph comparing his physique to the New York Aquarium's prize manatee. It was vicious enough to make a Roebling killer blanch.

"She must have been joking," said Cherub.

"This goes far beyond a joke. Stuy sunk everything he had into this stupid play. A bad review from Marka Watson would close it in a night. That's no game."

"You think he'd kill her over it?"

"Stuy couldn't hurt a fly. I mean that literally—I don't think he has the coordination. It's hard to imagine him hacking his friends to death."

"Even so, it's a possibility."

"Maybe. I don't know. These people don't make any sense when I'm sober."

I dug through the rest of the scraps, finding nothing of note. Cherub nudged open the steamer trunks and prodded his foot against a heap of women's undergarments and costume jewels. When he'd given up that bit of pointlessness, he nudged aside some of the ivy that blocked the window, took a look at the river, and sighed.

"What?" I said.

We'd only been reunited for an hour, and I had already lost the strength to keep the irritation out of my voice.

"Thinking about Gilly. As far as I know, she and I are the only survivors of the One-Eyed Cats. I'm sorry it had to go the way it did."

The mention of Slaybeck chilled me. I felt exposed and small, like a child caught scratching her name on the glass. It wasn't just what I had done to her—although smashing a bottle into a woman's skull was hardly the best etiquette—but that in the moment, it had felt so good.

"This is why you should never borrow money from a friend," I said.

"I'll have to remember that. Do you think she's still alive?"

"God, I hope so. I don't need any more blood on my ledger. I keep telling myself that the Mudfoots wouldn't have left if she weren't above water and breathing fine."

"That's probably true."

I reached to rub the side of his face, but when I raised my hand, I felt the weight of the bottle and the horrible impact as it slammed into Slaybeck's skull. I pulled away.

"It was the right thing to do, wasn't it?"

"I'm a little too close to the question to make ethical judgments. I will say that I'm pleased to no longer be trapped in a room full of curing fish. From where I was sitting, she gave you no choice."

"You're right. She was going to drown you."

"Not necessarily. Knowing Gilly, she'd probably have stabbed me in the heart."

Some women would hate a man for making a joke at a moment like that. I threw my arms around him and squeezed him as tight as I could. There was so much more I needed to tell him, so much more pain I could have let spill out onto that mossy green floor, but in the moment we were both almost happy, and I was not cruel enough to see that destroyed. It was so much more pleasant to take him by the wrist and say, "Do you know how long it's been since we had access to such a big bed?"

For half a second, he was confused. Then he understood. He fell backward onto the mossy bed and dragged me with him and, for a little while, no one was angry at all. He kissed me hard, and I kissed him back, and we were both struck with such pain that any thoughts of sex became laughable. Instead we stripped off our clothes and dozed, enjoying that feverish space between nightmare and true agony.

When I couldn't sleep anymore, I stared at the ivy that crisscrossed the ceiling and tried to ignore the stench of my armpit. He brushed his finger along my battered ribs, where the skin had turned waxy. Pain bloomed like ink in water.

"You won't get far with these," he said.

He snatched one of Marka's priceless black frocks off the floor and tore it into strips, then cinched them tight enough around me to squeeze everything into place. I could hardly breathe, but I no longer felt like my sides were packed with broken glass, and that was an improvement. He rested his hands on my waist. Even through the bandage, I felt their cold.

"I suppose I should get dressed, too."

"You may as well treat yourself to something nice."

"Somehow, I don't think anything from the Marka Watson collection is quite my size."

"You'd be surprised. She loved wearing men's clothes. Found them shocking or comfortable or both. See what you can find."

He rooted through the piles and found a ruffled white shirt and tuxedo pants with a lime green stripe down the side. He got dressed by the front door. As he pulled up his pants, the weeds beside his foot seemed to sway.

"What was that?" I asked.

"Nothing but trousers."

"Not your damned trousers—what was that by the door?"

I knelt in the weeds. They were tall, spiked things, with stalks as thick as my little finger. I patted their roots, finding nothing, then ran my fingers down the space between desk and wall. I discovered only dust.

"There was something here."

"I really don't—"

"You must have kicked it. When you pulled up your trousers, you kicked it . . ."

The desk was a heavy, hideous thing—closer to a sarcophagus than a work space—but there was a narrow gap between its bottom and the matted vegetation on the floor. Sticking my hand under, I felt a thin piece of paper. I gripped it with my fingertips and pulled it out.

"It's a note."

"Well I'll be."

It was written on Huntington stationery. The paper was cheap, the lettering gaudy. They had pads like this in every room and at a table in the lobby. We had all used them before.

"You kicked it under the desk," I said.

"Not on purpose. I didn't even know I did it."

He said it with the utmost conviction, but that's the way he said everything. I stared at him for a second or two, trying to work out if there were any reason he might lie. Finally, I felt ridiculous, and smiled.

"How about you tell us what it says?" said Cherub.

"'You've been utterly nasty and I won't have it,'" I read. "'Meet me tonight at the Pit, or I shall tell the world.'"

"That handwriting . . ."

"No one but a playwright would have the ego to let *G*s and *P*s take up half the page. It's Stuy. And it's dated today. He must have written it before he knew she was dead and slipped it under her door. It's just been waiting in the weeds."

Cherub ran his hand along my shoulder, a mournful look on his face.

"You won't make us go, will you? I hate the Pit."

"I'm sorry."

"Please, Gilda. Let's stay here. Rest awhile, wash up properly, see if we can find strength for a few hours' sin."

"We both know it would be minutes at most, and even for that, there isn't time. Get dressed and get moving and let's head for the Pit."

I slipped on Slaybeck's trousers and shirt. Cherub held open the door to the hall. Before I left, I took a breath in the doorway, taking in the scent of his body and the sight of the room. I understood why Marka had never let us see it. This was the sort of place where one retreats to die. As the door shut behind me, I felt a clammy certainty that someday I would end up somewhere like here.

TWELVE

Back in the hallway, the party had turned a corner. The voices were louder, like no one was listening anymore, and the laughter had soured. Eyes were glassy and faces were slick with sweat. The blonde in the choker was slumped at the top of the stairs. People stepped over her like she was a lump in the rug. Grass was already starting to cover her legs. As I passed, her eyes snapped open and fixed on mine.

"Hey," she said.

Cherub moved toward the fire escape.

"Hey!" shouted the blonde.

She got to her feet—I have no idea how—and shoved herself between Cherub and me. Her hair looked brittle and loose, like I could clear her scalp with a single tug. Her breath stank of rose-scented tobacco.

"You were in Marka Watson's room," she said.

"If you say so."

"Don't you just love what she writes? I've always said she's the funniest old bitch. You can ask anyone—I say it all the time."

I gave my blandest smile and turned away. She wrapped her hand around my arm. Her skin was softer than I could stand. She tilted her mouth toward my ear and hissed.

"Don't worry, I won't tell nobody," she said. "I always tell folks, you can trust Renette—that's me, I'm Renette. If you and your man want to sneak off for a little I don't know what, who am I to complain? I'll keep your *dark* secret."

"Very enlightened of you." Just as it was enlightened of me to not push her down the stairs.

Another dozen drunks poured into the hallway. The crowd congealed, and no matter how we weaved, Renette stayed on us like wallpaper.

"Personally I never go with the colored boys," she said, "but I know some girls swear by them."

Cherub's jaw was set. He couldn't say anything. I could.

"Please go away," I said.

The smile melted off Renette's face. It was replaced by a look that was both injured and angry, like a beaten dog who's about to bite.

"What did you say?" she said.

"Never mind."

Renette tugged, trying to drag me away from him. Her nails were sharp. I could not pull away.

"Go," I whispered to Cherub.

"I can't—"

"I've handled worse. Just get to the window."

But he did not leave. My stomach churned. I was not worried about what this woman could do to me, but I did not want to see what a hallway full of drunk whites could do to him.

Renette dragged me closer. Her face had taken on the streaky red of a used bandage. I tried to look meek. I'd had enough experience that year with wealthy drunks to know that, left alone, they tended to blow themselves out. But she showed no signs of slowing down.

"I'm out here trying to be friendly. I'm just trying to make a little nice conversation, and you tell me to go away?"

She was louder than the music now, louder than all conversation. Every eye in that hallway was locked on us. Even Jerome, Renette's erstwhile escort, was watching. He leaned against a doorframe, a bottle dangling dangerously from his fingertips, happy his date had found a new target for her rage. I felt Cherub, close but not quite touching. More than anything, I wanted his hand in mine, but the slightest touch would put him in danger. I kept my hands by my side.

"If you'll excuse me—"

She pulled me closer. Her eyes stabbed into mine. For a moment I thought she was going to hit me. I'd have known how to handle that. What she did instead was far more troublesome. A cloud came over her face, like she was thinking for the first time and didn't care for the sensation.

"I know who you are," she said.

"You couldn't possibly."

"I do. I do! Folks! Folks! Folks! Don't you know who this is?"

I tried to pull away, but the crowd had turned into a phalanx and Renette's hand was tight. Cherub stepped a little closer. We were back-to-back, ready to fight. It was not, I supposed, a bad way to be.

"Everybody, look what I found! This here is the fugitive detective, the woman who killed Marka and Bess and everybody. This is Gilda Carr!"

There was no getting away from it now. I tried to look tall, peaceful, innocent—everything the notorious Gilda Carr was not. Renette panted, waiting for the crowd to tear me to pieces, but they just stared, as still and lifeless as well-dressed ghosts. Finally, the silence was snapped by the crash of breaking glass as the bottle slipped out of Jerome's hand.

"Shut up, baby," he told Renette. "Let's go home."

Her hand unclenched. She whipped around and began screaming incoherent obscenities in his face. He looked over her shoulder, utterly bored with the entire thing, and said, "My apologies. The booze they've got over here—it makes her crazy."

"I've heard it has that effect."

But he wasn't looking at me anymore. He was face-to-face with Renette, matching her oath for oath. Nobody at the party seemed to care. It dawned on me the rich only wanted the spotlight on themselves. That's why they came to the Westside. It was so dark, they thought they'd shine. The crowd parted easily now, and Cherub and I attracted no glances as we climbed out the window onto the fire escape. He breathed heavily, letting his anger ebb. It was something he did well.

"I hate these parties," he said.

"I do too." I spat off the fire escape. It was a long way down. "The next time I tell you to run, you're going to listen."

"There's nothing in the world that could make me leave you behind."

There was no gallantry to what he said, only sadness—either because he wished he knew how to walk away or because he knew that eventually, he might not get the choice. I wanted to scream at him, to remind him that above all else, I could handle myself, but then he slipped his hand into mine and I found it impossible to say more.

We went down together into the night.

The alleys around the Huntington were lit up bright and patrolled by cops as skinny and fearful as the one we'd sicced on the Mudfoots. We bowed our heads and tried to look as beaten as Lower West street rats were supposed to be, and the police paid us no mind. After we passed the third patrol, my nerves were close to shattering. My pace slowed and I must have started shaking, because without saying a word, Cherub pulled me close. Pressed against his side, it was much easier to go on.

"There's something I should unload," he said.

"I don't think I can take on any more."

"It's not important. It's just . . . something I've been carrying around. You know I'm constitutionally incapable of keeping secrets."

Considering the recent revelations about the provenance of our boat, I thought, he'd been doing quite well.

"Let me go first," I said.

"Okay."

"I hate the boat."

He tried to pull away, but I didn't let him. As long as we walked like this I could not see his eyes, and that almost made it easy to tell the truth.

"What do you mean, you hate it?"

"I mean that given the chance, I'd burn it to the waterline. I hate getting sunburned on its deck and banging my head every time

I go below. I hate sleeping in dead air, having nowhere to put my things, living on canned food and stale bread, and trying to pretend it's all a wonderful dream. Everything in my house is hardwood, as solid as the earth, and I miss that in a way you cannot understand."

"I—"

"And I miss work. I am nothing without my profession, and that means I've been nothing for over a year, and it was all bad enough before this weekend, but you do not understand the horror of what happened there—bodies burst like rotten fruit, blood soaked into the cushions in the cockpit, so deep into the threads of every piece of rope that you could scrub the *Queen* for a decade and not get her close to clean. Even if we're still breathing this time tomorrow, I cannot go back to that boat. Not for ten seconds. Never, never again."

The echoes bounced off the empty street for a little while, and then there was quiet. I hadn't realized I'd been shouting. At some point, Cherub had slumped against the base of a platform that may have once been a loading dock. His eyes were closed. He didn't look angry. He looked tired.

"Anything more?"

"No."

My throat was sore. I'd have killed for something to drink, even just water, but I felt curiously free. This must be what it feels like after you throw yourself off a building, I thought, in the instant before death, when you are learning how it feels to fly.

"You could have said so," he said.

"Probably."

"I loved it so much. Every piece of brass, every stitch in the sails. First thing since the One-Eyes that felt like it was mine. I see . . . I see why you wouldn't want to spoil that for me."

"I'm sorry."

A smile crept across his face. It looked fake, like he'd put it on for my benefit. I stepped toward him, trying to find one to match.

"You're not the one who needs to apologize," he said. "I trapped you there, and I never saw it, and . . . it's all boats, isn't it? Not just the *Queen*?"

"All boats, I think. But especially the *Queen*."

He threw his arm around my shoulder and pulled me tight.

"Oh well," he said. "I love you more than any river. And if the *Queen*'s the mess you make it out to be, I don't think there'd have been any going back anyway."

I returned his hug, so hard my ribs screamed beneath their bandages. I might have vomited, but instead I said, "I love you."

"How convenient! I love you too."

I took his hand and we walked on. I felt like I'd had a bullet removed. I breathed without pain. And then I remembered.

"You had something too?" I said.

"I hate the bird."

I laughed. There was nothing else for it. I bent double, and he laughed too, huge whooping laughs that blended into a kind of hellish harmony and echoed loud enough, I hoped, to scare the hell out of the cops.

"What did she ever do to you?" I said, wiping my eyes and trying to get my shoulders to stop quaking.

"Nothing! All she did was shit and squawk and eat and shit and shit some more. Made the boat her own personal cesspit. She had those wet stupid eyes, and the stump of her leg was always oozing, and every time I saw her, I wanted to break her neck and drop her off the stern."

"Why didn't you?"

"She was your bird."

"She was, wasn't she? Not ours. Mine."

"Your bird. My boat."

We kept our arms around each other, kept walking down the block, neither of us willing to ask the question that had suddenly become impossible to ignore. If the *Queen* was his boat and Grover Hartley was my bird, it was hard to imagine we'd ever been anything at all.

The sky was black, and dawn seemed like an impossibility. I don't know what time it was when we reached the crudely constructed amphitheater known as the Pit, but from the gate we heard the murmur of a packed house. That night the Zhins were fighting rats.

At the main gate, Cherub stopped. He'd never frequented the Pit. He loved rats too much. The browns, the blacks, the healthy, the dying, young and pink or old and frail. In his gangster days, he'd made an art of trapping them, taming them, and treating them with the indulgence of a doting grandparent. Theoretically, he had taught them to race, but that business was as illusory as the *Misery Queen*'s ferry service. He loved the rats for the same reason he loved his boat—they gave him a chance to play. There was no playfulness here.

"The way they treat those poor rats. A sensible man would set the place on fire."

I glanced down the steps at the few dozen people sprinkled around the bleachers. They were weary, distracted. Nothing to fear.

"We needn't both go inside," I said.

"Didn't I just make a strikingly romantic speech to the effect of 'I'll never again leave you behind'?"

"This is different. I'm leaving you."

It was supposed to be a joke, but there was nothing funny there. I brushed his cheek. He pressed against my touch, a cat demanding more. So many hours on the run, and he was still days from needing a shave.

"If Stuy sees both of us," I said, "he could spook. You know how skittish he is."

"How do we even know he'll be here? Even the strictest masters of etiquette don't expect you to keep an appointment with a dead woman."

"He loves the fights. And he has nowhere else to go."

I said it as confidently as I could, but I deceived neither of us. Cherub squeezed his fists and managed not to call me a fool.

"Watch the gate," I said. "The Mudfoots could come crashing in any minute, or the police, or god knows who else. I need you here."

"Watching you walk away, it's like losing a limb."

"I know. But I generally come back."

I started down the stairs, acid in my throat, feeling like I was consigning him to death all over again. Every few steps, I glanced back. He was always there.

The third time I looked over my shoulder, my foot missed a step. I had just enough time to think, "Oh, hell, falling again," when a hand shot out, grabbed my arm, and dragged me back to standing. The grip was steel. Garish muscles bulged beneath the sleeves of the man's uniform, and the badge on his chest gleamed like a spotlight.

"Y'all right there?" he said. His voice was mushy. His face was, too, like he'd been a boxer before he sank into life as a cop.

"I am fine."

My heart was in my throat, but I managed, I thought, to keep my voice from shaking. The cop stared hard. There was no telling if he was comparing me to the description of notorious killer Gilda Carr, or if he was simply trying to divine if I was a boy or girl. High on the concourse, Cherub strained, ready to take a beating on my behalf.

"Could I escort you to your seat?" said the cop. After a tortuous pause, he added, "Miss?"

"Thank you. I'm sure I can find it on my own."

He gave a sharp nod and left me to it. I watched my feet as I descended, avoiding every suspicious patch of wood, not willing to risk another fall. I did not glance back. Unless the cop's brain had been pulped in his prizefighting days, he would eventually realize why my face had looked so puzzling. If I could find Stuy first, all would be well. But I glanced up and down the crooked bleachers, and Stuy was nowhere.

At the foot of the stairs was a low wall and a drop to the fighting square, whose floor was a grayish mixture of sand, sawdust, and blood. At its center, a burly husband-and-wife fighting duo—Jiho and Yoojin Zhin—stood back-to-back. Their hair was shaved down to fuzz, their bare legs shone with grease, their fists were clenched. The bell rang, and they smiled. Men dragged barrels to the middle of the catwalk. They hoisted them onto the railing and tipped them over. Hundreds of rats crashed to the floor, a living wave, screeching and chattering as they flooded the space. They had been brutally starved. Some charged at the Zhins. The rest formed into knots, tearing at each other, gnawing the flesh off their cousins' bones.

As smooth as molten silver, the Zhins grabbed rats by the fistful, tore them in half, tossed them aside, and reached down for more. Rats climbed their calves, but the grease stopped them from getting a firm grip. A shake of the leg and a stomp of the boot, and another rat was dead. Normally, it would have disgusted me, but on that long weekend, such horrors were commonplace.

In the front row, dead center, a man in suspenders leaned over the edge of the pit and screamed for blood. His dangling belly threatened to burst out of his shirt, and his hair was wild. It took a moment's staring to recognize the Casino's impresario, Roy B. Sharp.

After another glance confirmed that Cherub was where he was supposed to be, I slid down the aisle and rapped my knuckle on the wood beside Roy. He flicked his eyes at me and sneered.

"No autographs," he said. "I've got forty minutes till the last set, and I'm making 'em count."

"I wouldn't dare to intrude."

"And yet, here you are."

Here I was. If someone had asked me why, I don't think I could have explained. My life was threatened from every angle, and I risked exposure to pester a third-rate pianist. Yes, I'd made a promise to Screaming Minnie, but I had broken promises before. The question of Roy B. Sharp's middle initial had gotten hold of me. I had to know, and that desire was one of the few parts of me that I loved.

"What's the *B* stand for?" I asked.

"It stands for bugger off, bitch, or I'll throw you in with the rats."

Some people just don't know how to make friends. Before I could seize on a proper response, I spotted Stuy staggering down the steps on the far side of the aisle. I squeezed past Roy, giving his ankle a firm stomp as I did so, and caught Stuy's wrist before he slammed into the railing. He was as drunk as a person can be, smiling like he'd heard a joke for the first time.

"The fugitive!" he shouted. Heads turned our way.

I slammed him into the nearest empty seat. It was slick with fresh blood, but he either didn't notice or didn't care. He seemed to slouch in every direction at once, like a condemned building in the second before it collapsed. We were right under the post that held one of the lights. It spun silently, shadows dancing so fast that Stuy looked like a sputtering candle. I felt sick.

He pulled a pint of red gin from his overcoat and waved it in my direction. I shook my head. He looked surprised.

"Why'd you want Marka to meet you here tonight?"

"Why shouldn't I? She always had a taste for violence."

"I saw the note. You were blackmailing her."

"Oh, not really. Just considering it. It would never have worked, anyway. By the time I wrote that note, my poor victim was already dead."

He gulped, looking ill. I moved half a step back. If he vomited, I did not want any of it to get on me.

I produced a page torn from Marka's marbled notebook. When Stuy saw it, he got a little more pale.

"Is this what it was about?" I asked.

"Please, if you value me at all, do not subject me to those words."

"'If you're looking for hilarity, a staged reading of the telephone directory will provide more amusement than *Ready, Willing, & Mable.* The theatrical equivalent of an oozing boil, Stuyvesant Wells's latest atrocity has but one thing to recommend it: it may yet end this so-called playwright's career once and for all.'"

His cheer drained away. The liquor that had been propping him up began to drag him down. I'd never seen him—or any of them, really—looking so authentically sad.

"Not my best notice," he said.

"Did you know it was coming?"

"I had an inkling. A friend in the *Sentinel* city room saw it and told me to brace for the beating of my life."

"Would you kill her for it?"

"You think I'm as thin-skinned as all that? It's all part of the game, you know. Marka savages me in print; I get her back at the dinner table. She was only fooling around."

Somehow I doubted he ever got her back. Below us, Jiho Zhin tore a rat in half. Its spine popped like popcorn.

"What was the secret you were threatening to tell?" I said.

Stuy squeezed his temples, feigning agony, as though spilling someone else's secrets wasn't his favorite thing in the world.

"Marka had troubles," he said at last.

"Do tell."

"It was something to do with birds. Can you imagine that, birds? The woman never gave a damn about a bird unless it could be turned into a hat. But the last few weeks, it was all she cared to discuss."

"What kind of birds?"

"Garbage birds, the whaddaya-call-'em, seagulls. Every time I poured her a drink, it seemed like, she was on about them. Said she'd gotten hold of a story, something real. That woman never chased down a story in her whole life. A critic. Pah. Rats are more evolved."

He slumped onto the knees of the spectator behind him. The woman gave Stuy a swift kick in the spine, which got him sitting straighter than he had all night. If it hurt, his face didn't show it.

"What was the story going to be?"

"She was terribly mysterious about it. It was awful to watch—a woman her age playing ingenue. But she dropped hints. 'It will turn this District on its ear,' she said. Who cares? But she was hell-bent on it. She started to attract attention."

When he said it, he pointed to the concourse, where a pair of Peacekeepers were taking in the spectacle. I sank a little lower in my seat as Stuy sang, in a honeyed tenor, "And everywhere poor Marka went, the law was sure to go."

"When did they start following her?"

"As soon as she got on this gull business. She talked to everyone—the Roebling people, the Van Alen people, the city, the gamblers and hoods who hang out at the Casino—and when you talk to everyone, you get attention."

"That still doesn't add up to a mortal threat."

His hand lurched up to touch my face. I was too surprised to flinch. He pressed a clammy thumb to my cheek, and pain snaked across my face. I didn't even remember getting hurt there.

"Have you seen yourself, dearest Gilda?" he said. "You've had their attention for a day, and your face looks like a rotting peach."

"You're holding something back, and I don't have the time. What made you write that note?"

He sighed in a way that could only be called theatrical.

"Last night, after I'd finished making my donation to Ugly La Rocca's blackjack tables, I went to see Marka at the Huntington. I was going to give her a talk about the finer points of stage drama, to help her better understand my intentions with the piece, to—"

"To beg her not to run the review."

"Precisely. I spotted her on the sidewalk. She walked east, into the dark. It was unusual, maybe scandalous. I followed."

"I didn't know Marka had ever been to the real Westside."

"She hadn't. You could tell by the way she walked—hesitant, unsteady. Not clomping at all. That's why she had her guide."

"Who?"

"Your paramour. Our Charon. Young Captain Stevens was leading her by the hand."

My stomach sank like a shot bird. I looked up toward the concourse. Cherub was not there. The wind off the river felt suddenly numbing. I forced myself to keep talking.

"That's not possible."

"Our loved ones get up to all sorts of things, dearest, when we're not there to watch."

"Where did they go?"

"In the dark, it felt like a mile, but it was only a few blocks. Varick and King. An old pillow factory. When they got there, Marka slipped a cigar into Cherub's hand. They went into the building. They were in there a long time."

"You didn't go inside?"

"Skulking is your job, detective, not mine. All I know is that when they came out, Marka looked drained of blood. They started back toward the District, and I tried to follow, but I tripped on a bit of foliage and made quite a racket falling down. I was caught."

"I can't imagine she was happy to see you."

"She was like ice. I'd never seen Marka so still. It was terrifying. I tried to make her tell me what was going on, told her I was her friend, that she could confide in me."

"What did she say?"

"'A third-rate speech from a third-rate playwright.' Not a bad line, but when she tried to light her cigarette she was shaking too much to guide the flame. We were close to the District by then, and she told Cherub to take me back to the Casino."

"How did he seem?"

"Like Marka. Subdued. Frightened. Not like himself at all."

Constitutionally incapable of keeping secrets. Like hell. Since I found him at the Mudfoots', Cherub had looked wrong to me—like a picture that's just out of focus. I felt for him, tended to him, stole him a fistful of sausages, and he had been lying to me the whole time. I felt like I might break in half.

"And Marka?" I said.

"I don't know where she went. I invited her here hoping to leverage whatever secret she had into quashing that review. Instead, well, she died."

He was quiet for a while. In the ring, most of the rats were dead, and those remaining had no fight left. The Zhins stood in the center, their chests heaving, streaked with blood. The bell rang and a fresh batch of rats was dumped into the pit. This time, the fighters did not smile.

"Those bodies on the *Misery Queen,*" said Stuy, "that was everyone in the city who could make me laugh. They're all gone now."

"Murder will do that."

"But what's going to happen to me?"

I had no answer. From the top of the bleachers came screams—not of terror, but of indignation. The crowd shuddered apart, and

Cherub came barreling down the middle of the aisle, stepping on hands and laps and anything else that got in his way. He looked like a fool, and in that moment, I didn't find it cute at all.

"Stop, goddamn it!" shouted the cop with the lumpy face. When no one stopped, he drew his club and advanced down the aisle. Roy B. Sharp refused to get out of his way. They traded unpleasantries. I scanned the place for a way out and saw nothing to give me hope.

"What is it?" mumbled Stuy, his eyes mostly closed. "Is something interesting going on?"

Cherub tripped over the last step and crashed into me, not quite knocking me down into the ratting pit. I shoved him off me.

"What the hell are you doing?"

"Koszler's here, up on the concourse, with a half dozen cops. They'll be here in no time. They—"

But of course, they had already arrived. Before Cherub could finish the thought, the lumpy-faced cop shoved Roy aside and lunged for us, swinging his club. I don't know if he was aiming at Cherub or myself. Perhaps he wasn't aiming at all. I yanked Cherub toward me. The blow caught Stuy in the face. The playwright tumbled off the bench, his hands clutched over his face, blood gushing through his fingers, screaming a ragged scream. I knew too well that no amount of booze could dull that kind of pain.

The cop seemed surprised by what he'd done. He looked at me, hurt and angry at the same time, like what happened to Stuy was my fault. Maybe he was right. I didn't have time to ponder it. Koszler was on the concourse and other cops were moving down the aisles.

Koszler planted his fingers between his lips and loosed an earsplitting whistle. The cop snapped to attention. He whipped his club at us again, but his feet weren't set and he was still distracted by Stuy's screams. Even as he lashed out, his wide eyes showed that he knew he was in trouble. Cherub stomped on his knee as hard as he could, and before he could regain his balance, I threw all my weight into his chest. The cop fell backward into Roy, and they tumbled together into the fighting pit.

Rats swarmed over the cop, tearing at every patch of exposed skin. For a moment, there was no sound but their chittering teeth, and then everyone—the Zhins, the crowd, the cop—began to scream. The audience rose up as one, everyone running in every direction, firming into a wall that the cops could barely pierce. It would be a moment before they reached us, but there was nowhere we could go.

Roy B. Sharp flung a hand over the lip of the wall. The bandleader was hanging by his fingertips. I leaned over the wall. He was red with fear.

"Help me, goddamn it," he barked.

"Leave him," said Cherub, pulling on my arm. "For Christ's sake, they're on top of us!"

I got closer to Sharp, until I could see the sweat that floated on his pancake makeup like grease in a hot pan.

"What's the *B* stand for?"

"Who cares?" shouted Cherub.

"Tell us, Sharp, or you fall."

Sharp's arms strained as he tried to heave himself over the lip of the pit. I grabbed his wrist, ready to tear him loose. He quit trying to climb.

"Nothing," he said. "It stands for nothing."

Cherub and I gripped his arms and pulled until he flopped onto the sawdust on the bleacher floor.

"Thank you," he said. "I can't—"

"Shut up. What's your real name?"

"You can't be serious."

I pressed my heel onto his right hand, just hard enough for him to know that I was. In the aisles, polished black clubs gleamed in the spinning silver light. They swung sharply, smashing anything foolish enough to get in their way. The crowd fractured. People staggered past us, clutching handkerchiefs to cut foreheads and broken noses, as blood streamed down their chests.

Cherub pressed himself to me.

"For god's sake, can we please run?"

I pushed my boot harder onto Sharp's hand.

"Tell me," I said, "or you don't play piano anymore."

"Mervyn. Mervyn Melody. I changed it when I started out because, well, it's just so obvious."

As he said it, a shadow fell across his sallow face. I ducked, and felt a club slice the air behind my head. I shoved Cherub toward the pit. He vaulted over the edge and I scrambled after him. There was no time to cushion my fall.

I thudded onto my hands and knees. The sand stung my palms. The rats swept up my legs.

I rolled onto my back, kicking frantically. Some fell, but more climbed on. The Zhins looked up from the fallen cop, whom they'd been trying to aid, and stared helplessly as the starving vermin climbed my arms, my neck, my hair. They didn't even bite—it was as if they were simply trying to suffocate me. Before the rats flooded into my mouth, the air was split by a strange whistle. It was not Koszler. It was musical, playful—a song whose melody I had forgotten, but which was so familiar, it made me dizzy.

Cherub was down on one knee, his hands cupped around his mouth, pouring out a series of unearthly tones that simply hypnotized the rats. They ran to him. He greeted them with an easy, cheerful expression that fell for only one moment—as he looked at me, and I saw the terror in his eyes. The message was simple.

Run.

The crowd howled as I got to my feet and limped across dirt that was littered with blood and shredded rat. Some of the audience was impressed, thinking this was all part of the show. The devotees of the sport, however, simply wanted our blood. I slammed into the arena's far wall and scrambled up a coarse mesh net to the lip of the pit. There were no bleachers here, no fans, only a sheer drop to the sidewalk and the true Westside night. I straddled the wall and, for the first time, looked back the way I'd come.

On the bleachers, Stuy was curled into a ball, clutching his handkerchief over his seeping wound. Beside him was the heaving form of Roy B. Sharp, né Mervyn Melody. A half dozen cops were scattered across the seats, holding back the crowd. At the center,

Emil Koszler leaned on the fence, smiling softly as he stared across the bloody sand. He snapped his fingers, sending two of his men clambering over the wall. They landed softly in the pit. At first, I thought they'd come to tend to their fallen brother, but no—they were there for Cherub and me.

"Run!" I said.

Cherub did not look my way.

He was in the center of the pit, rats clumped at his feet, dipping lower and lower and his song pitched higher and higher. The animals were completely still. With long strides, the cops crossed the sand. I tried again.

"Hey, idiot!"

That got his attention. He glanced up, saw the cops, and bolted. Freed from their spell, the rats scattered. Some fought each other; others charged at the cops. There were too few of the animals left to bring the policemen down, but Koszler's boys lost a step trying to get out of the rats' way. Cherub threw himself at the net. The wall shook. He climbed fast, not even pausing as he vaulted over the top. He landed on the sidewalk as easy as a cat. I did not have his grace, and so I lowered myself as carefully as I could. Just before my head slipped below the fence, I caught a final glance of Koszler. He had not moved; his expression had not changed. He would catch up with me, we both knew, somewhere down the line.

I landed, gently enough, beside Cherub. I did not let him catch his breath. With a fist tight on his wrist, I dragged him into the dark.

THIRTEEN

"Two dozen rats! They were in bad shape, poor bastards, ribs stick-ing through and hair falling out. I haven't done the call for two years now—I didn't think it would still work. But I got them, goddamn it, and I held them, too."

His exaltation fell away, and he was silent, waiting for my praise. I gave him nothing. Whenever I tried to speak, I saw him and Marka, marching merrily these same empty streets, sharing something he preferred I didn't know about. For perhaps the first time in my life, I was too angry to speak. He felt it. By the time the District's lights were out of sight, his joy had died, and he knew a fight was coming. Perhaps thinking he would have an advantage if he began on the offensive, he chose to start it himself.

"You see what happens when I leave you alone?"

"Excuse me?" The words dripped from my mouth like venom.

"Not the police, of course. If they're coming, they're coming, and there's not much one can do to change their minds. But getting stuck on Roy B. Sharp—perhaps if I'd been there from the start, I could have dissuaded you from that particular insanity."

"I made a promise. Screaming Minnie saved my life."

"As though promises are so holy. I've watched you break thousands of them. You hung back and risked a cracked skull for the sake of a fixation."

"And just what about my fixations do you find so objectionable?"

"They tend to get us hurt. Someday . . ."

"What? Someday *what*?"

My voice frightened him. He stepped back, his hands up, asking for peace. It was far too late for that.

"Tell me what you were going to say," I said.

"Someday one of your fixations is going to get you killed."

"I suppose that's why you've been trying to keep me from my work."

"Quitting work was your idea! You needed a break, you said. Couldn't sleep more than an hour at a time. Crying for no reason. You were worn down to nothing."

"And thank god, I'm doing so much better now."

I stomped down the block, trying to crack the sidewalk with my heels. Cherub followed, as obedient as a hungry dog. I hated him for his loyalty, for his cheer, for how simple he thought life could be. I needed silence. For a block or two, he was smart enough to give it to me.

"I don't know why we're fighting," he said. "We should both be dead, two or three times over. That we're not is a stupendous miracle. I can't see any reason why we shouldn't just embrace, and kiss, and get on with our lives."

"Think harder."

Even more than most people, Cherub didn't like being yelled at. He toiled to make other people happy. When it failed, he felt like a martyr. He opened his hands, looking for someone to take his side. Nothing was there but broken windows and a squat, malformed oak.

"Wait," he said. "I know this block."

"Yes. You do."

"Where are you taking us?"

"Varick and King. The pillow factory."

His smile slid off his face like it had been stuck with cheap glue. When he finally spoke, it was with a voice I hardly recognized.

"I don't think that's a good idea."

"You've been there before?"

"No."

In the years we'd known each other, Cherub had often irritated me. He had occasionally infuriated me. But that was the first time I ever really wanted to punch him in the jaw. Because I am a lady, I spat at his feet instead. He squirmed.

"Lie again and I'll spit in your eye," I said. "Stuy saw you here."

"That motormouthed drunk doesn't know what he's seen."

"He saw you, Cherub. You and Marka, alone on some secret mission. You took her there and she gave you a cigar. Why did you lie?"

"I didn't lie. I just didn't mention it."

I slammed my fist against his chest, catching him right above his heart. He stood still, his jaw clenched tight, like he was trying to trap whatever he was going to say next.

"You've been lying this whole time!" I yelled. "What did she tell you?"

"That the birds were dying. That she'd gotten a message to meet someone at the pillow factory who would tell her why. Offered a cigar if I got her there safe."

"You'd betray my trust for a cigar?"

"It wasn't for the cigar! I wanted to make sure that stupid woman didn't get herself killed."

I had to work very hard not to hit him again. On the whole of Manhattan Island, there were perhaps three people whom I trusted: Hellida, Bex Red, and Cherub. To have that trust broken didn't just irritate me—it felt like my entire world was tipping sideways, and I was about to fall off.

"So all night, you've known what we were after?" I said.

"I was trying to steer you away from it. Whatever trail Marka was following led to her death. There is something out there that tears people apart. I didn't want it to get you."

"I will say this clearly, and for the last time: I have never needed your protection, Cherub Stevens, and I never will. If you have any respect for me, any love, stop acting as my shield. Help me or get out of my way, but let me do my work."

I was really shouting now. The buildings beside us were completely obscured by moss and vines, which absorbed the echoes of my words like they were thirsty for them. The moon gave just enough light to see Cherub looking furious and frightened all at once. I hoped he was scared of me.

"You know, for most people 'I was trying to save your life' is a compelling explanation for a little white lie."

"You are not in love with most people. You are in love with me."

His eyes flicked away.

"Aren't you?"

There was a deadly pause. I truly did not know what he would say, and I wasn't sure which answer I dreaded more.

Finally he spoke.

"I don't just love you. You're the breath in my lungs, the food in my belly. Why else would I worry like I do?"

"I never asked for your fear."

He held open his hands. A silent apology. An admission that there were some things he simply couldn't change. It might have been good enough. It would be a while before I could be sure.

We kept walking, our step heavy, our feet silent on the moss.

"So what's in the pillow factory?" I said.

"I don't know. That's the truth."

"You went inside with her."

"I was her guide, not her partner. All I knew is she had this address, and she needed a Westsider to help her get there. I went as far as the front hall. The way it stank . . . I've been around enough death to know the smell. She went on without me. When she came out, she could barely stand."

"Why didn't you ask her what she saw?"

"Sensible people don't want to know those things."

I didn't have to explain that sense was not something I was burdened with. I kept walking, and like always, he followed behind.

Our destination was a cast-iron building as white as bleached bone. Faded paint advertised, "Logan Pillows . . . Soft!" The doors and windows of every other building on the block had long ago been broken or stolen or simply disappeared, but the old pillow factory was boarded shut with fresh yellow timber. We used metal scrap to pry out the nails. The boards fell away.

The stench was worse than I'd imagined. Why death had to smell so sweet, I would never understand.

Moonlight spilled over the threshold, enough to show a long, bare hallway. Our footsteps died on the concrete. It was rare to find a floor on the Lower West that had not cracked or sunk into the earth. This one was as pure as if it had been poured that morning.

"How long was Marka inside?" I asked. My voice sounded strange in that place. I could not tell if it was the building, or if I was simply afraid.

"Perhaps twenty minutes."

"And after she sent you away with Stuy, where did she go next?"

"I don't know. South. It wasn't in the District, or if it was, she didn't want us to know. She only told me she'd see me at the boat. She did."

"And when she got back to the boat . . ."

"She was her old self. Jolly. Almost shouting. Told me, 'Get on the river quick, before the sun comes up and spoils the fun.' I got us underway. We were just pulling into the current when the Mudfoots dropped in. After that, well . . . I guess I missed the real show."

"When you were taken, the ship was adrift?"

"Effectively. Merc and Yoshi acted like they knew their way around a boat, but they were hopeless."

"Did you notice any other ships closing with the *Queen*?"

"No, but I was preoccupied with getting my eye bashed shut. You sure you want to keep going with this?"

"I have no choice."

"Then allow me to open the door."

The hallway had a single exit, a pair of rusted metal doors that looked like they would be fused shut, but which glided open with a gentle pull. Beyond was the factory floor, a broad room whose ceiling was high enough that it could not be seen. Grimy windows let in enough moonlight to show shattered machinery crowded against the walls. The scent of death was thick enough to touch, and it soaked us to the skin.

"Never knew it took so much junk to make a pillow," said Cherub.

We stepped into the room. My foot found something soft, white. I assumed it was a pillow, and in a sane world, it would have been. But when I moved my foot the thing made a squelching sound. I ran my fingertips across its surface. They came back coated not quite in blood, but rather in a thick ooze streaked with pink and fatty yellow.

It was a bird, or it had been once. It was closer to putrefaction than the poor creatures housed in Lady Birdlady's morgue. It was so soft, so close to bursting—it was hard to believe it had ever been able to fly.

I stepped backward and landed on another bird. Behind it was another, and another, and many, many more.

Seagulls, filling that great room from wall to wall. Thousands of them.

"Dear god," said Cherub. "You understand, of course, that we should run away."

"I understand."

Trying to disregard the stench, I knelt. The birds were patchy, their limp feathers hanging from wrinkled skin. Many appeared to be not dead, but simply shifting in their sleep. A closer inspection revealed that the illusion of life was caused by writhing maggots. It was an unpleasant sight.

"I've seen others, dead like this," I said. "These seem worse."

"I can see why Marka was upset."

"Maybe."

"What do you mean, maybe? You think she could look at this without being bothered?"

"The woman didn't give a damn about birds. She had a story, she said, that would shake the District to its roots. I don't know if this would have been enough."

"Good god. I hope you're wrong."

Covering his nose with his shirt, he took a long breath and scanned the room. He pointed halfway across the floor.

"A break in the mess. Could be a trail."

We picked our way toward the spot and found a bloody footpath where the birds had been cleared away. We walked along it, crossing a room that was not as silent as it should have been. Between our breaths, we heard the rustle of shifting feathers. I hoped, rather desperately, that it was the maggots, or a family of curious rats, and nothing more.

Our trail led us to a heavy steel door. It was not quite closed. I tugged the handle. It glided open to reveal total black and a stench powerful enough to compete with the heap of rank birds.

"Don't go in there," said Cherub.

I stepped forward.

"Oh. You're going in there."

Of course I was. I wanted to be in my bedroom on Washington Square, buried under every quilt I owned. I wanted to shut off my brain and sleep for a year, but my mind did not know how to turn off, and so I was here.

The room was small—a vault or old storeroom, probably. I could feel the walls close on my shoulders.

"Got a match?" I said.

"No."

Of course not. No one could reasonably expect such a stroke of good fortune. I walked on, the stink twisting around me like a shroud. One step, two steps, and then my foot bumped into something solid. I ran my hands along it, discovering smooth metal corners. At the top of the column I found a cage made of wire, perhaps the size of my torso. At its base was a crank.

"It's a Bourget Device."

"Strange place to leave such an expensive toy."

"Whatever Marka found, there must have been a lot of money in it."

"Can you think of any other reason to butcher all those people?"

I didn't answer. The crank was heavy. I could feel the resistance of the gears inside the machine.

"Well?" said Cherub. "Do you want to turn it on?"

"No."

I spun the crank. Gears groaned, plates spun, and the light

flickered on—dim at first, then almost blinding as the plates whizzed to full speed. The wire of the cage became a web of shadows, making a chessboard of the little room, throwing sharp lines across the things that hung there. They were not birds.

They were men.

Twelve of them.

Thick leather straps secured them to the walls. Gags had been shoved deep into their mouths, but nothing covered their eyes. Their clothes were gone. In some places, their skin hung like loose cloth. In others, it was pulled so tight their bones had nearly erupted through the surface. Their flesh was the sickly pale of a sliced potato, even for those whose features suggested they had once had dark skin. Their hands hung slack; their palms were stained with dried blood where their fingernails had dug into their flesh.

Whatever killed them must have been slow, and it must have hurt.

Cherub and I stood there for a long time. I heard him fighting to calm his breathing, and I did the same. If I hadn't, I'd have passed out. After a while, his hand found mine. There was no sense pulling away.

"Who were they?" he said.

I forced my feet across the floor and inspected the nearest man. After he died, his gag had slipped loose, revealing a toothless mouth and a black tongue. Where the light did not touch, his skin was much darker—almost brown. It almost looked healthy. His hair was brittle and his face was spotted and scarred. I did not recognize him, but I knew him all the same. His was the same face I recognized from every street corner and saloon in the Lower West. On particularly bad mornings, it was not far from the face that greeted me in the mirror.

"He was one of us," I answered, and Cherub understood.

I touched the pale part of my forearm. I could not tell if my skin had always been so dry, so pale. It did not look much better than his.

The light was spinning faster and glowing brighter. Beneath the stench of death, my tormented nose detected something new: the crisp, autumnal odor of a bonfire.

Something inside the machine clicked as it reached full speed. The smell of burning grew unmistakable. Wisps of smoke curled up from the places where the light touched the man's flesh. On my own exposed skin, I felt the heat rise. I itched terribly and had a sudden urge to scratch until I reached bone.

"The light," I said. "Turn it off."

Cherub hadn't needed telling. He was already there. He jabbed his finger through the Device's cage but couldn't reach the button that turned it off. I got no closer. The smoke pouring off the corpses burned my eyes. I squeezed them shut, and the light seared straight through the lids.

Cherub darted out of the room. For an ugly second, I thought he had deserted me, and then he came back with a dead bird.

"Pick a feather," he said.

I tore the longest, toughest feather from the corpse and stabbed the sharp end through the light's cage. It took three tries, but I found my mark. The plates of the Device slowed. The light died.

Choking on smoke, I found myself unable to step forward, afraid I might clatter into one of the dead men. Cherub's arm wrapped around my waist and dragged me into the comparative peace of the bird-strewn factory floor. We tumbled forward, stomping on dead gulls, all fatigue banished by the certainty that another minute in that place would mean death or madness. We crashed out onto the sidewalk and did not stop running until we collapsed onto the soft moss that blanketed the street.

I spat until my mouth was dry and my jaw ached. It didn't help. I would taste that charred flesh for the rest of my life.

"That room," said Cherub. "That room."

I wrapped both arms around him, pressing my head into his chest. His heart was pounding like Screaming Minnie's rhythm section. He nestled into my hair. After a while, my skin stopped itching and we were both able to breathe.

"I'm sorry for everything," he said. "Mainly for being a fool."

"You weren't the only one."

"Those poor bastards. What happened to them?"

"You saw the way their skin smoked when the light got going. Did you feel that itch?"

"Everywhere the light touched. I suppose this means Gilly really was telling the truth. It wasn't liquor that poisoned them."

"It was the lights."

Those lights. Those glittering miracles that were on every street corner of our blighted District, hanging above the marble in every respectable bar. If they could do *that* to a room full of prisoners, well—such knowledge certainly would be worth killing for.

"God knows what they've been doing to us," I said.

"God and Vivienne Bourget."

The bitter flavor of rosemary flooded my mouth. I closed my eyes and remembered a night a year prior, when I sipped strange cocktails in a strange bar. Marka had heard scandalous rumors about the floor show of a third-floor cabaret just north of Spring Square, and she'd dragged the entire gang there for a look at the late performance. The act was nothing new—once a person strips fully naked, there's not much more they can do—but the drinks were bizarre. The bartender had attempted to mask the sweet burn of Ida Greene's gin by steeping it with every herb in her garden, and the result was something that tasted of grass clippings and looked like mulch. Still, it was novel, and I drank more than my share.

I was toying with a sprig of rosemary, trying to signal the waiter to bring me another round, when Ida Greene sat down beside me and announced that she had a woman for me to meet.

"I'm not in a sociable mood," I said. I waved my sprig at the dance floor, where Marka and the others were reenacting the performance, proving once and for all that stripping should be left to the professionals. "Look. My friends have deserted me."

"Then aren't you lucky I'm here."

She raised an eyebrow in the direction of the waiter, who sped off to find us more drinks. I sat silent, afraid of looking a fool in front of Mrs. Greene. There was something about this woman, from her impeccable bone-colored wardrobe to the way her eyes stabbed out from behind her spectacles, that simply screamed, "I do not need you." After a lifetime of thumbing my nose at authority figures, I had a perverse desire to impress her—which of course meant that I never impressed her at all.

The drinks arrived—three of them. They looked cleaner and colder than the ones I'd been served when I was alone. Mrs. Greene crooked her finger, and our guest sat down then. It was the first time I'd seen Professor Bourget since the day the lights turned on. She'd looked old before. Now she looked ancient, her skin spotted and scarred, her posture crooked. She appeared to be wearing the same outfit she'd sported at the ceremony in Spring Square, and I wondered if this was the first time since then that she had emerged from her lab. She did not touch her drink.

"Well?" she said, eyeing me like I was feces smeared on her wall.

"I finally convinced the professor to take a tour of the District," Ida Greene said. "I thought it was important she understand just what her Devices have enabled—what joy she's brought to all our lives. I couldn't let her pass through without introducing the Westside's most unusual detective."

There was an unfamiliar tension in Mrs. Greene's eye. I realized that she was asking for my help impressing her guest. It was not the first time I'd been called upon for this ambassadorial work—Marka expected a similar routine every time I met one of her friends—and I slipped easily into the role of the mysterious Lower Westsider.

"I specialize in tiny mysteries," I said. "The little things that keep you up at night, the minute questions that—"

"Ida told me," said Bourget. "Sounds a terrible waste of time."

"That's just what I like about it."

She grunted. Mrs. Greene stared at her, reminding her to play nice. Bourget put on a scientifically accurate imitation of a smile and launched into a speech that wasn't merely wooden but petrified.

"You're precisely the kind of person I had in mind when I devised the Device. A girl who's lived her whole life in the dark, who doesn't understand how bright the world can be. I hope my achievement has brought some joy into your life. Please, uh, please continue to patronize the District."

She stood up abruptly, bumping her hip on the table, and sailed away. Ida Greene pushed away her drink—it was untouched, as was the professor's—and gave a shrug that could almost be considered apologetic.

"Geniuses are no fun," she said.

I couldn't disagree. She left me alone with three free drinks. The first few sips were pleasant enough, but the taste soured as I realized that somewhere along the line, I'd become a tourist attraction. I left the drinks on the table and went home to the boat.

Outside the pillow factory, Cherub squeezed his knees to his chest. He looked washed out, almost frail.

"You'd think it'd get easier," he said. "I've been around death my whole life. I've seen enough corpses, lost friends. At a certain point, you'd think it would just be a matter of throwing a little more misery on the pile. But I cannot take much more of this."

"I'm sorry."

"It's not your doing."

He smiled. I saw how much work it took, and I knew that he was doing it for me. I didn't hate him anymore.

"When Marka left you with Stuy," I asked, "she walked south?"

"Toward the Bourget Works, now that you mention it."

"Then we'll have to do the same. The professor will have some questions to answer. Are you sure . . ."

"What?"

"You don't want to run anymore?"

He shook his head, smiling still.

"Some things are so horrible, you can't run away."

And just like that, we were together again. Despite the aches that filled my body and the taste of death that lingered on my tongue and the lies we'd told to each other, it was a good enough way to be. He stood up and helped me do the same, and we headed south—past the tail end of the District, where Bourget's Device stabbed the belly of the sky.

FOURTEEN

The Lower West was not asleep. Even away from the lights of the District, we heard the unrefined noises of citizens gambling, drinking, gorging, and fornicating. We did not mind. It sounded like home.

Still, it was not an easy walk. My sides ached. I was thirsty and hungry, desperate for a cold glass of anything and twenty hours' sleep, but as long as I kept moving, I did not fall.

We were turning a corner when something made Cherub yank me into the shadow of a caved-in building with rusty blood on the floor and hooks dangling from the ceiling. For a moment, I feared he had been seized by an inconvenient flash of lust, and then I heard the song.

It was "Moonlit Melody," one of the old Westside tunes. A pretty name for a song that was either about gutting a woman or making love to her or doing a little bit of both. Few gangland anthems touched on anything more sophisticated. Whoever sang those ragged harmonies was not far away.

"Mudfoots?" I hissed.

"They don't like coming this far inland or this far south. Of course, for special circumstances . . ."

The song grew louder. Hearing it made me feel fifteen again, a girl huddled up to her windowsill, listening to the world pass by. It was a strangely pleasant sensation. I pulled Cherub close. I was surprised to find that, for all the venom we'd passed back and forth that evening, it felt comfortable to have him in my arms.

The singers passed our abattoir. One voice soared above the rest—a voice so light and pure that it was hard to imagine it could have been born on the Westside. I snuck a glance through the cracked doorway and recognized the woman with the white braids and silver coat. She and her friends appeared to have acquired a sense of purpose. I was not so sure that was a good thing.

She sang:

And I saw her there
And I seized her hair
And I kissed her
With my knife

And then they were gone. It took a long time before I was ready to let Cherub go. When we stepped out of our shelter, the street was empty. For the rest of our journey, there was no sound from the city, and no words from me.

The Bourget building was tall, brick, and windowless. Aside from the gleaming Device on its roof, it was dark. There was no way in aside from a shuttered loading dock and a small iron door. Both, naturally, were locked. I jiggled the doorknob and then, just to have something to do, jiggled it again.

"How do ordinary people go through life without burglar's tools?" I asked.

"I'll show you. I've never tried this before, but who knows . . ."

He stepped past me, curled his hand into a fist, and did something it would have taken me hours to consider.

He knocked.

Heavy feet shuffled. The door eased open. Light poured out over the shoulders of a massive man with a gleaming shaved head, a leather butcher's apron, and a cloth mask stretched tight across his mouth. His voice was flat, with only the faintest hint of irritation.

"Yes?"

Cherub looked dazed. I don't think he expected knocking to be so successful. He fumbled for something clever to say, and came up with "We're, uh, here to see Vivienne Bourget."

"Professor Bourget is occupied."

The door began to close. Cherub wedged into the awkward space between doorframe and attendant. The big man sighed. I began to grow bored.

"Perhaps you might return at a more conventional hour?"

"I'm afraid it's urgent."

"What could possibly be—"

"The pillow factory," I said. "Twelve dead men and a whole lot of birds."

He showed no sign that he knew what I was talking about, but death on that scale was apparently a question for the higher-ups. He let us inside. The anteroom was spotless white. There was no sound but the whirring of the Devices on the walls and behind closed doors. The air was terribly cold. He sped across the floor, not glancing backward to see if we were keeping up. Smoked glass doors opened onto a staircase, which led down to a low-ceilinged chamber that may have been the cleanest boiler room in New York. Another pair of doors brought us through a laundry room filled with racks of leather aprons, white shirts, and masks. Even here, it was not warm.

We went around corner after corner, up stairs and down, through little rooms and big rooms. Unfamiliar machinery made unusual sounds, but there was none of the commotion of manufacture. People with the same shaved heads and tight masks as our guide hunched over gleaming steel tables. Every surface sparkled, and every room was lit with more Devices than was necessary. I swore I could feel them burning through my skin. I'd have liked to slip through the shadows, but there were none to be found.

Only once did we see anyone speak. A pair of workers strolled down the hallway toward us, and as they passed I caught a fragment of what could be called conversation.

". . . still wants me to quit. Says she doesn't trust it. Says she—"

"Who the hell cares what she says?"

"That's what I told her. Think I'd give up a chance like this, just for . . ."

And then they were gone.

At last, once my internal compass was thoroughly scrambled, we arrived at a door. Like every other one we'd passed, it was unmarked, and it looked like it had weight.

"Where do you come from?" I asked our guide.

"Excuse me?"

"I'd have noticed a troop of bald men parading in and out of the District every day. Do you sleep here?"

"Sometimes."

"And the rest of the time?"

He stared, his eyes as cold as the hallway, and finally decided I was too harmless to worry about.

"The professor has a private dock."

"I've never seen it," said Cherub.

"That's because it's private. You wouldn't see it, unless you knew where to look. You'd be surprised what you can get away with on the water."

And with that cryptic statement, he pulled open the door. Behind it was a small space with white paneled walls, a bare workbench, and a pair of Devices dangling from the ceiling.

"Our waiting room," he said. "Sorry it's not more comfortable."

"I've endured worse. The professor?"

"I'll fetch her."

"We'll come too."

He shook his head. I stepped to him, preparing to explain that no power on earth could compel me to wait in this dull little room. He planted his palm on my chest and shoved hard. I thudded onto the floor, rattling every part of me that was already bruised or broken, and before the taste of pain drained out of my mouth, the man was gone and the door had slammed.

"That door is locked, isn't it?" said Cherub, helping me to my feet.

"I'd almost be disappointed if it weren't."

We tried it. We got nowhere. Cherub applied himself to the

lock, wiggling his pinkie in the keyhole, accomplishing nothing. I ran my hands along the underside of the desk, then picked the stool up by its feet. Neither revealed any secrets.

"Think that stool's heavy enough to break the door?" said Cherub.

"No, but it'd make a handy weapon for when our masked friend returns."

"Give it here."

I tossed it to him, and he practiced looking threatening. His breath steamed from his mouth. If I didn't know better, I'd have thought he was having fun.

"If it's Bourget who comes through the door," I said, "try not to break her neck."

"No promises. I'm in a neck-breaking mood."

I traced a wall panel with my fingertip. A gentle press, and it popped open. A drawer slid out, clicking into place with the faintest tinkle of glass.

Not glass. Crystal. Dozens of the delicate crystal sheets that powered Professor Bourget's Devices, still wrapped in their crinkly brown paper, ready to be slotted into a machine to banish the dark. I pulled one free and unwrapped it. It was like opening a penny candy. The crystal looked clear, but as I moved it closer to my eye, I saw it was traced with twisting red strands that flowed across each other like they were alive. Perhaps they were. It had never been clear just how these marvelous machines worked. All that mattered was that they turned on the lights. We did not consider how, and we certainly never asked at what price.

I replaced the crystal and closed the drawer. I opened another and another, finding tens of thousands of dollars' worth of the crystals, but it wasn't until I reached the fourth drawer that I discovered a surprise.

Her skin was white with the faintest background of blue—the color of the coldest, hardest ice. Her lips were purple, squeezed in a permanent scowl, and her eyes were wide. Not a curl was out of place. Our guide had been correct, in a way. Vivienne Bourget was occupied and would remain so forever.

Cherub set down the stool. He sighed and gave my shoulder a squeeze. I placed my hand on his.

"Another body on the pile," he said.

"Are you all right?"

"Should I be?"

"I suppose not."

Another sigh.

"What?" I said.

"It's just . . . I never take you anywhere nice."

I wanted to shut the drawer, but my hands were limp. Cherub was not the only one who'd had enough of bodies. I wanted, more than anything, to flatten myself against that cold tile and let it suck the heat out of my back, draining me of everything until there was nothing left but sleep. But I stayed upright, my eyes on the corpse.

"Her skin," he said, "it doesn't look like . . ."

"No. Not like the men we found. She died a more traditional death."

"What do you mean?"

I tugged at the high white collar of her work shirt, revealing the only color anywhere in that entire room: a copper bruise on Bourget's neck, about the width of my thumb.

"She hanged herself," I said. "Or someone did it for her."

"I'm going to say something that may be controversial, and I don't want you to get upset."

"Yes?"

"These people are bastards."

"You are not wrong."

The professor's work clothes matched those of the man who'd brought us in—from the thick leather apron to the clunky black boots. Her gloves were missing, though, and her fingernails were scorched, like their tips had been held in an open flame. I rifled the pockets of her apron, feeling that old familiar panic rising in my chest. It didn't hit as hard as it had in the pillow factory. I felt sluggish, and I couldn't be sure if it was from cold or hunger or simply being sick of arguing with the man at my side.

I dug my hand under her hip—it was too soft, like putty, and the touch made me want to vomit or scream—and searched until I found a ring of keys. I snapped them off her belt.

Footsteps sounded in the hall.

There were too many keys on the ring. I picked one at random and tried to open the door. It did not fit. My fingers were too numb to keep trying. Without a word, Cherub took the keys from my hand. With his eyes closed, he chose a key and plunged it into the lock. It fit tightly. The door swung wide.

"Very nice," I said.

"I've always been a lucky fool."

We slipped down the hallway, walking slowly to keep our feet from echoing. As we approached the first corner, Cherub held me tight. I did not pull away. I was too tired to remember whether or not I was angry. All that mattered was that he was the only person on earth whose touch I could stand.

The hallway stretched out before us, long and bare, sloping sharply down. If it had an end, we couldn't see it. There were doors—black iron and gleaming steel. We tried all of them, and all of them were locked. There was shouting, indistinct but very angry. It was impossible to tell if it came from behind us, from ahead, or from the other side of the walls. We walked faster.

"Did we come this way before?" said Cherub, his voice a rasp.

"No. But it's the way we're going now."

Heavy footsteps echoed from every direction, as though an army was bearing down on us. Abandoning all pretense of caution, we ran. It was no longer possible to see where we'd entered the hallway, and there was still no sign of an end—just that same long slope into the earth. We reached another door. It was wood this time, pale around the edges and scorched black in the center, like someone had tried and failed to use it for a fire. Cherub tore at the knob, but it gave him nothing. The sweat on my neck was cold.

"This way, fellas!"

The shout came from behind us, I believe, but it echoed so

violently that we heard it again from every side. The words were calm, the voice of someone who knew they couldn't lose.

I looked up. Two bumps protruded through a white ceiling tile. I pointed, and Cherub saw too.

"Get me up there," I said.

He let me climb onto his back. I shoved aside the tile, which was as thin as newspaper, and found the end of a ladder that stretched up into the pitch dark. I gave it a sharp jerk. It slammed down, making an unmistakable racket. I pulled myself into the nowhere between the walls and Cherub followed. We dragged the ladder up behind us and, with shaking hands, replaced the ceiling tile.

"Where the hell are we?" he asked.

"I don't know, but it's better than where we were."

"Are you sure?"

"Of course not."

We climbed for a long time. The footsteps and shouting fell away, and still we went up. It was impossible to tell how far underground we'd been led before we found Bourget's body, and it was even harder to say how far up we were going now. The air was cold, and it was all I could do to keep my numb hands moving, rung after rung after rung.

"Do you think they killed her?" asked Cherub.

"Do I think who killed whom?"

"Bourget's people. Do you think they were the ones who hanged her?"

"Perhaps. Probably. I don't know. I can't think anymore. I can't theorize. It's too much death, too much fear."

"I'm sorry. I'll let you get back to your climbing."

"Don't apologize. Keep talking, please, about anything at all."

I swear I heard him smile. After a moment, he spoke again, in that same cheerful, easy voice that he once used to greet passengers on the *Misery Queen*. I knew how much that cheer was taking out of him, and I was grateful that he would spend his strength to entertain me.

"Have I ever told you about the time I ate a bad clam?"

"A dozen times."

"Would you like to hear it again?"

"More than anything."

It was a story that got longer every time. He ate the bad clam at an underground saloon, just north of the Battery, and was struck immediately by an urge to vomit. He fled to the street and emptied his guts into the gutter, which would have been simply embarrassing had there not been two people sleeping there: Cordelia Eastman and Bilge Rat Blake, a pair of notorious confidence tricksters whose loathing for each other was exceeded only by their seething hatred of everyone else. Understandably upset, both at being woken from their slumber and being covered in regurgitated seafood, they chased him up Broadway, through the Thicket, and all around the seediest quarters of the Lower West, a mad odyssey that ended only when he tricked his pursuers into turning on each other. Blake stabbed Eastman in the eye; Eastman broke Blake's neck; and Cherub slipped away.

"It was," he concluded, "a very bad clam."

The story distracted me so fully that I did not notice we were running out of room to climb. The ladder stopped a few inches below a rough wood ceiling. Beside it, there was a narrow ledge and a small white door. The door was locked, but one fierce shove solved that problem. I eased myself off the ladder, crawled through the door, and sank to the floor as my muscles seized. Cherub followed, showing no sign of discomfort as he helped me to my feet. His hands were rough and his eyes were soft. I hoped he had enjoyed getting to tell his tale.

It was a workroom, not so different from the ones we'd passed through downstairs, but with wood and iron standing in for silver and steel. The room was lit, not by a Device but by a pair of lanterns hung from the ceiling and candles burning in holders on the wall. Beside our hatch, a locked door led to a proper set of stairs.

Across from the door, a window ran from ceiling to floor, showing the river and the District, gleaming white. One wall was given over to a street map of the District, with paper flags showing the location of every Bourget Device. There were many more than I had imagined.

"They made so many of them," I said, "so fast."

"People have been waiting for light."

"They've been dying for it."

A bank of meters bobbed with the flow of whatever crystalline force controlled the lights, and a little wood-and-glass box was labeled with a brass plaque: "Master Control."

It had a single dial. Its cables ran into the walls, through the building, and—one assumed—north into the city. I gave the knob a gentle twist. It may have been my overworked imagination, but as I did so, the lights in the District seemed to pulse.

"Oh my," said Cherub. "That is an impressive little knob."

"We could kill every light in the District from here."

"Shall we?"

"I don't know. There are several thousand drunks strung out along that waterfront who have no idea how dark the Lower West really is. Take away their lights, and god knows how they'll misbehave."

"Then why haven't you moved your hand?"

I looked down. My hand was tight on the dial, ready to spin it all the way off. Before I made up my mind, a sound echoed across the little room that set my stomach churning. Someone was coming up the stairs.

FIFTEEN

"Perhaps you'd like to join me in hiding?" said Cherub.

"With pleasure."

He darted underneath a workbench and I followed suit. It was a great beast of a thing, made from a single piece of thick, scarred wood. We pressed ourselves against the wall. A rack of carefully organized tools dug into our backs. The door opened. We tried not to breathe.

A man's shoes gleamed under the flickering yellow light. Wingtips. Surely not factory issue.

"Better come out, Miss Carr. Nowhere to go but the window."

Oliver Lee, as friendly as ever. We pressed harder against the wall.

"It's like playing hide-and-seek with my four-year-old. Your feet are sticking out."

He ducked under the panel and smiled. Not a hair was out of place, and even in that dim room, his teeth seemed to shine.

"I'm alone, you know," he said. "Unarmed."

"A Roebling man never goes anywhere unarmed," I answered.

"I lobbied for special permission. Hard to play the nightlife impresario with a bowie knife on my hip. Had to fill out, oh god, I don't know how many forms, and the result is that you have me outnumbered and entirely at your mercy—assuming you still have the strength to fight."

"I'd rather not."

"Good. That's very good."

He offered a hand, but I refused it. Cherub and I crawled awkwardly out from under the table. Lee stood in front of the window, the light of the District playing around his face like a halo. I detected a slight flush around his cheeks. Perhaps I wasn't the only person for whom the evening had been a trial.

"You were supposed to let me sort this out," he said. "Not cause any trouble. Don't you wish you'd played along?"

If he was going to banter, I deserved to sit down. I dropped onto the stool. As soon as I left my feet, I remembered how tired I was. There was no question of being clever. It was time to get to the point.

"We've been to the pillow factory."

"All the way in?"

"All the way."

His brow tightened. The lines in his forehead were shallow. This man was not accustomed to worry.

"Unpleasant sight, isn't it?" he asked.

"What did you do to those men?" said Cherub, staring at the floor. I wondered if Lee recognized this as fury or mistook it for Cherub being shy. Part of me was afraid that Cherub would choose this moment to loose his anger on Lee. Part of me wanted to see it happen.

"I didn't do anything," said Lee. "Well, I signed the form authorizing the experiment, so from a corporate perspective I may be responsible, but—"

"Experiment?" I said.

"It's quite difficult for me to have a conversation like this, with a detective, mind you, not knowing precisely what she already knows. I'm dealing with company secrets, you see, and I'd hate to give anything extra away, you understand."

"I know everything Marka Watson knew and a few things more."

It was a bluff, and it seemed Lee bought it. He gave a little shrug.

"Poor woman," he said. "To die like that, simply for asking too many questions. She was just doing her job. You are, too."

He lit a cigarette off the nearest candle. I couldn't understand why he was chatting instead of raising the alarm. Perhaps he enjoyed his voice too much to stop.

"This summer, Professor Bourget began to suffer headaches. Dizziness. Rather inconvenient incidents of vomiting. She grew quite pale and found herself unable to get out of bed for days at a time. She became convinced that her Device was the culprit, and she asked my permission to run an experiment to test them. I thought it sounded awful, but she was adamant it would save lives."

"The Devices hadn't been tested before they were installed?"

"She assured us they were safe. I don't argue with genius."

"How did the experiment work?"

"It was quite simple. She wanted to understand the effects of prolonged exposure to the light. I secured a dozen derelicts and confined them to the pillow factory vault. We took their clothes, which were worse than rags, and we fed them better than they'd ever had in their life."

"But you strapped them to the walls," snarled Cherub.

"Yes, well, science is complicated," said Lee. "They developed headaches, dizziness, fatigue. They grew as pale as snow, stopped eating, stopped moving. One by one, they died. It was all quite sad."

"The light killed them," said Cherub.

"That was Professor Bourget's conclusion, yes."

"The same lights that burn at every corner of the District. That have been installed in hotel rooms and restaurants and saloons . . ."

"The very same."

We should have known the Devices were poison. From the first moment they spun their miraculous light across this District, we should have known they were too beautiful to be anything but deadly. In a land where nothing worked, anything useful must have a price. But we had been in the dark so long. We had not wanted to know.

"Gilda, I think we should throw this man out the window."

"It's a thought," I mumbled, staring over Lee's shoulder at the strip of sin that hugged the river, seeing the croupiers, janitors, cooks, prostitutes, trombone players, and countless other Westsiders who had flocked to the District for money and society and a good time. All of them, poisoned by the light.

"Does Van Alen know?" I said.

"I certainly didn't tell him," said Lee. "Aside from heroin and cheap muscle, the Devices were the Roebling Company's main contribution to this experiment. My supervisors would crucify me if I got us tossed out over this kind of mistake."

"Why don't you take them down?"

"Why on earth would we?" He seemed genuinely perplexed.

"Because they're killing people," said Cherub.

"Oh, just a bit. Professor Bourget was confident she could find a solution before the onset of fatalities. We had absolute faith in her work—she was a true visionary, and they are so rare—and we saw no reason to shut things down."

"You mean you didn't want to stop making money."

"Obviously. We are businessmen. What other function do we have?"

Cherub's hands squeezed into fists. I gestured for him to calm down. He walked to the window and tried to breathe.

"I think you're exaggerating the problem," said Lee. There was the faintest note of panic in his voice, as though I was not the only one he was trying to convince.

"Really?"

"Our test subjects were under constant exposure to the light. Professor Bourget found daylight lessens the effect and slows the, well—"

"Poisoning."

"If you want to use such an ugly word. The professor spent more time under those lights than any of us, and it took her over a year to start suffering symptoms. She estimated that it wouldn't be until fall that the people of the District started to die, and even then it would only be the true degenerates—the ones who rarely saw daylight and never left."

He cranked open one of the panels in the window, letting in a welcome gust of soft, warm air. He flicked his cigarette outside. It took a long time for its orange glow to be swallowed by the night.

"Come here," he said. When I didn't move, he spread his arms and smiled. "Please, Miss Carr. If I wanted you dead, you would be dead. I simply want to have a look at your hands."

I held out my hands. He touched them. His palms were soft and almost feverishly warm. He leaned forward, so low that for a moment I thought he was going to kiss my wrist, and took a long look at my cracked white skin. When he stood, there was a sickening gleam of sympathy in his eyes.

"Yes?" I asked, although I had a very good idea of what he was going to say.

"You suffer from headaches," he said. "Crippling ones, nearly every morning."

"They're called hangovers. A reward for anyone who drinks too much red gin."

"I can see why you'd think that. But it's not just the headaches. You have dizzy spells. You are tired all the time. Your jaw aches. You hardly eat. No matter how much sun you get, you stay pale."

My mouth was dry. I felt as if I were at the top of a cliff, and I wanted him to go ahead and shove me off.

"What is your point?"

"You must spend every night under those lights."

"Days, too."

"I'm surprised you can still stand."

There it was. In a way, it was almost a relief. I'd spent so long feeling wretched without knowing why. I'd blamed liquor, Marka, Cherub, myself. It was much more satisfying to blame Oliver Lee.

"You're here just as much as me," I said. I found it impossible to raise my voice above a whisper. "It's hardly fair that you look so good."

"You should see me in the mornings. I'm nearly as pale as you, been suffering terrible rashes. I'm turning gray. On the rare occasions I see my children, they have to look quite hard before they recognize me. Makeup, hair dye, nice clothes, and low lighting—that's all I am now."

There was no sadness in his voice, only resignation. I'd have felt sorry for him, I think, if he hadn't so recently had me confined to a cage.

"Is there a cure?" I said. I did not dare hope that his answer would be yes.

"Professor Bourget made great strides toward a treatment, but—"

"But she's dead now."

"My. You really do know everything."

"Did you kill her?"

"You don't think much of me, do you?"

"I don't trust anyone who shines their shoes."

In that little room, his laughter sounded like a shot. Cherub squeezed his hand on the window frame, like he wanted to tear it loose from the mortar. Lee lit another cigarette.

"It was Marka who killed her. Not literally—get that hungry look off your face—but she drove her to it. I was at the Casino last night when I got a message that there was a problem at the Works. I came quick. Marka was here. She'd backed Bourget into that corner and was just about screaming at her. She called her a murderer."

"She was," muttered Cherub. Lee shrugged, and continued.

"I'd never seen Marka so self-righteous. I was genuinely afraid she was going to hurt the professor—a frail old woman!—and so I pulled her away. She told me everything. The pillow factory, you know, and the poor, pitiful, poisoned people, but really she was just like you, just like me—terrified by the knowledge that soon she would die."

"What did the professor say to all that?"

"She was stone. I reminded Marka that nobody's ever solved a problem after one A.M. and convinced her to go back to the boat. We left the building together. I was nearly back at Spring Square when one of the professor's assistants caught up with me and told me she'd hanged herself, right there. I cut her down myself. Such a stupid waste."

He pointed at the hook where the lanterns dangled from the ceiling. Ash tumbled from his cigarette. He wiped it away with his arm, then scowled at his sleeve. I didn't understand how a man on the brink of hideous death could still be concerned with his clothes, but I'd never understood worrying about one's appearance, so perhaps it was simply beyond me.

"Did you kill Marka and her friends?" I said.

Lee chuckled, sort of, like the question was so ridiculous he couldn't help but be amused.

"I should like to know just how, and why, you think I might have committed such an act."

"You have the full resources of the Roebling Company at your command. You would need nothing but a boat, an ax, and the help of a few large, unpleasant men. As for why, well, you have as much to lose as Professor Bourget if this secret comes out. I can think of no better reason to kill."

"If I were as mercenary as I'm sure you think I am, I would have."

"But?"

"This is embarrassing, Miss Carr. I've been trying to keep my personal feelings out of this, but you do have a knack for drawing out people's secrets. I loved Marka Watson."

He said it so earnestly. I was astonished—it was the first heartfelt thing I'd ever heard pass his lips. I goggled.

"You did *what*?"

"Pathetic, isn't it? From the first day I saw her, I was captivated. She was so tall, so elegant, so strange. So perfectly unlike my wife. Why do you think I was always asking myself along for drinks with your gang?"

"I thought you were just a boor."

"Perhaps I am. But it was always for Marka. Simply to be near her. Every moment I spent in her presence, it was like pumping myself full of electricity. The only time I ever felt alive."

"Did she know?"

"Perhaps. I never said anything. I'm not delusional, Miss Carr. I know she'd have had nothing to do with me, and Roebling

Company men are expected to be good family types. I would never blow up my marriage for . . ." He shook his head, imagining something unspeakable. "In any case, no. I would have cut my own throat before laying a hand on her."

That uncomfortably earnest expression had not left his face. It was becoming harder to look at him, and so I let my gaze drift away to the window, to the lights.

"Could it have been one of your employees, acting on his own to protect the firm?"

"It's certainly possible. The Roebling Company encourages initiative. My background is business—not criminal. I find murder distasteful, and wholesale slaughter like what happened on your boat not only in poor taste but bad for business as well. That kind of baroque butchery, well, I find to be very Westside. But when a Roebling man kills, he does so quietly, cleanly, and with approval from higher up."

"You think it was someone in Van Alen's organization?"

"Or the local criminal underworld? Sure. Why not? The thing is, I don't really care. My concern is ensuring that what Marka was planning on handing to the *Sentinel* doesn't make it out into the world."

He wiped his eyes with the heels of his hands. When he'd finished that, he once more looked like the devil's maître d'.

"So you're going to kill me, too?" I said.

"Probably not! Here's what I'm thinking—and at the moment my bosses know nothing of any of this, so understand that I am not stating official company policy, but merely my own opinion. Marka, despite her charms, wasn't much of a reporter, was she?"

"I wouldn't know. I tend to stick to the sports pages."

"Sensible girl. She was a critic who stumbled on a story. I don't think she was working this alone. She had a source, or sources, slipping her documents, blueprints, a confession—I don't know what. I want their names."

"So you can have *them* killed?"

"What do you care? You'll be alive."

"I'm beginning to fear that you don't think much of me."

He laughed, and I didn't like it. He tossed his cigarette into the night and shut the pane. He tried to walk away from the window. Cherub blocked his way. Lee leaned down to speak to him, as though he were talking to a child.

"Still want to hurl me through the window?" he said.

"More than ever," said Cherub.

"It's a bad idea."

"I don't care."

"Really, though! I can help you. I'll get the police off your back, bring Koszler to heel, get the thousand-dollar bounty off your head. I'll even return that boat of yours and pay for it to be cleaned until it sparkles. I'll solve your every problem, and all you have to do, my dear detective, is your job."

Lee was not merely posturing. His voice still held that earnest note. He really wanted my help.

"What about the lights?" I said.

"You are not the only one who does not want to die. I have hopes that simply turning them off will be enough to let us heal. There was a thirteenth member of our little experiment whom we released halfway through. His symptoms lessened. He remained addled, fearful, perhaps a bit mad, but he survived. If we can't sort out a cure in, say, the next two weeks, I'll order every one of them taken down."

"It is not easy for me to trust you."

"So what? You do not have another choice."

I nodded. He exhaled. And then I reached for the little glass box labeled "Master Control."

All color drained from Lee's face. For the first time, I saw his makeup. I held the box above my head. It had almost no weight, but it was deadly cold. Its cables dangled like heavy braids.

"No," he said.

"Those lights are poison. You said it yourself. I'm not waiting around for a cure."

"Think what's going to happen when those lights go out. There are thousands of people out there, drunk, entitled, and far from home. How many of them are going to get hurt? How many will die?"

"How many will die if these lights stay on?"

He took a step toward me. I made like I was going to drop the box, and he stopped walking.

He squeezed his fists. He squeezed his jaw. It appeared he was attempting to look tough. His eyes were fixed on me, on the bauble in my hand. He did not see Cherub inching around behind him, or the wrench clutched in my lover's hand.

"It's a pointless gesture," he said. "Stupid, even. Bourget was not the only genius working in this facility. Even if you break that connection, they will have the lights up again in an hour, maybe two."

"Then why do you look so afraid?"

"Because these things aren't stable! God knows what they'll have to do to get them working again, how much more they will *hurt*."

"But you'd still turn them back on?"

"It is my job."

Cherub swung the wrench. Lee's eyes lost focus. He swayed. He collapsed.

Cherub stared at the red smeared across the head of the wrench. He opened his fingers and let the tool clatter to the floor. His mouth formed silent words. I think they were "Oh god, oh god, oh god." He squeezed his eyes shut. I don't think it did any good.

"Two days ago we were respectable parasites," he said. "Now look at us. Can't even have a simple conversation without the other person getting their head bashed in."

"Is he breathing?"

Cherub knelt beside Lee and, with great effort, placed a hand on his chest. He nodded. I was mildly horrified to find that I wouldn't have minded if the answer had been no.

I tossed the little glass box gently from hand to hand. The cold left my palms red and numb.

"What do we do with this?" I said.

"He's right. The dark would be dangerous."

"But it would be the kind of danger we understand."

Cherub smiled, and I smiled too, and between us there was no pain. I raised the box over my head and was about to smash it against the worktable when it occurred to me that he needed this more than I did. I placed it gently in his hands.

"Be careful. That's Roebling Company property."

"Terribly valuable, I'm sure."

He tucked the box against his cheek and spun like a shot-putter. The cables twisted and stretched and were about to snap when he released the box. It sailed over Lee's shuddering body, straight toward the great window that looked out over the Lower West. Glass shattered. Cables snapped.

Across the District, every light went out.

SIXTEEN

The door led to a narrow stairwell. We descended as quickly as the darkness allowed. We met no one on the stairs. Through the walls we heard pounding feet, unintelligible conversation, the odd shout, and the thumps and groans of uncooperative machinery. The people trapped in the bowels of that strange factory must have been terrified. I would not weep for them.

The stairs ended at the street. We were up the block from the factory's main entrance, where panicked scientists and engineers stood in a clump, using lighters and matches to hold back the night—surely the darkest they'd ever seen. Welcome to the true Westside, I thought. If they saw us, they showed no interest, and so we slipped away.

"Where now?" said Cherub.

"I don't know. I ran out of ideas hours ago."

But in that moment, for the first time since my last nap on the *Misery Queen,* I was certain I'd think of something. The night was cool, the darkness like ice against my forehead. My spine straightened and my headache drifted away. My feet were so light, I wanted to run, but the persistent ache in my side reminded me what a bad idea that could be. So instead, we strolled, arm in arm, like we had always done. And between our footsteps, between the slap of the river, I heard soft feet scuttling in the darkness and a snap that might have been a switchblade.

Westside sounds. Even after only a few minutes of darkness, the villains who owned this land were coming home.

At first there were only a few of them, and they were little more than children. Skinny and scarred, missing teeth and patches of hair, they seeped up from the street itself. Once they'd have paraded in gutter finery—sunken top hats and stolen silk—but in today's Westside, there was nothing for them but rags. They were joined by old men with deep scars, grinning women with long knives, and others who had watched their neighborhood be taken away from them, brick by glittering brick. With every step, there were more—ten, twenty, too many to count—and they kept picking up speed, until we had to run to keep from being trampled.

"We need to get out of here," hissed Cherub.

"I think that door has closed."

Trying to leave would have only drawn their attention. As long as we kept with the pack, we were part of it. I could not tell if we were passing or if we truly belonged, but that was a puzzle for another time.

I pulled him close, my fear steady and familiar, almost a comfort. As his body molded against mine, I had a dangerous thought. I had come to the river worn as thin as old lace. Life on the *Queen* had just made it worse, and for that I'd blamed my friends, my lover, my bird, my booze. I'd denounced the entire concept of waterborne transportation and cast suspicious glances at the river itself. And the entire time, the lights were there, on the land and on the party deck, burning me from the inside out.

"What if it wasn't us?" I said. "What if, on the boat, when we were miserable—"

"I wasn't miserable."

"When I was miserable, then. If it wasn't because of who we were, if the lights were to blame. We could go back to how things were. Happy, simple. Just you and me."

"On the river?"

"Who knows?"

"That would be nice."

There was no hope in his voice. I squeezed his hand tighter, and he pulled it away.

"The lights weren't the problem," he said. "It was us, dearest. It was us, the whole time."

"And what does that mean?"

He sucked in another deep breath. It looked like it hurt. I braced for the words I'd expected one of us to say for a year or more: "It's done." Perhaps that would be better, if he really didn't want me anymore, if . . .

I swallowed. We were close to the Boardwalk. The air smelled of violence. Cherub and I, thank god, would have to wait.

A figure at the front of the mob turned to face the pack. It was the white-haired woman, her long silver coat fluttering like a cape as she ran backward at an astonishing clip. Her eyes were black pits and her smile showed every rotted tooth. But her laughter and her speed belonged to a much younger girl. Every few steps, she snapped at one of her people. They peeled off, wordlessly, to bring her unspoken message to some other quarter of the growing mob. Give her a boat, and she could have been Amelia Slaybeck. Give her a black dress and a permanent headache, and she might have been Gilda Carr. She carried no weapons and wore no uniform, but she was unquestionably a general, and this was her war.

"The dark," muttered the warrior at my elbow, a round-faced boy with close-cropped hair and an exquisite pair of sideburns. He tossed a club from hand to hand. The wood was fresh, well-polished. It had not yet tasted blood. "She finally got the dark."

Beneath the moonlight, the river was a silver ribbon. Against it, we saw the shadow puppets of a hundred or more well-dressed tourists, wandering from dock to dock, trying to beg a ride home. We were too far away to hear them, but I could imagine their voices, slurred from education and champagne. I had learned to walk among them, and part of me wanted to warn them against the coming storm, but I did not want to betray the Westsiders. They were my home, too.

Just before her wave crashed over the dock, the white-haired woman stopped. The mob stopped with her, barely contained, like water about to boil. Men in top hats and boaters stepped uneasily to the front of the tourist crowd, hands shooing their women back. Now Cherub and I moved, slipping sideways, trying to slide away without being seen. I did not have an appetite for another fight.

We were nearly out of the pack when the silence broke. A tall man, whose impeccably tailored dinner jacket only made him look gangly, waded into no-man's-land. The moon lit up the ringlets at the back of his head, and he looked for a moment like a gigantic, beautiful baby. He lit a cigarette.

"If you're looking for a boat, you'll have to wait your turn."

The white-haired woman approached him.

"That's all right," she said. "We're not leaving."

He smiled, the same way he'd been smiling at women his entire life. For perhaps the first time, it did not go as he expected.

I don't know where she got the hammer. It was a magic trick—her hand was empty, and then it wasn't. One swing, and the man with the curls was on his knees, blood in his hair, his fingers still gripping his cigarette.

It was a match on dry kindling. The Westsiders hurled themselves at the tourists, screaming things that were not words but were simply the purest expressions of long-buried rage. In groups of two or three, they swarmed anyone who looked like they might have money. They tore pearls from necks and wallets from coat pockets, but robbery was not the point. They weren't even trying to kill. They had spent a year and more watching these people infest their neighborhood, swallowing their anger every time another shipload of tourists was vomited upon their shore. This was their chance to tell the world how bad that hurt.

The Eastsiders did not try to fight. They ran in every direction, smashing headfirst into their cousins, lovers, friends, and neighbors, tripping and falling and becoming that much more appealing targets for the Westside wrath. The District's best customers were caught in a noose, and the noose tightened fast.

I had Cherub by the wrist, or perhaps he had me. We spun away from charging Westsiders, ducked blows and leapt over the bodies beginning to litter the ground. We headed east toward Spring Square, but we were swimming against the current, and we had not even escaped the Boardwalk when our path was blocked by a screaming man.

"Help me, somebody help me . . ."

He was curled in a ball on the ground, surrounded by four boys who seemed intent on stomping him into a paste. They took turns on his hands, his gut, his face. They neither laughed nor shouted. They were too intent on their work.

"Bastards," said Cherub. "That's no way to fight."

"Forget them. Look what's coming next."

I pointed past the Boardwalk, to the muddy rubble of Spring Square, where the forces of law and order were preparing a charge. Roebling men clutched knives and knuckledusters; Van Alen's guardsmen balanced nail-studded clubs on their shoulders; and the men of the NYPD twirled their nightsticks. There was no one directing them, so for the moment they remained a muddle, but in a moment or two they would find their nerve, and the situation on the Boardwalk would grow much, much worse.

Cherub did not care. Pummeling an unarmed man was an offense to gangland honor—a concept I'd always considered moronic, but which meant quite a bit to him. He pulled away. I followed, not because I had to, but because in that moment I realized that risking one's life to save someone else was hardly more stupid than doing so to learn a bandleader's middle name. Cherub was kind. He cared, even when it was a mistake.

That is a beautiful thing.

We had no weapons. Beyond that, we had both run out of fight hours prior. But I'd spent my youth deflecting the misplaced aggression of boys who thought they were tough. They did not frighten me.

We slammed hard into the biggest of the boys. He stumbled over his victim, landing face-first on the Boardwalk, looking so stupid that his friends forgot immediately that they were supposed to be fearsome. Cherub lunged at one of them, growling like a rabid dog, and their resolve crumpled. They broke ranks and melted into the fray.

The heap at our feet began to cough. I stuck out a hand and dragged up something that looked like a very sick fish. His hair was wild and his shirt was beyond repair. His glasses had been smashed to dust. Only once I caught the stench of his cologne did I recognize Marvin Howell.

We dragged him to the edge of the Boardwalk, in the uneasy space between the ongoing brawl and the slowly congealing mass of law.

"You," he snarled. "I should have guessed this was your doing."

"You're welcome. For saving you, that is."

"*Saving* me? You're the reason I was almost killed!"

"I turned out the lights. I can hardly take credit for the rest."

"Gilda Carr, under the authority granted to me by Glen-Richard Van Alen and Ida Greene, I hereby place you under—"

"Shut up," said Cherub. Howell shut up. He looked grateful for the opportunity. This man was not comfortable being in charge.

"What are you doing out here?" I said.

"Van Alen sent me to see about the lights. Ida Greene said he asked for me specifically, that he's been quite impressed with my work, that—"

"Wait. He's in the District? Glen-Richard Van Alen is here?"

Howell nodded, smirking as he reveled in knowing something I did not.

"Since spring. Took private rooms at the top of St. Abban's. He heard we were running an impressive operation, and he wanted to see for himself. He liked it so much that he decided to stay on for the rest of the season."

I wasn't looking at him anymore. I was seeing past the riot, past the cops, to the cupola at the top of St. Abban's. I could almost see the power bottled up there, stored like water behind a fragile dam. Here was deliverance. Here was hope. Here was Glen-Richard Van Alen, a killer with principle, the last of the great New York brawlers, emperor of the united Westside. Here was a man who trusted me, who'd known my daddy and liked me better. Here was the only man who could turn those lights off for good.

"Take us to him," I said. "Now."

Howell massaged his scalp, trying to reclaim his center part.

"I wouldn't waste his time with you."

I liked the way he said that. There was a snarl in his voice, a little blood. For the first time, I could see the gangster he had been. Luckily, I knew how to snarl back.

"You've had quite a beating, Howell. The only reason you're still conscious is because your body is working overtime to hide the pain. But if I do something like this . . ."

I dug my thumb into a gash on his cheek. Howell's mouth fell open; his skin blanched. He did not make a sound. I felt vile hurting an injured man. But even as the guilt welled up in me, I remembered the thirst I'd felt on the Long Pier that morning, when Howell's friends left me to rot in the sun, and I pushed a little harder.

I withdrew my hands. He slumped to the ground. I waited until he was breathing normally and whispered in his ear, "Will you take us to Van Alen now?"

He smiled, and I knew something was wrong. He didn't hit me; he didn't bite. Instead he screamed.

"It's Gilda Carr!"

Six of the hardest-looking Westsiders looked our way. They were men and women, most older than me, with the scars and limps and never-healing wounds that marked a lifetime winning tougher fights than this. They carried chains. Behind us, the line of police had become impenetrable. We were stuck in the middle, and the middle was getting small.

Howell kept yelling.

"The butcher of the bay! The girl that killed Marka Watson! She's got me. She's got me. Save me and you'll have the thousand-dollar—"

Cherub seized Howell by the collar and smacked him hard. He stopped yelling.

"Camembert, I thought you were better," said Cherub.

"None of us were."

Cherub let Howell fall. The six strolled our way, as steady as the tide. The one in the front of the pack twirled her chain, then cracked it on the Boardwalk like a whip. Cherub found my arm. His grip was firm, and when he spoke there was an unsettling note of courage in his voice.

"I'm tired of running," he said.

"As am I."

"But you've got work to do."

And then he screamed—a sickening yowl, a sound humans are not meant to make, a sound New York had tried to forget. The war cry of the One-Eyed Cats. And it meant, as it always had, that Cherub was about to do something gallant or dumb or both.

I seized his arm. He broke away and hurled himself into the six, punching and kicking and laughing like he'd never had so much fun. Even on his best day, they would have been stronger than him, but he fought for something they couldn't understand, and that put him on top—at first, anyway. His laughter stopped when he took the first blow to the face, yet he did not fall. He leaned back on his heels as his six opponents formed a ring around him, their chains rapping dully on the dock.

Every part of me wanted to go after him, but then he caught my eye. There was misery there, and fear, and a warning.

"I gave you this chance, dearest. Don't waste it."

Taking my eyes off him felt like an amputation, but I did it. I ran. Behind me, the dull smack of metal on flesh melted into the din of battle, but I knew it would ring in my ears for the rest of my life. The riot had splintered into little knots of violence—two lean Westside women tearing the dinner jacket off an unconscious tourist; a pair of Eastsiders pummeling a boy who'd lost his knife; a woman in a scarlet gown standing in the eye of the storm, her mouth gaping as blood streamed down her ruined face—and I was able to escape without attracting much interest. Several Westsiders spotted me, but none bothered to attack. It was obvious I had nothing to steal.

When I reached the mud of Spring Square, I risked a glance over my shoulder. Cherub had fallen back from the pack. He yowled one more time and ran into them at full force, crashing through like a bowling ball, carrying a pair of them off the Boardwalk and down to the water below.

And then he was gone. The Hudson had taken him home.

A line of cops and Peacekeepers stretched across the width of Spring Square, their features hidden by the dark. It was no longer possible to tell who was NYPD and who belonged to us, and I suspected it didn't matter anymore. They said nothing; they did nothing. They were waiting for a signal, but from where I could not see.

Dress shoes squelched in the mud. Howell lurched toward me. He was standing straighter now, and that made me like him even less. He raised an arm, signaling the cops. They paid him no mind.

"Bastard," I said. The word was inadequate, but in that moment it was all I had.

"Can you blame an old soldier for trying to hang on to a job? Do you know what a miracle it was that Ida Greene took pity on me, took me in, taught me her business? Do you really think I would let you and Cherub spoil that?"

"Quite truthfully, I do not care."

He reached out, trying to wrap me in a bear hug. I twisted away, but he managed to get hold of my wrist. He threw his other arm high into the sky and screamed to the police: "I've got her! Gilda Carr is right here. I've captured her and—"

I slammed my elbow into his gut. He staggered backward, coughing like he was going to throw up, but he kept his footing. He would have grabbed me again, I think, had the police not chosen that moment to charge.

They swept across the mud in a flying *V*, pounding hard enough to rattle the glass panels on the darkened Device. Howell kept waving at them, kept yelling that he'd captured the killer detective, but either they did not hear him or they simply weren't interested. The wave swept around us. All except two cops, who hung back like we were a rock that snagged them. Their uniforms were wrinkled, their shirts untucked. Their faces were mottled with stubble and sweat, and their buttons were not shining anymore.

Howell made a last, desperate attempt to smooth out his hair. He had just begun his monologue about how he'd captured Gilda Carr when the bigger of the two cops—a human refrigerator with sleepy, bulging eyes—cracked his club across Howell's mouth. Howell didn't merely collapse, he disintegrated, falling unconscious to the mud.

"That's enough," I shouted, but the cop did not stop. He pounded Howell's skull until it looked like a burst tomato. While he attended to that gruesome work, his partner dragged me away from the fray.

I suppose I was screaming something to the effect of "Let me go, you stupid bastard, let me go," but he did not release his grip until we were at the base of the great light in the center of Spring Square. He hurled me to the ground and stood back, wiping sweat from his eyes.

"Would you stop screaming, you ungrateful bitch? I just saved your life. Why don't you be smart and get the hell back to the Eastside? You're safe. Do you get that? You're safe."

I saw, to my shock, that he was right. I had escaped the battle, and it was proceeding without me. At the water, the lawmen crashed across the Westsiders with an insane fury. The white-haired woman had formed her side into ragged ranks, but no amount of desperate brawling would stop the Peacekeepers and cops from pushing them into the river. In a minute or two, it would be over. I hardly cared. The only person in the District who mattered had gone into the river. I would get him back. Van Alen was here. He would save Cherub. He would save all of us. I just had to get in the door.

The Casino doors were blocked by about five hundred pounds of cop, and so I went around the side. The screams from the river sounded very far away. The kitchen entrance was barred. No lights shone. I rounded the building's back corner and worked my way down the sidewalk until I found the fire escape.

La Rocca hadn't exaggerated when he said it was mostly rust. I grabbed hold of the ladder and a chunk came off in my hand. I climbed anyway. It wobbled, but held. I was almost feeling optimistic when I reached the top and discovered the fire door was locked from the other side.

There was no time to waste on self-pity. I straddled the fire escape and eased myself onto the window ledge. It was barely wider than my hand. The street was very far away. Making myself as small as possible, I crawled along the wall, planting one hand in front of the other. Once, I recalled, I'd had a paralyzing fear of heights. What a luxury that seemed now.

The farther I got from the fire escape, the harder it was to keep going. I kept at it, trying to hold an image of Cherub clinging to a pier down the river, or washed up on the bank waiting for me to find him. I tried not to imagine what he'd look like if he drowned.

I was halfway to the window when a bird shit on my head.

I craned my neck and saw the rear end of a seagull dangling off the building's roof. With a hop, she dropped to the ledge and met me eye to eye. It took a long second before I recognized her, and even longer before my brain could admit that it was true.

Grover Hartley had returned.

I might have swooned, but at that altitude it didn't seem the intelligent thing to do. I inched closer to the bird. She cocked her head. She did not look well. Her plumage looked greasy, with the unhealthy color of a chain-smoker's fingertips. Her eyes were the yellow of rancid fat.

"I doubt I look much better," I said.

My voice startled her. With a few quick hops, she was at the corner of the ledge.

"Bird," I called. "Damn you, come back here!"

She stood on the corner, staring into space like I'd never existed at all. I crawled all the way to the end of the stone. She swayed in the wind, testing it, waiting for the right gust to take her away. I reached for her. One motion, and I'd have her back.

But why?

I could stuff her under my shirt, I supposed. If the struggle didn't send me toppling off the side of the building, I could try to get her inside. Taking her with me would do her no favors. I was a woman pursued, a woman who couldn't go home, and the man I was trying to save never liked the damn bird anyway.

I withdrew my hand. She hopped off the ledge, spread her wings, caught the air, and soared. For a moment, she was a white dot against the darkness, and then she was gone.

I stood up, keeping my back pressed against the rough wall, and cracked the window with my elbow. The shards fell a long time before I heard them smash.

"Right," I said. "Now the next part."

I knocked the glass loose, trying to clear enough space to haul myself over without being too badly cut. It was a minor concern. My legs were starting to shake, and I just wanted to get inside. I was about to start climbing when the window fell open.

I lost my grip.

And somewhere far away, deep in my overtired brain, I had a simple thought.

You are going to fall.

And I would have, if Ugly La Rocca's thick, leathery hands hadn't grabbed me by the shoulders and dragged me over the sill. He cradled me so carefully that I didn't sustain a single cut—and then he threw me to the floor.

"You. You are a serious goddamned problem."

"Thanks for the hand."

"Do you know the trouble you've got me in? After that scene you pulled with Koszler—"

"What scene? He beat me half to death."

"They're going to take my Casino, you get that? Send me back to working the tunnel, or worse. Every time I see you things get worse. Do you have any idea what's going on outside?"

"A fight. Eastside versus West."

"Who's winning?"

"The police."

He sank into his desk chair and lit a cigarette. He slumped so low, the end of it nearly singed his shirt.

"I've got five hundred people down there, important people, and they're scared to death of the dark. We opened the wine cellar, been passing out champagne to keep them happy, but the store is almost gone."

His face looked like a boiled steak: lumpy and far too pale. His hair was thin and his moustache looked like it would only take one hard jerk to pull it loose. I'd never seen him looking so, well, ugly.

"You get headaches?" I said.

"Comes with the job."

"Dizzy spells? Nausea? How often do you vomit?"

"Takes a lot to keep this place running."

"It's not the work. It's the light."

"How do you mean?"

I told him about the pillow factory, the experiment, and the death of Bourget. I told him I was the reason the lights had gone out, and that if they came back on, they would be more dangerous than ever. I think he wanted to argue, but—like me—he was simply too tired. Once the news had sunk in, he held out his hand. It quivered like a freshly hatched bird. He closed his eyes.

"Did you know?" I said.

"Of course not."

"You're the link between the Roeblings and St. Abban's. You work with both sides. I don't see how something like this could be kept from you."

"I'm a glorified bartender, pouring drinks and dealing cards—dangerous enough to give the people downstairs a thrill without actually making them afraid. Nobody tells me a damn thing."

"Then who was Marka's source?"

"Nobody at St. Abban's. You know Van Alen. There are no secrets from a man like that. Something like this, if he found out? He'd have burned the District to the ground. It must have been the Roeblings. The Roeblings alone."

"Not Cornelia Prime or Marvin Howell?"

My voice caught slightly on Howell's name. I wondered how long he would be lying in the mud before anyone noticed he was gone. I wondered if anyone would care. I tried to put those thoughts out of my head, but they would not stay quiet long.

"They don't have the wit," said La Rocca.

"What about Ida Greene?"

"Maybe." He stubbed out his cigarette and slapped his hand on the desk. "I am so sick of that woman! She came to see me this week, you know? Very official. Told me she's been on special assignment from Van Alen himself. He asked her to check up on the District. She didn't like what she found."

"I saw her taking notes at the docks. She didn't look impressed."

"Irregular. That's what she called it. 'The entire situation is too irregular, Mr. La Rocca, for it to survive. And I want you to know that when this ludicrous arrangement collapses, I will see that Mr. Van Alen knows you are to blame.'"

Even through his accent, his impression of Ida Greene was spot on. I wondered if he'd been rehearsing.

"Why you?" I said. "Why not Howell and Prime?"

"They're her pets. Why else would two inexperienced young idiots be put in charge of the entire operation at St. Abban's?"

"I had been wondering."

"Me, though, I'm Van Alen's boy. I never wanted to be anything else. But Van Alen isn't what he used to be. He's been fading for a long time. Someday, he'll be dead. When that happens . . ."

There was a tremor in La Rocca's voice, and he couldn't meet my eye. He looked like he'd lost twenty pounds during the course of our conversation—like someone had poked him with a hatpin and let out all the air. I sloshed liquor into a glass and watched him press it to his lips and take the smallest possible sip.

"She'll do everything she can to make sure that when the old man goes, she takes his place."

"Won't you do the same?"

He forced a rickety smile and gave a little nod. I'd seen La Rocca take men's heads off with a single swing of his ax. That he no longer looked fit to lift the weapon didn't change how dangerous he could be. He fit in this office, fit like he never had before. If Marka had threatened that, I didn't doubt he'd have killed her for it—even if he had to hire someone to do it.

"Van Alen's the reason I'm here," I said. "I need to see him."

"And ask him to do what? Blow up the District because you say please?"

"You just said—"

"If he knew the truth, he'd do it. If he knew for sure. But what kind of proof do you have?"

Every wound on my body. Cherub, lost beneath the docks. Blood and bone soaked into every surface of our home. That someone might question me, after the night I'd had, made me want to scream, but that would be wasted breath.

"The bodies at the pillow factory," I said. "Twelve derelicts bleached as white as paper. Might that get his attention?"

"Perhaps, if you could get him to see it. But he won't leave his apartments for anything."

"Why not?"

He shrugged the way only he could.

"How should I know?"

I took a long swig of his drink. It didn't even burn. It only made me warm, like slipping into a perfect bath. I slid the glass across the desk, just out of reach. I did not need too much more of that.

"Don't you see him?"

"Not since I started here. Booze, gambling, cigars. I've become unclean."

His voice cracked on that last word. La Rocca had told me once that he saw Van Alen as somewhere between a father and a god. To be cast out must have hurt more than he could say.

"Who does he see?"

"Runners from uptown—representatives of the people handling the schools and the clinics, the candle distributors and midwives and everyone else. But from the District, the only people who cross his threshold are Howell and Prime. And Ida Greene, of course.

They won't let you in without something hard—something you can put in the old man's hand."

If only Marka had been a better reporter. If only she'd taken a single conclusive page of notes, or written down her interviews with her source, or left behind anything for me to use. As investigators, we were sloppy. We made a perfect pair.

"The last time I saw Marka," I said, "I was on the boat. She'd gone out but came back to give me a bottle."

"That sounds like her."

"She was always very free with drinks. She knew I needed it. She stood over me, her hair straight and her pearls dangling, as calm as a nurse. She even tucked me in. I drank half the bottle and passed out hard. Had a hideous dream—I won't bore you with the details, there's nothing worse than other people's dreams—but it ended with Marka tucking me in again."

"Riveting stuff."

"It was no dream. She was back on the boat, about to set sail, and she came to see me. Marka couldn't stand to touch another person, and she took a moment for me."

"To make sure you were all right?"

"To hide something. Under the mattress, maybe, or beneath the bunk. That's why she was there."

I said this with certainty, but in truth I had nothing but hope. I tried to conjure up an image of Marka crouching beside my bunk, slipping a sheaf of incontrovertible evidence beneath my mattress. I replayed that imagined moment again and again, pressing it against my brain firm enough that it almost seemed true. There was something on the boat. There had to be, because if there wasn't, I had nothing left.

Not that it was all that much. But because I believed it, for that moment at least, La Rocca believed it too. He stared in awe, like he'd just witnessed a moment of genius, and perhaps he had. In all the Westside, there was no one better at lying to herself than Gilda Carr.

"I have to get back to my boat," I said. "You're going to help."

"What will it take?"

"Seven hundred fifty dollars."

He laughed so hard that the scar on his cheek flushed red.

"What makes you think I have seven hundred fifty dollars to give away?"

I nodded at his safe. The laughter stopped.

"That's Roebling Company money," he said. "They'd cut my throat for a dime. I'd hate to see what they'd do for seven hundred fifty dollars."

"Who cares? We've been dying all year. Will you really refuse a chance to tell the Roeblings to go to hell?"

He rubbed his temples, pressing his knuckles against them with the practiced hand of someone whose headaches worsened every day.

"I don't want to die, Gilda. I never have."

This time, he didn't shrug and he didn't smile.

He stood up.

He opened the safe.

SEVENTEEN

A pinprick of light, fickle as a firefly, bobbed above the sludgy cur-rent of Morton Creek. I grabbed a chunk of masonry from the nearest decomposing wall and pelted it at the glow. I was answered with a particularly foul curse. Whoever wielded the pinhole lantern tore off its shade. The naked light was almost blinding. I fought the urge to cover my eyes.

"Gilda Carr!" called Slaybeck. "Go straight to hell."

Her foot was braced against the prow of a black canoe. At her feet, her crew rowed, sweeping her across the dead water with perfect quiet. She looked good up there, and I think she knew it.

"I have your money," I answered.

"Keep it. River's turning. We have to go."

"I need your help."

"Do I hear anguish in your voice? Don't tell me the great Gilda Carr has come to beg!"

Her laugh echoed off the banks of the canal. The lantern keeper dropped the light's cover. The canoe disappeared. The laughter went on.

Reaching the creek had required another grueling march. The pain in my side was total. If it had been consistent, I might have been able to ignore it, but it came in irregular waves and never failed to surprise. That summer I'd woken up with some of the most crushing hangovers in the history of mankind, when the *Misery Queen*'s cabin was my own private oven, my mouth was taut with thirst, and even the slightest movement of my head sent shocks of pain from my forehead to my gut. I'd survived them all. I could get through this, too.

With another silent stroke, the Mudfoot canoe pulled alongside me. The rowers looked little different from the Westsiders who'd been beaten on the Boardwalk for the crime of trying to reclaim the territory that was being stolen from them. I wanted to reach out and touch them, to remind myself that they were still real, but another breath, and they would be gone. And so I shouted my last, best offer—the one I knew Slaybeck could not refuse.

"I'll let you hit me as hard as you want."

"Hold!" she cried.

The rowing stopped. The boat drifted toward the bank. It slammed into the dirt and resisted the current's attempts to tug it back into the creek. With an easy leap, Slaybeck came ashore. She had a scarf wrapped around her mouth and her hair was still slicked down with thick, black grease. There was dried blood on her neck. She inspected me like she was trying to decide if I was too rancid to eat.

"I don't like hitting women in the face."

"I don't particularly care about my face."

"That shows."

"I don't feel good about ambushing you the way I did."

"Neither do I. I'm one of those people who hates getting hit in the head."

"You have to understand—"

But I suppose she didn't, because before I could finish my simpering apology, she smashed her fist into my much-abused ribs. She put her entire body behind the blow.

Bone crunched. It hurt like nothing I'd ever known.

Without warning, my legs stopped working. I may have passed out for a moment, because the next thing I knew, I found myself curled in a ball at Slaybeck's feet. When the roaring in my ears died down, I heard myself screaming. I was far enough away from what was happening to me that, for a moment, all I could think was how stupid I sounded.

Slaybeck pulled the wad of Roebling money out of my trouser pockets and tossed it to one of the boys on the boat.

"Thank you," she said. "That's the most fun I've ever had getting paid."

She stared for a while. My hands tensed, not sure where the next blow was coming from, but after a few breaths she shook her head.

"You're not worth the shoe polish," she said. "Keep the pants. I hope they bury you in them."

"Please," I groaned.

"Whatever it is, no."

"It's Cherub. There was a fight at Spring Square, and he ended up in the river. I don't know if he came out."

Slaybeck crouched in front of me. She pulled the scarf off her mouth. She ran her tongue over teeth that were ragged and black.

"What makes you think I care whether Cherub Stevens lives or dies?"

"You could have killed him for welshing. You broke your own rules to let him live. You care."

"I've done him enough favors tonight. The boys and I are clearing out. Our Westside is dead."

I grabbed her by the collar and pulled her close. Before she could wrench herself away, I let loose an earsplitting yowl—my best imitation of the war cry of the One-Eyed Cats. It cut through Slaybeck's armor. Years on the river fell away, and she was once again a tough little girl who liked to climb trees.

"I haven't heard that in years," she said.

"It's what Cherub screamed before he threw himself off the Boardwalk, a killer wrapped in each arm. The last charge of the last gang."

"Your point?"

"If we can get him back, our Westside will live a little bit longer."

She dragged me to my feet. I acted like it didn't hurt. A couple of the Mudfoots stood on either side of her, waiting for her move. They were older than the kids who once followed Cherub into battle, but they were children still.

"What do you need?" said Slaybeck.

"Do what I paid you for. Take me to my boat."

The rowers slapped their oars into the Hudson like they were trying to hurt it. With every thrust, the boat rose up like a bird about to take flight, then slammed down hard enough to rattle my many loose bones. From the middle of the river, the District looked as black and lifeless as the rest of the Lower West. Only the shifting figures on the Boardwalk gave it away. Past the Eastside, the sky was turning gray. This long, stupid night was nearly done.

The rower at my elbow—one of the bald girls—watched Slaybeck like she was a god.

"Where were you headed?" I asked her.

"Upriver. Anyplace. As long as there's water and other people's money, the Mudfoots will be just fine."

She smiled as she said it, and that broke my heart. These pirates were worse than an anachronism. They were a dream—the type forgotten the moment day breaks. That they had managed to survive so long without being stamped out by the police or vigilantes or the cold reality of capitalism was a Westside miracle. They had no idea how out of step they were with the rest of the world. Away from the Lower West, they were doomed. I knew it and I think they did, too.

As for what that said about me, well, I had other concerns.

We found the *Queen* on the Jersey banks, where she'd gotten wedged in the poles of an abandoned shad-fishing barge. The rowers maneuvered the canoe alongside, and Slaybeck fixed a grappling hook to drag us the last few yards. Before we were secure, we smelled the massacre. One of the Mudfoots vomited over the side of the boat, and his fellows looked like they were on the verge of joining him.

"What in hell could smell like that?" asked Gowdy.

"It's not your problem," I said. "Aren't you a lucky boy?"

The canoe slammed into the side of the *Queen*. I stumbled, and Slaybeck looked amused.

"Have you got a plan, or are you just going to thrash on my boat like a dying fish?" she said.

I got to my feet. Slaybeck held the line that joined us to the *Queen*, rising and falling with the canoe like she was part of the river.

"I'm going aboard. You're going to find Cherub. He went in the river near Spring Square, so if he's still alive he—"

"Don't you dare explain this river to me. If he lives, we'll find him. You want us to bring him here?"

"I won't be here long. Drop him at Spring Square and tell him to find me at St. Abban's. I have an audience with Glen-Richard Van Alen."

She looked at me like I was a child describing an upcoming trip to the moon.

"And just how are you going to get there?" she said.

I patted the hull of the *Misery Queen*.

"I'll sail."

Laughter rippled across the canoe. I might have felt embarrassed, but there was no room for that now.

"The way she's fouled in those poles," said Slaybeck, "it'd take a team of master sailors to get her loose."

"I've lived on the *Queen* for over a year. I know her."

"Let me leave a couple of my boys to help you."

"What I'm here for will be easier if I'm alone."

The wind picked up, as though the river itself were endorsing my plan. There was a chill in it, a first hint of autumn, and though I may have imagined it, I thought I saw Slaybeck shiver. I held steady.

"Give me a boost and row away," I said. "Tell Cherub to meet me at St. Abban's at dawn."

She shrugged like she'd never cared less about anything in her entire life. She slapped the shoulder of one of her boys and before I quite knew what was happening I was being launched into the cockpit of the *Misery Queen*. I landed with my customary lack of grace. Behind me, oars bit into the river. The canoe sprang away and I was alone with death.

A day in the sun had dried the blood and gristle that streaked every surface. That was the only improvement to the tableau. The bodies of Distler and Barron slumped across each other like exhausted lovers. The birds had been at their heads, and skull shone through. The last time I'd been here, my shock was total, and it was impossible to consider the true horror of this death. Now, I was calmer, but no matter how hard I tried to remind myself that these had been people, that I had drank with them, laughed with them, liked them and loathed them in equal measure—there was simply no way for it to ever make sense.

I stared down into the galley. The tooth I'd found rolled back and forth at the foot of the steps, glinting in the moonlight. It wasn't the tooth or the blood or the bodies that had me terrified. It was the way the ship's boards creaked along with the river's caress. It was the way that sounded like home.

Cherub and I had built a kind of life here, something I'd never thought I could do with any man. I'd learned he liked his coffee to be mostly sugar; he'd finally grasped that I liked to be left alone in the mornings. We had risen together and gone to bed together and in between, we were a pair so tightly matched that the rest of the world fell away.

It was not something I'd ever thought I'd wanted, but once I had it, it felt so natural that I'd go hours without noticing how badly I wanted to scream.

I fought that urge again as I climbed belowdecks. The galley was dark. I dug through the debris, found a book of matches, and lit one. The little room was a mess. Plates were smashed, papers were scattered across every surface, and rotted fruit littered the floor. As I let my eyes drift across the wreckage, it occurred to me that this was not so much worse than how we usually kept the space.

It was us, the whole time.

Us.

Lazy and overworked. Giddy and gloomy. Drunk and hungover and drunk again. What we'd built here had been nothing at all, or at least nothing good. It had been misery, yes, but I grew up on the Westside, so this had been the most tolerable misery I'd ever known.

I stepped over the trash and shoved open the cabin door. The bed where I'd passed my last night of decent sleep was still there, the sheets rumpled like I'd just gotten up. If it weren't for the blood dripping down from above, it would have looked inviting.

I ran my hand along the mattress and, for the first time, let myself wonder what might happen if Cherub and I were still alive when next week began. There was no coming back here. And whatever we had, I wasn't sure it would work on dry land. I wasn't sure I wanted to try. If it had been us, if every problem had simply been us, there was nothing to do but say goodbye.

I flipped the mattress. It was not hard finding what Marka had left behind: a small notebook with a marbled cover where white and green swirled in a nauseating way. I opened the cover and found a surprisingly elegant sketch of a dead seagull. I was surprised she'd known how to draw. On the next page, she'd written, "It's the most ridiculous thing, of course, to be so worried about these birds. Stuy calls them flying roaches, and I'd have agreed with him except I've always found a certain beauty in the cockroach, and seagulls are simply trash. But the thought of them dying like that is keeping me up nights, and since I bought the notebook I may as well use it, and anyway there might be a play in it or a story or something, god, I don't care—I just need something new."

I flipped through the notebook and found that within a page or two, Marka dropped her ironic pose. She stopped writing in sentences, simply bulleting information and making notes in shorthand when she was doing interviews. Whatever she was looking for had her terrified, because nothing but fear could make Marka Watson act like a real reporter.

The spine of the book was cracked, falling open to a page where she'd written, "Headaches constant. Nausea worse. Dizzy all the time. How long till I'm like them? Meeting w/ source. She promises a cure."

After that, there was nothing else.

I understood how sick she'd felt. I'd felt it too. How stupid we were, how proud. If we'd been able to talk about it, we might have solved this mess before blood was spilled. But for all our chatter, we'd never really talked at all.

A plain white envelope lay beside the notebook. Inside were four brown paper packets, all empty, that I recognized as the sort used to wrap Vivienne Bourget's marvelous crystals. With them was a note in ragged handwriting that read: "All four at once—*jam them in!*—and you will be made whole." The letters were smeared.

Whole. A lovely thought. I could see why Marka fell for it.

I kicked the cabinet beneath the bunk. It splintered, and I kicked it again. I wasn't angry, exactly. I was impatient, my hands shaking too hard for me to bother with the latch. Inside, I found my bag, right where Cherub had stashed it, and down at the bottom was my little pouch of burglar's tools. I gripped it, feeling the metal cold and hard through the leather, and for the first time in a day or a week or a year, I knew precisely who I wanted to be.

I passed back through the cabin and cockpit and grabbed hold of the rail that ran the length of the ship. I squeezed it as tightly as I could, but my hand shook. After a long, slow walk, I stepped onto the party deck. The bow had smashed into the shad-fishing barge, tangling the lines and breaking the rail. Every pulse of the river shoved us harder against it. Above my head, rope and canvas dangled as limp as drying pasta. The Mudfoots' message—"Cherub Got His"—was a smear of red on the crumpled sail.

The bodies, well. Their condition had not improved. Broken glass was scattered throughout, and the blood sparkled under the thin moon. Beneath the funk of death, the tragic odor of spilled liquor clung to the wood.

I stepped over a heap of shattered bone—ribs? The ribs of someone I had smiled at, drank with, loathed?—and inspected the Bourget Device. Its cabinet hung open. Its crank spun uselessly. The panels were closed tight and the door to the crystal compartment was fused shut. The moonlight glinted off something wedged in the cabinet's corner. I tugged it out and was rewarded with a bottle of Diana's Fire secreted by Marka or Bess or one of my other doomed so-called friends.

Leaning against the Device, I forced myself to look at the horror behind me. I uncorked the bottle and raised it high.

"You were all bastards," I said. "Witty, talented, overeducated, and cruel. Thank you for the distraction and the booze. I'm sorry you're dead now."

I drained half of it, savored the almond heat in my throat, and smashed the bottle on the deck. The spilled liquor slid toward starboard. The blood it touched gleamed like wet rust.

I flipped through my burglar's pouch and withdrew the miniature chisel and hammer. Three hard blows and the Device's crystal compartment fell open. There, as expected, were four blackened crystals, jammed in a space meant to hold only one, overloaded by the surge of poisonous light that butchered Marka and her friends—the surge provoked by the source's lie.

The boat had told me everything it had to say, but I was not finished with it, although god knows I wanted to be. It was time for the last voyage of the *Misery Queen*.

I stepped across the party deck's vile mess and leaned over the bow of the ship. Setting Marka's notebook by my feet, I placed my hands against the barge and gave a hard shove.

We did not budge.

I planted my feet and pressed harder, sending spasms of pain racing up and down my sides. I accomplished nothing.

"We won't be having that," I told her. "You have tortured me enough."

I kept pushing. I gave a shove for every time I'd smashed my forehead on her bulkheads and my little toe on her doorframes. I shoved for every spell of seasickness, every hangover that had been amplified tenfold by the hell of sleep belowdecks in an airless room. I shoved for every useless piece of nautical lingo she'd forced me to pick up, for the stupidity of saying "line" when you meant "rope" and "deck" when you meant the goddamned "floor." I shoved until my hands shook from the pain in my sides, and still we did not move.

Breathing heavily, I inspected the mess above my head. Every line was caught. I pulled uselessly at the nearest length of rope and felt the *Queen* nestle tighter against the barge.

"Damn. Sweet god damn."

Even if I had the skill and the time, there was no chance of getting the *Queen* sailing. She had won again. I could only laugh. I leaned on the rail and cackled at the wadded rope that had me chained to that damned barge. Laughing hurt, and that made me laugh even more.

My laughter echoed across the wide, quick river, and was answered by the splash of oars. I felt the gentle nudge of a boat bumping into the *Queen*'s stern.

"Slaybeck?" I shouted into the wind. "You were right. This boat will never sail again. Thank you for coming back."

But the voice that answered had none of the easy ferocity that comes with a life on the river. It was cold, sharp—as shocking as a length of exposed spine.

"You've made a mistake, girl. You're speaking to the NYPD."

All laughter died. I snatched up the notebook and grabbed the neck of the bottle of Diana's Fire. I looked up and he was there, leaning cheerfully against the cabinet of the Bourget Device. In the moonlight, his skin looked like dry ice. His lips were apple red.

"A liquor bottle, again?" he said.

"It worked before."

"I'm disappointed. You're running short of ideas."

Koszler planted his cane on the deck and strolled across the mess of bodies and blood.

"What brings you to the *Misery Queen*?" I said. "If you're looking for a pleasure cruise, I'm afraid we're out of service."

He said nothing. This man was too brutal for banter. He simply advanced. The broken glass in my hand looked fearsome, but it would be useless in an honest fight. I was no match for his strength.

But he wasn't counting on strength.

He pulled a stubby little pistol. He cocked the hammer and pointed it at me. My stomach lurched. The world dropped away. The sensation was strange, but not surprising. I'd had guns pointed my way before.

"Drop the bottle," he said.

I let it fall to the deck.

"I've always wondered where the Westside ends," he said. "On land, it's easy to tell. Cross the fence and your sidearm is useless. Safer to leave it behind. But on the river, who can say? We're practically touching Jersey. Do you think my gun will fire?"

I shrugged. He sneered, and I remembered what my father told me when the Westside began to reject firearms, when every gun in the Lower West rusted to pieces and failed to fire.

"We're better off without them," he'd said. "A gun is a crutch. The man that pulls one has already given in to fear."

My father had been wrong about nearly everything, but he was right about that. The longer Koszler held that pistol, the more frightened he seemed to be.

I took a step toward him. His gun hand twitched, but he did not fire.

"Step back."

"I'd rather not."

I took another step.

"I don't think that gun will work," I said. "And even if it does, I don't think you really want me—"

He pulled the trigger. Fire burst from the muzzle. When my ears stopped ringing, I realized I felt no pain.

"That was an experiment," he said. "The next I aim at your navel. Then your kneecaps. Then, an hour or two later, your face."

"I see."

"I like the way you pale when you realize you're wrong. I do want you dead. I've wanted it so badly for so long, though, that I can't let myself have it all at once."

"Then what are you waiting for?"

"Nothing at all."

He leaned harder on his cane. The gun shifted, just a little, until it was pointed at my waist. I felt the heat of its gaze on my stomach. I did not want to get shot. I did not want to die. Somewhere in my overheated, overtired mind, I found an idea.

"Would you like to know who killed Marka Watson?"

He didn't shoot me, so I kept talking.

"You're standing in her blood. Don't you want to know how it got there? You haven't always been a rat, Koszler. Once you were just a cop. Haven't you any curiosity left?"

It was interesting, watching uncertainty take hold. His eyes narrowed. His mouth did, too. He looked intensely uncomfortable in a way I was very familiar with. He'd heard a question and needed an answer, and god damn anything that got in his way. In that one sense, he was quite a bit like Marka. He was even a little bit like me. I hated that, but I could use it, too.

"Who killed her?" he said.

"I don't share secrets with men who wave guns. Put it away."

"Like hell. I'm not as dumb as I used to be."

"Of course not. I heard what you said at the Casino. You've read every word Marka Watson ever wrote."

A smile seeped across his lips. His fingers squirmed against the butt of the gun.

"Nice touch, wasn't it? Rich bastards'll believe anything you tell them, as long as you let them think they're the smartest people in the room. I've gotten good at talking to people like that."

"So have I. But we're still Lower West at heart. We're not afraid of how ugly things can get. Do you know what Marka was after when she died?"

"Something to do with birds."

"Bourget's Devices are poisonous. Killing people, killing birds. The District's bigwigs knew about it. Profited off it. One of them killed Marka to keep the press and the police from finding out."

I waved the notebook. His eyes flicked toward it.

"If you were just another prick with a badge, you wouldn't care about this. But you don't like loose ends. What happened to Marka Watson—that's going to keep you up at night, isn't it?"

He chewed his bottom lip.

"If there's any cop left in you at all—"

"I'm all cop."

Maybe he meant it. His voice had gone soft, and some of the hate had ebbed from his face. He was staring at that book like it offered something he needed—answers, fame, salvation. I wasn't sure and I didn't particularly care. It was too close to dawn for me to be giving anyone the benefit of the doubt.

"Toss it on the deck," he said. "I'll look later. It won't change anything for you."

"Oh well. A girl has to try."

I tossed it, like he said. Only I threw it a little too hard and a little too high, and for once in my life, my aim was true. It slammed into his elbow, knocking him just enough off balance that when he pulled the trigger, the bullet went wide.

I crossed the deck.

He leveled the gun at my chest.

I kicked his cane. He smashed onto the deck, groaning like a dying pig. His gun slid away.

"You stupid—" he said.

He didn't have time for anything else. I picked up the cane and cracked it against the side of his face. It made a soft, wet sound. I kept hitting until one of his teeth skittered across the deck.

He was still breathing, but it didn't sound like it was doing him much good. I kicked the gun into the river, picked up the notebook, and grabbed my bag.

And then I set the boat on fire.

EIGHTEEN

It was easy. What luck, at the end of that endless day, for something to simply *work*. A chest on the party deck held cleaning products, seldom used and extremely flammable. Once, on a rare dry night, Marka and her friends had considered drinking them, but the scorching chemical odor scared them away. I emptied them across Koszler's quaking body and the rest of the deck, dropped a match and let them burn. Some women might hesitate before setting their home on fire, but between my loathing for that boat and the sudden need to disguise a murder, it was a choice easily made.

A murder.

It had been two years since I'd committed that particular sin. Something about the river brought out the worst in me. I'd killed a woman in the Hudson, as it happened, just a few hundred yards away. I'd let Cherub take me to the water to get away from her, and it had failed even worse than I'd expected. I would always be in that river, and I would always be on the *Misery Queen*.

The fire swept across Koszler's body. He thrashed, flinging sparks across the deck. Noises escaped his throat that couldn't quite be called screams. I stayed until he wasn't moving anymore, until the smoke began to taste of barbecue, and then—perhaps a few minutes late—I pondered my next move.

I could have waded ashore, fought my way across the wilds of Jersey, and found a way home. But that would have taken longer than Cherub had. I returned to the cockpit, coughing on the smoke, trying not to slip on the blood. As I smelled my former home turning to ash, I allowed myself the faintest feeling of pride. The *Queen* had broken me, but I had won.

At the stern I discovered how Koszler had gotten here: the saddest boat on the Lower West, ready to take me home. It had been blue, once, but most of the paint had flaked away. Its oars were chipped and it sagged in the water like a drunk trying to stay on his feet. It was occupied by a single man. When he saw me, a broad smile spread across his broad face. Otto Conforto was pale with fatigue, there was a smear of dead bird on his shoulder, and his hair cream had given up hours before, but that didn't stop him from enjoying that I looked worse.

"I need a lift," I said.

"I'll bet you do."

With a long, lazy motion, he pushed the little boat away from me. Another few strokes, and the Hudson's current would catch him, and I would be alone with a ship that was looking less and less seaworthy with every belch of flame.

"Wait, goddamn it!"

"Now now. That's no way to talk to an officer of the law."

Another stroke. He was suddenly quite far away. The water between us was black and infinite. I considered jumping, but I couldn't have swum a yard. It was simpler to beg.

"Please," I shouted. "I know how Marka Watson died."

"I don't care. You can't shove someone into a room full of dead birds and expect them to do you a favor!"

"Hundreds more will die, thousands even, if I don't get back across this river."

"Let 'em!"

"You'll die too!"

He stopped rowing. I could no longer make out his face, but I knew he was smiling still. The fire was making the back of my neck sweat, and the smell had turned from the pleasant scorch of charcoal to something chemical and vile. There was a pop as something flammable burst. The flames soared.

"You stubborn bastard! Help me!"

"But it would be so much more fun to watch you burn."

The heat emphasized his point. The crackling of burning wood grew closer. Smoke billowed out from the cabin. In a few moments, I'd be forced to jump into the river. It would ruin the notebook and do no favors for my latest set of borrowed clothes. I'd thrash around for a minute or two, and that would be the end. I wasn't having it.

Perhaps I was overestimating Conforto. I'd imagined him as a kindly tough simply because he'd never attempted to cut my throat. But that didn't mean he was above simple, honest greed.

"How'd you like to make a thousand bucks?" I called.

He turned his little boat around.

I promised I would not try to escape. He answered by chaining me to the oarlock and lashing me to the bench. As long as I kept my wrists still, the handcuffs barely hurt.

He rowed languidly, like we were a couple enjoying an afternoon on the water. With every stroke, he let off a satisfied little grunt. I hated him for how much fun he was having, but for what I'd done to him, I didn't blame him for wanting to rub it in.

"Where's the cop?" he said, like the question had just occurred to him.

"He slipped on the blood. Hit his head. Rolled into the water. I suppose he drowned."

"And of course, you did everything you could to save him."

"I lit the fire to guide him back."

He thought that was terribly funny.

"I heard shots."

"And you didn't rush to the aid of your brother lawman?"

"He told me to wait. I hate to disobey an order." He gave another pull at the oars. "I wonder what the Jersey cops will make of that wreck. Do they even have cops over there?"

"Not that I answer to. How did you know I was on the *Queen*?"

"Koszler had us watching the water. We saw the river rats

approach the wreck and leave in a hurry. He had an idea they'd left you on board."

"Clever man."

"He was a savvy detective, I will say that. Not much for conversation, though."

The current was strong. The river seemed endless. I looked north and south, saw no sign of Cherub or the Mudfoots. The weight on my chest grew heavier. I'd gambled everything and I was losing badly. I tried to believe that things were on the verge of turning around, but the deeper we got into the river, the harder it became to hope.

"Let's hear about this reward," said Conforto.

"They've been shouting it from every street corner. A thousand dollars for the dread detective Gilda Carr. Take me to Van Alen, and the money is yours."

"But Van Alen ain't the one who offered the reward. That was Koszler, and Koszler is . . ."

"Yes."

"I don't know Van Alen personally. Hardly seems fair to expect him to honor another man's debt."

"He's an honorable man. Once I tell him what I have to tell him, he will sort all this out."

"Honorable or not, you think I can just kick down his door asking for money?"

"You could have with Barbarossa."

The name hit him in the gut. Perhaps he'd hated Barbarossa, perhaps he'd loved her, but by the way his voice dropped, I could tell her death had left a hole in his life.

"Barbie was a peach," he said, finally.

"She killed for fun."

"Naw. She might have enjoyed it, but she never killed anybody without a good reason."

She never killed without reason. I wonder if, when this long weekend was done, that would be the best anyone might say of me.

"Take me to St. Abban's, then, and take the reward?"

"St. Abban's. Sure."

Really, he didn't have much to lose. If they didn't pay him, he could kill me at his leisure. And he had to get back to land somehow, so my death was on his way.

After that, there was nothing to say. Conforto kept rowing. Above his shoulder, a warm glow tinted the silver sky. In the water, Westside bodies floated in the surf. Each pulse of the river pushed them deeper into the mud. There would be more downriver. I prayed that Cherub was not among their number.

"Hell of a fight," Conforto muttered.

"We've seen worse."

"Not by much."

"Were you there when it finished? What happened?"

"Cops pushed the Westsiders into the river. Some of them swam away. Some didn't. The rest got beat senseless and tossed in the cages at the Long Pier."

A few people in tattered evening wear slumped on the docks. Some lay flat on the wood, dead or simply exhausted from pain. The blood that stained their clothes had begun to dry. I wondered what they would do with their ruined furs: toss them, give them to the servants, or simply set them on fire. A ring of police guarded them from whatever danger might remain in the Lower West, but the starch had gone out of the cops. Their uniforms were torn and bloody, their expressions dazed. Like the tourists they protected, they just wanted to go home.

And then the lights flared on, and everyone came alive.

They spun up all at once, steel grinding against steel. They were brighter than they had ever been—pulsing, flaring, their color no longer a cold white but a dirty gray, like snow on its fifth day in the gutter. Dawn's slow creep was no match. The Boardwalk's remaining shadows were driven away, and cheers went up as the revelers realized there was time yet for another drink, another needle, another hand of cards. They had collected the anecdote to end all anecdotes—the time they were attacked by the vicious hoodlums of the Lower West—and they had survived. Surely, they deserved another round.

A hot spike of pain formed behind my right eye—or had it been there all along?—and whatever strength I had left seeped away.

"We have to turn them off," I said.

"Yep."

"You feel it, don't you? The weakness that comes with the lights."

"I'm just tired."

He looked it. Conforto had not changed clothes since his dip in the cabinet of rotting birds. He'd attempted to blot the filth out of his rainbow silks, but he'd only succeeded in smearing the mess around. After every stroke of the oars, he shifted his gut, fighting to keep his lowest buttons from popping free.

"Barbie never made you wear a uniform," I said.

"Hell no."

"So why put up with it now?"

"I gotta work. Without it, I'd fall apart."

"But that doesn't mean your work has to make you so sad."

With a final grunt, he slammed the little boat into the base of the Long Pier. The rowboat sagged, as if exhausted by its journey and hoping it might lie down and get some sleep.

"I hate boats," he said.

"Me too."

He grabbed a length of rope and tied us tight. He looked at my handcuffs. He looked at the ladder we'd have to climb.

"You can trust me," I said. "I'm too tired to run."

Twenty minutes prior, I'd have been lying, but the light of the Devices had hit me like a shot of mercury. I was going nowhere.

He unclasped the cuffs. I flexed my wrists and climbed. The cages were jammed with the bloodied survivors of the Westside army. The light bleached their skin white. They slammed on the bars as we passed. I wondered if they took me for a trespasser or one of their own.

"What will happen to them?" I asked.

"If they're lucky, trial. If not . . ."

We stepped onto the Boardwalk. Conforto slapped one end of

the cuff around his wrist and put the other back on my arm, where it settled neatly on the red mark it had left before.

"Couldn't we dispense with the iron?"

"When we get to St. Abban's. Until then, I'm a guardsman and you're nothing."

The crowd was thick. Conforto had muscle enough to barrel through, but he stepped gently, muttering "Excuse me" and "Beg your pardon" to people bred not to notice we were there. Only when we reached the police cordon did he shove straight through.

"Bastards," he said, quite low.

"You hate them, don't you?"

"The cops or the Eastsiders?"

"Aren't they the same thing?"

He snorted, nodding his head.

"We should have never let them in here. They've got their half of the island, we have ours. Theirs is safe, happy, bright. Ours is hell, but at least we never had to share. Now they want that, too."

We trudged across Spring Square. The square had been rubble before the police charged across it. Now the rubble was slightly smaller. A deep buzzing came from the great light at the square's center, like the hum of ten thousand cicadas. Even glancing at it sent spikes of pain through my forehead. It seemed incredible that it could spin so quickly without shaking itself to pieces. Bourget's engineers had done their work well. I scanned for Howell's corpse, but it was gone.

"Did you know Marvin Howell?" I asked Conforto.

"By sight. He never had time for the guards. Something happen to him?"

"A cop beat him until his skull cracked. It was, well . . . you can imagine. I thought I'd find his body, but it isn't here. I guess they got rid of it."

"Then the old joke's true. What's the only thing a cop ever cleaned up?"

"What?"

"Evidence."

I didn't laugh and neither did he. There must be someone, I thought, who would mourn Marvin Howell. I did not want it to be me.

St. Abban's rose above the square like an obelisk over a crypt. Its brick shone white and its windows were like mirrors. A dozen guardsmen stood, arm in arm, before the door. They took a long look at Conforto before they let us pass.

Inside, the place had the atmosphere of a palace under siege. Clutches of panicked people stomped down steps and huddled at corners. There was no light but what streamed through the stained glass. In the darkness, I felt closer to whole—like a pane of glass that's spiderwebbed with cracks, but not quite ready to break. I worked very hard not to shake as I climbed the stairs. Conforto let me rest at the first landing. He stared at me with a look that could have been pity but was probably indigestion.

I rounded the corner and prepared to climb on. He grabbed my elbow and held me back.

"Van Alen's at the top of the stairs," I said.

Iron bit deep into my wrist as Conforto dragged me across the landing. He yanked open a door, removed the cuff, and shoved me inside. It was Ida Greene's office—the room where I once matched wits with Cornelia Prime. The room faced east, and there was no light but the soft gray of dawn. Chalk dust hung heavy in the air.

"We had an agreement," I said.

"You agreed. I didn't."

"Van Alen trusts me. One word from him and the lights go off for good. We'll be rid of the slummers and the cops. The Lower West will go back to what it's supposed to be."

"Maybe he trusts you, but I don't. You're gonna wait here."

"For what?"

"You promised me a reward. I intend to get it."

"And you shall. After I—"

He slammed a fist on the doorframe. I stopped talking. He looked like he wanted to scream, but instead he forced himself to speak slowly.

"Andrea Barbarossa was the only person on the Westside who ever gave a damn about me. Since she died, all I've done is get kicked around by you and Van Alen and a thousand other people who weren't fit to wipe her ass. Ida Greene's the only person in this city with money and sense to match. I'm gonna find her at the distillery. I'll get my thousand bucks, and then I intend to retire."

"And just where would someone with eight fingers and no appreciable skills choose to retire?"

"Far from you."

He slammed the door so hard that the windowpane shook. I heard his key turn in the lock, and simply had to laugh. I had my burglar's tools back. No Catholic school in the world could hold me.

I opened my pouch. The pick felt both delicate and powerful—like a scalpel. It took only the slightest pressure to pop the lock. I placed my hand on the door but did not turn the knob.

Pencils. I was thinking of pencils.

The loss of the Blue Streaks had nearly broken Cornelia Prime. I'd been so confident when I pointed to Oliver Lee, but just because he had one in his jacket at the Casino didn't mean he had stolen them all. The lights of the District were back on and more powerful than ever. Hundreds of lives were at stake, including my own. This was no time to be looking for pencils, and yet I felt their pull.

Perhaps that was madness, as Cherub had said, but I preferred to think of it as humanity, or what passed for it on the Lower West. As long as I put pencils over my own life, I was still myself. It was something I did not dare lose.

I searched the desk. The left-hand drawers held meticulously organized papers connected to the day-to-day running of the District: shipment of grain into Ida Greene's distillery, Casino ledgers, tallies of death by heroin and alcohol in the dives along the District's northern reach. None of it mattered to me.

I opened a drawer on the right side. A dozen sky-blue pencils, all marked with that proud gold *C. P.*, rolled gently toward me. I picked one up. It felt expensive. I wondered just what it could do.

I pulled out the note from the envelope I'd found on the *Misery*

Queen. On one of the reports in Prime's left-hand drawer, I scribbled, "I am so goddamned tired." The lead matched. As near as I could tell, this note had been written with a Bishop's Blue Streak. Not necessarily one of Prime's—everyone in the outfit had them—but at least that meant I was in the right building.

I closed the drawer. It shut with a soft click—not the sound of a closing drawer, but the faint tap of something falling somewhere unseen. And within me, everything clicked together as well. I opened the drawer again and ran my fingers along its back seam. There was a gap, a small one, just wide enough for a pencil to fall through.

I opened the bottom drawer and, after much awkward maneuvering, managed to remove it from the desk. Inside the desk, in the deepest part, I found a heap of Bishop's Blue Streaks. Oliver Lee hadn't been stealing them—at least, not in quantity. They had gotten lost all on their own.

I let out a shuddering breath, knowing at least one more tiny mystery was closed.

NINETEEN

The carpet stopped at the top of the stairs. I peered down a long hallway whose warped wooden floor rose and fell like an uncooperative sea. Light dripped from the keyhole of a heavy wooden door. On a table beside an armchair, a candle burned. A woman gazed at the thin book that rested in her lap. Ida Greene was on guard. Every time I saw her, she looked the same—white dress pulled tight, eyes flashing behind her tortoiseshell frames, cigarette nestled in her holder—but I was never prepared for the shock she sent through my spine.

I could not explain why I feared her. Maybe because she was one of the few people I'd ever met who made me feel dim. She dressed sharp enough to cut, and while I normally looked down on people who wasted time on clothes, something about her wardrobe made me ashamed of mine. I didn't realize how badly I sought her approval until Ugly informed me that I'd lost it. To get to Van Alen, I would have to choose not to care.

I stepped into the hallway. She did not react until I was at her feet. At last she reached for a bookmark, nestled it into her book, and closed the cover. Now she looked at me. I hoped I did not seem scared.

"How did you get in here?" she said.

"The front door. They're good for that, once in a while. I need to see Van Alen."

"He's resting."

"I'm jealous. Will you wake him, or shall I?"

"He needs his sleep. He is useless without it, and tonight it is my task to see that the madness you have unleashed on our District does not disturb him."

She set her book on the table and stood, smoothing her dress as she stepped between me and the door.

"Why didn't you run, Miss Carr?" she asked.

"I've been running all night."

"You could have fled to your town house, gone upriver, bribed a guard, and escaped to the Eastside. I know how resourceful you can be. Why come back here?"

I thought of Cherub tumbling into the river, and the thought made me shake, and so I banished it from my mind. I rubbed my hands, trying to warm them. The skin was dry enough to crack.

"Do you really think I killed those people on the boat?"

"Of course not."

"Then why order me handed to the NYPD?"

My voice cracked, and I hated myself for it. Mrs. Greene shrugged.

"I'm neither judge nor attorney. I don't concern myself with the law. My entire function is to see that Mr. Van Alen's wishes are executed properly. In order to discourage the police from taking an interest in the work we do here, it was important that a suspect be found. You fit the role."

It was all just business. I was a mark in her ledger, and I either helped balance the books or not.

That stung more than anything anyone had said all day.

I wanted to kill her. It would have been such pleasure, I thought, to tear the glasses from her face, snap the stems off them, and stab her with them until she wasn't smiling anymore. But that would have been exactly what she expected, and I was tired of proving this woman right.

"Did you know about the lights?" I said.

"What about them?"

Her head tilted, her lips pursed in an expression of the mildest curiosity. If she did know anything, if she were responsible for Marka's death, there was no sense trying to talk it out of her. It was foolish to expect her to make a mistake—she had never made one before.

Except . . . she had.

"Do you trust Prime and Howell?"

"They are among our brightest rising stars. Why?"

"Well, first, Marvin Howell isn't going to rise anymore. He was beaten to death by a cop in Spring Square during this evening's unpleasantness."

"Why?"

"He misjudged the situation. Lost his temper. I thought you trained them better than that."

Her finger rubbed against her knuckle hard enough to redden the skin. That was the biggest reaction I was going to get out of her.

"But his mistake was nothing compared to Cornelia Prime's," I said. I pulled a fistful of pencils from my bag, opened my hand, and let them fall. They clattered like hail.

"What does this have to do with pencils?" she said.

"Somewhere between very little and quite a lot."

She stared at the ground, like she knew she ought to pick up the pencils but felt it would be undignified. I wondered if this was how she looked when she was scared.

"Explain," she said.

"For the last few weeks, Cornelia Prime has been losing pencils. It's had her scared to death, so frightened she actually tried to hire me to help her find out where they were going. She was convinced they were being stolen, but they were simply falling out the back of her drawer into her desk. Did she tell you about any of this?"

Mrs. Greene shook her head. There was something about the smallness of the gesture that was terribly sad.

"What's your point?" she said.

"That you are fallible. You misjudged Howell and Prime. You may have made other mistakes as well."

"Such as underestimating you."

"It's not something I recommend."

"Well. What would you have me to do to make amends?"

"Get Prime here. La Rocca too, and Oliver Lee, and if you can find the bastard, Otto Conforto. Anybody else you can think of who wants to skin my hide, bring them as well."

"Lieutenant Koszler?"

She smiled when she said it. She must have heard about the beating he gave me. I wonder how it had made her feel.

"If you can find him, he's more than welcome to join the party."

"And what shall I tell this illustrious group?"

"That if they're not here in thirty minutes, I cut Van Alen's throat."

She stepped back from the heap of pencils, pressing her braids against her head.

"That's thirty minutes from when I see them, or thirty minutes from right now?"

"Just go."

Shaking her head, she walked down the hall. When she reached the steps, she called back, "Good luck with the door. Mr. Van Alen's got the only key."

But I'd already drawn my picks. My little instruments slotted into my hands so naturally, it was like they'd never left. As I closed my eyes and felt the tumblers yield, the years fell away, and I was a girl without a care.

There was a key in the lock. I turned it. I leaned against the wood. One strong shove forced it open enough for me to squeeze through. I locked the door behind me and confronted a scene that made me retch.

I hadn't expected luxury. Though he styled himself an emperor, Van Alen lived like a monk. The first time we met was in the lamp room of a lighthouse on the far Upper Westside whose only comforts were a pair of lumpy couches and the hundred candles he used to protect himself from the dark. Those quarters were immaculate. At St. Abban's, Van Alen lived in squalor.

The door had been blocked by a mound of rotting meat, fly-specked dishes, crumpled papers, and soiled clothes. As I shifted the heap, scuttling sounds came from deep within it—mice, rats, or something worse. An overflowing chamber pot produced a predictable stench. Heavy carpets, tacked clumsily to the ceiling, blocked the window, but the space was not dark. A half dozen Bourget Devices provided blinding silver light. They were arranged in a circle around a battered wingback chair that faced the covered window. That's where I found my man.

When I'd met Glen-Richard Van Alen, he had the thick chest and quick temper of a street brawler who refused to admit that he had long since rounded life's final turn. I had seen him angry, hopeless, gloating, shot. I had watched him grow addled and frail. But that morning was the first time he ever seemed broken.

His eyes were glassy, his skin as soft and wrinkled as the bare flesh of the dead birds. His legs were piled with soiled blankets. Drool trickled from his slack mouth, leaving a wet spot on his shoulder, and his breath came in shuddering gasps. What remained of his hair was as brittle as straw, and his scalp was covered with an archipelago of oozing cuts. He did not notice I was there.

I shook his shoulders and felt bones rattling loose beneath his skin. I clapped in front of his face. He did not blink.

"Wake up, emperor. Your people need you. And I need you more."

He breathed. That was all.

I kicked his legs off the ottoman and sat, staring into those empty black eyes. The cold light of the Devices assaulted me from every side. I felt it penetrate my clothes, my skin, my muscle, my bone. It didn't hurt. It just made me so desperately tired.

I tried to turn them off, but the switches had been removed, their holes plugged with iron. Perhaps I could have pried them open with one of my tools, but the mere thought of lifting my little chisel made my arm feel weak.

"These lights are killing us," I said. "Killing everybody. We have to stop it, but I just . . . I just don't know how much longer I can care."

I stroked his hand. His flesh wrinkled under my thumb. When I withdrew it, the skin did not snap back.

"I killed a cop. Emil Koszler, remember him? Ugly bastard. Deserved to die. Doesn't make it right. It was him or me. For so long, it's been them or me, and I keep choosing me, and I wonder if the world would be better off if I'd stop."

He said nothing. Dying men make wonderful listeners.

"Cherub wouldn't say so. He'd tell me that if I wasn't smart enough to run, I should keep fighting until I was spent. I'm spent now. He's going to have a hell of a time forgetting me, but one day he'll manage, and then he'll be free. He can get another boat. Another . . ."

There was no point talking anymore. I had too many sins to confess. I let my eyes close. I luxuriated in the dark. What a treat, I thought, to feel sleep stealing up, wrapping itself tight around you. It was the first time in so long that something was closer than my pain.

Someone banged on the door. A smile curled around my lips as I decided they could go to hell. How clever I was to have locked the door. Someone threw their body against it. My heart beat a little quicker at the thought that it might be Cherub, come to keep our rendezvous, but no—it was only Ugly. He sounded fearful. That was new.

"You're not fooling anyone. We know you're in there. You sent out invitations for the world's worst party and everybody came and goddamn it, you have to open the door."

"Is Cherub with you?"

A pause. I asked again, as loud as I could manage.

"Is Cherub Stevens outside that door?"

"No."

So that was it. The Mudfoots hadn't found him, or they betrayed me, or . . . it didn't matter. I'd lost him and saved him, only to lose him again. That knowledge would have broken me if I could feel anything at all.

I smacked my cheek. The sting barely registered. Half falling, half under control, I tipped off the ottoman and got to my feet. I could hardly see through the glare of the lights, but I did not let myself sit back down.

I looked at my hand and found it empty. I was supposed to be holding a knife to the great man's throat. There was no telling where my knife had gone. On a table at Van Alen's elbow, I found scraps of molding bread, filmy cups of cold green tea, a notepad covered with lewd drawings, and piles of twisted paper that had once held Bourget's crystals. I swept my arm across the table, tearing through the mess until I found a cardboard box marked with the symbol of the Bourget Works.

I unwrapped the crystals. When they caught the light, color streaked across them, dancing from one to the other like something alive. Their weight was negligible—I could hardly feel them in my hand. I could have crushed them to dust. Instead, I did something insane.

My guests shouted, kicked, and smashed their shoulders against the door, but the wood held. There's simply no defeating the architecture of a New York school.

When I finished my work, I opened the lock. I leaned against the curtained window, enjoying the rough fabric against the nape of my neck, the faint strength that came from being outside the ring of lights, and watched my audience pour in. First Oliver Lee, whose makeup was running and whose bloodied suit had finally begun to wrinkle, and a Roebling man who was as tough as boiled beef, with a razor in his left hand.

Prime came next. Her face sank when she saw the state of Van Alen, the wreck of the room. She cast a helpless look at me, asking me what the hell had happened to him. I wanted to soothe her worry, but all I could offer was a cold, pointless shrug.

La Rocca staggered in like he was at the tail end of a bender. There was almond liquor on his breath, but I don't think he was drunk. It was the lights that took it out of him, the same as they were doing to me. He slumped against a wall, using everything he had to keep upright, and covered his eyes with his hand.

Last, of course, was Ida Greene. She'd recovered from our encounter in the hallway. Her armor was firmly in place, and even without words, everyone in the room treated her like she was in charge. Hopefully, I could convince them otherwise. She shut the door and I locked it, then slipped the key into my bag and returned to the window. I'd made my final play. Maybe it would work. Maybe I would die. All I knew was that soon, I would be able to rest.

"Did we make it in thirty minutes," asked La Rocca, "or did you already cut the old man's throat?"

"This is patently ridiculous," said Lee. "She doesn't have a knife. She doesn't even have a clock."

"I've got something better."

They didn't seem to care. They couldn't see what I saw—that one of the Devices was whirring a bit faster than the rest, that its light had turned the sickly gray of a dirty linen. They could not feel how it was beginning to squeeze. On the table, papers quivered like they were being tickled by a draft. I did not know how long I had.

Lee turned to Ida Greene. She expelled a thin trail of smoke from the side of her mouth.

"We warned you about her," said Lee.

"I recall."

"She is an erratic presence. She should have been dealt with a year ago. Let the police have her and let us get on with our work."

Once, I'd have been confident that Ida Greene would defend me. She would say that she liked me because I was erratic, that I'd been useful in the past. She would make a crack about how silly Oliver Lee looked wearing a tuxedo at dawn. Instead she shrugged, saying nothing at all.

I was too tired to be disappointed.

The infected Device glowed brighter. It seemed to have a grip on my heart, slowing it down, squeezing it tighter with every beat. Its sickness had spread to its brothers as well. Their light pulsed unevenly, like a dying man's heartbeat. Was I the only one who could see?

Lee elbowed his brute in the gut.

"Throw her out the window. I'll buy you breakfast."

The very large man stepped toward me and I thought I was finished. But as his foot touched the floor, sparks leapt from one Device to another. The Roebling man jumped back. At last, I had their attention.

"Have any of you visited the *Misery Queen*?"

"We received a full report," said Cornelia Prime.

"But did you see it for yourself? I've witnessed more than my share of horror on the Westside, but this outdid it all. People turned to hamburger. I didn't know you could do that to a human body. One of you perpetrated that atrocity. One of you alone."

"That's not possible," said La Rocca. "One person couldn't—"

"Until quite recently, you were all happy to pretend that Gilda Carr, the mad detective, had done it by herself."

I smacked my hand on the table. The lights surged. My audience stepped backward, pressing their backs to the wall. It was wonderful to see them so afraid.

"What have you done to them?" said Ida Greene.

"The same thing Marka did to the Device on the boat. The thing one of you told her to do. The thing that stripped the flesh off her bones."

"Turn them off, and we can talk."

"Turn them off yourself."

Nobody moved.

"Fine. Then we'll talk now."

"What is it you want?" asked Prime. She was doing a valiant job of trying to look as unruffled as Ida Greene, but her panic showed. "Your freedom? That can easily be arranged. A few words to the police and we can find someone else to blame."

"The Mudfoots, perhaps," said La Rocca.

"Or the hoodlums who instigated the attack at Spring Square."

"You could be a witness instead of a suspect. You woke up on the boat, saw whoever it was chopping Marka and her friends into chum, and were so scared you dove into the water."

The Devices were not quiet anymore. For a year, they had lit our nights in perfect silence. Now, their plates scraped against each other. The glass rattled. There was a smell like searing meat.

"Just say yes," said Prime. "Say yes and you can go home."

Twelve hours prior, it's all I wanted. But without Cherub, home was an impossibility. I shook my head.

Oliver Lee broke. He twisted at the doorknob, pounded on it, threw his shoulder at the wood.

"For god's sake, help me!"

No one came to his aid. Their eyes, even those of the Roebling man, were on me.

"You might not want to pound so much, Oliver—the Devices don't look too stable." I looked at the rest of them. "These lights are killing us. Your headaches, your nausea—these are the reason why. They're killing everyone in the District, a little at a time."

"If we'd known, wouldn't we have stopped them?" said La Rocca.

"You'd think. But turning them off would cut into your bottom line, and you all like money too much to jeopardize that over something as piddling as mass murder. Marka knew, and—"

I doubled over coughing, hacking until I thought I was going to throw up.

When I righted myself, the room was coming apart.

Gleaming silver traced the corners of the room and the lines on the carpet. The burning smell grew sickening and the walls began to float away. Beyond them was the brightest light anyone had ever seen—a perfect silver void.

"God in heaven!" shouted Lee, but his god was nowhere to be found.

Prime, La Rocca, and Mrs. Greene stood back-to-back in the center of the ring of lights. The sparks were constant now, a greasy shimmer that flowed from Device to Device, growing thicker and louder with every passing moment. Van Alen was in the middle of them. The light shone off his flat eyes. It looked like he was trying to smile. The Roebling man was apart from the group, standing behind an empty chair, trying to decide if he wanted to run or fight or simply go berserk. It would be interesting, I thought, to see what he chose.

"This is the gift you gave Marka Watson," I said. "A light show, a headache, and a very messy death."

My voice sounded clearer than it had for days, like all the scratches in my throat had been smoothed clean. The walls drifted farther apart from each other. I looked down and saw my feet no longer touched the floor. This was troubling, yes, but in a distant way. Mostly, I felt free.

Marka must have felt this, I thought, in the moments before she died. She'd been desperate for relief from whatever was weighing her down, and for a few seconds there, she must have believed she was getting it. I hoped she died happy. I wondered if I would do the same.

"Please Gilda," said La Rocca, a sob in his voice. "Turn them off."

"I don't know how."

The walls fell away, and there was nothing but that magnificent silver. Frozen breath streamed out of our mouths as we rose farther from the floor, floating in a glittering nowhere, waiting to learn how we would die.

"What is this place?" said Mrs. Greene. No one answered, because no one knew. Her voice was hoarse. Even she could only take so much.

The Roebling man lost patience. He flung himself across the chair, tipping end over end in the air, and seized the base of one of the machines. His hands fused to the metal. He screamed like someone was tearing out his throat. When he dropped the machine, the skin tore away.

"Dear god," he yelled, clutching his bloody palms to his chest, spinning uselessly in the air. Again, no god answered.

"One of you told Marka to do this," I said. "You knew what would happen, and I think that means you know how to fix it. Do it now. Give yourself away and save your life and ours."

There was just one light now, streaming from every surface, from the void around us, from all the Devices at once. Inside the one I'd overloaded, gears popped. The plates tilted, spinning more and more unevenly, and the light took on the sickly tinge of rendered fat.

La Rocca and Lee grabbed either end of a table that held two Devices and flipped it upside down. The Devices crashed to the floor but did not break. Their spinning plates shredded the wood. The light got brighter still.

Lee grabbed me by the wrist and used my weight to pull himself toward Van Alen. He grabbed the blankets, and Van Alen groaned like a creaking door. Lee pushed off the chair, sailing toward one of the Devices, and used the blankets to grab it. With a guttural oath, he hurled it out of the room, into the sparking nothingness. It rebounded, flying past his head, bouncing off the walls that were not there, spraying cold light that cut his suit to pieces and bloodied the skin of his chest.

I drifted gently across the room, watching my victims struggle. They screamed at each other; they screamed in pain; they fought their weightlessness; they tried to disarm the Devices. In that bright room, only three people were calm.

Myself, soaking in the light.

Van Alen, doing the same.

And Cornelia Prime, floating in her corner like a snake waiting for its moment to strike. Her fists were clenched against her hips. Her jaw was locked tight. Besides me, she was the only person watching the sabotaged Device.

She was the only one who knew.

The plates in the Device split, and Prime snatched the blanket from Lee.

The top of the Device opened like a cracking egg.

Prime leapt across the floor, the blanket wrapped around her fist.

Light spilled out the color of liquid gold.

All around us, the endless light turned to black.

Everyone stopped breathing, stopped moving, except for Cornelia Prime.

She smashed her fist through the Device's cracking top. The air filled with the smell of her melting flesh. She pulled her arm out of the Device. In the mess of scorched blanket and burning skin, she clutched a fistful of copper wire.

The machine screamed.

With her other hand, Prime flicked through the wiring, seized one piece with thumb and forefinger, and tore it loose.

For a moment as long as the deepest breath, we were nowhere. The room was gone, and so was the light, and so was the void. And then our eyes opened, and we were back at St. Abban's watching Prime sink to the floor, her ruined hand pressed between her knees. No one else could move. The other Devices spun down slowly. Their light died, and there was nothing but the dawn.

"Get her!" said Lee. "She's the one—the one that knew. The one that did it! Somebody grab her!"

But he didn't do it, and neither did anyone else. Ida Greene crouched beside Prime, stroking her hair. I knelt on the other side. Her hand smelled like scorched rubber. It was too burned to bleed. Prime looked up at Greene, her mouth forming unspoken words, tears frozen on her face. Greene smacked her across the mouth. Prime did not fight it. She held there, waiting for another blow. I didn't have any interest in watching any more pain.

I pulled out the note I'd found on the *Misery Queen*.

"Did you write this?"

Prime nodded.

Something inside Ida Greene broke. She leaned closer to Prime and asked the only question that mattered.

"Why?"

"I knew Marka from around," said Prime. Her voice was brittle. "When she noticed the seagulls dying, she came to me. I told her she was imagining things, that even if it were true it couldn't possibly matter, but after she left, I began to ask questions of my own. I began checking the paperwork that passes between us and the Roeblings. I found notes about construction—some kind of project at the old pillow factory on Varick. I went to see for myself. And I found . . ."

"I know," I said. "What next?"

"I talked to Bourget. She told me everything. She was very matter-of-fact about it, you know—like it was all just another in a series of fascinating discoveries. She was the one who told me what would happen if a Device overloaded."

"Why didn't you tell her to turn them off?"

"I didn't have the authority."

"Then why not tell someone who did?"

"She swore she would fix it and, I didn't . . . I didn't want to rock the boat. The District was my project. I'd staked everything on it. It was essential that it thrive. The lights were a crucial part. I didn't . . . I didn't want to disappoint you."

It wasn't me she was talking to. I don't think anyone on earth cared about disappointing me. She was staring up at Ida Greene like a kicked puppy. Ida Greene just looked away.

I rapped the floor, and Prime turned back to me, her eyes swollen with tears.

"How did it end?" I said.

"Marka had this harebrained theory that it was bootlegged liquor making the birds sick, making everyone else sick, too. To prove her wrong, I asked her to meet me at the pillow factory. And, poor thing, she came. I told her everything. I begged her not to print anything, to wait until Bourget had a chance to correct her mistake. I tried to explain that revealing this secret would be destructive for everyone. She said I was a fool if I expected a reporter to pass on such a scoop. And so I gave her the crystals and told her they would heal her."

"You tricked her into killing herself."

"I told her to use the crystals when she was alone. I didn't mean for anyone else to die."

"You must not have known her. Marka couldn't stand being alone."

"Are you going to unlock the door now?" asked La Rocca.

"Not until we decide what to do with her."

"Give her to the police," said Lee, who was curled in a ball, pressing the dozen cuts that lined his chest to the blanket, staining the floor with his blood.

"There's no need for that," said Mrs. Greene.

Lee banged a fist on the carpet.

"Marka Watson deserves justice. She made everyone else in the room fade into the wallpaper. Prime should hang."

"Justice and the gallows have nothing to do with each other," said La Rocca. "A Roebling man should know that."

"It's true," said Ida Greene. "On the Westside, we handle our own."

"Fine!" said Lee. "I don't care. Just let us out of here so I can get some goddamned bandages."

I stood, and the whole world seemed to slip one way and then the other. I let myself slide down the side of Van Alen's chair. The upholstery stank of stale urine. It was a bracing smell.

I stared across the floor at Lee and forced myself to ask the final question.

"What about the lights?"

"That's company property. They represent a significant investment in research and materials. I can't simply—"

"Stop it. They stay off."

I was having trouble sitting upright, but my voice was loud enough to be heard.

"You're all pathetic. I can't talk to any of you without being told that you aren't simply criminals, but honest businessmen. Cold-blooded, sober, rational. Yet as soon as you don't get your way, you throw a tantrum, razors in hand. You've all made a fortune off this place. None of you give a damn about how many people died along the way."

"Miss Carr—" began Ida Greene, but I cut her off. It shocked her. It shocked me, too.

"Go home and count your money. You're selling cheap liquor in a country where liquor is illegal. I'm sure you'll find a way to make that pay."

I gripped Van Alen's chair and dragged myself to my feet. I nearly slipped again, but a hand reached out to steady me. Van Alen had me by the wrist. His skin was as dry as paper, but the grip told how powerful he had once been.

"Good god," said La Rocca. He grabbed the blankets from Lee and packed the least bloody around the old man's legs.

"I didn't know he was still in there," said Mrs. Greene.

Van Alen's mouth worked up and down. He wheezed faintly. I leaned close and heard him speak.

"Koszler."

"Heard that, did you?"

"Nothing in the world like killing a cop."

He smiled like he was remembering a long-lost summer fling. He let my wrist go. La Rocca lit the fire to make Van Alen tea. The air had become oppressive. And so I unlocked the door and went away.

TWENTY

I found Cherub in the hallway. He sat against the wall, his arms around his legs. His sodden clothes clung to his skin. When I opened the door, his head rose and his eyes went wide.

"I got here late. I took the wrong stairs, I got lost, I'm sorry, I . . ."

I helped him to his feet.

"What did you see?" I said.

"Bright light, streaming from under the door. Metal clashing. Screams. Nothing out of the ordinary."

Tears collected in the corners of his eyes. I brushed them away. More took their place. Behind us, Oliver Lee and his bodyguard were helping each other through the doorway. Ida Greene was comforting Cornelia Prime, and La Rocca was seeing to Van Alen. I was sick of all of them, so I led Cherub to the stairs.

We stepped out of St. Abban's to find the sun shining brightly on the bloody wreckage of Spring Square. Birds pecked at the blood spattered across the great light's base. Whatever had happened back in Van Alen's quarters had caused it and all its brothers to go dark.

We walked to the river. There was no discussion—it was simply what people in the District did when there was no money to spend or gin to drink. The Boardwalk was crowded with people looking for a way home, but the rising sun had sapped their anger. They were simply hungover and tired.

Across the river, a column of pale smoke twisted into the sky. I pointed it out to Cherub, and he hid his disappointment when I told him it was the wreckage of the *Misery Queen*.

"I'm sorry I ever got that boat," he said. "I'm sorry I brought us here."

"You didn't do it alone. I wanted . . . I wanted so badly for this to be paradise—the paradise you thought it was—that I forgot to mention when I became miserable. I hid in parties, in gin, in the hunt for that damned bird."

"You weren't the only one who hid."

I felt tears coming. Normally I'd have fought them off, but I was so uselessly tired. This was the moment I'd been trying to avoid all weekend, all summer, all year. I'd been so afraid of it that I'd smashed into it headlong.

"I didn't think it would end precisely like this," I said, "but I should have known it wouldn't go well."

"We're finished, then?"

I nodded. Hearts broke. The sun rose a little higher in the sky.

"You're pure joy, Cherub Stevens," I said. "It's not just that I don't deserve that—I don't even know what to do with it. For the things I've done, if I'm going to atone, I have to be alone."

The words stuck in my mouth like concrete. I got them out anyway. He scratched some of the dried blood off his cheek. His mouth opened and closed once or twice, but he could find nothing to say.

That night, the lights of the District turned back on. Whatever damage I'd done had been repaired. They spun out their icy light as clear and silent as ever. Few visitors from the Eastside were there to take in the sight, but no one doubted that the crowds would return.

They may have, if it weren't for the fire.

The Bourget employees fought it, sweat streaming across their masks, their leather aprons providing some protection from the heat, but it was a stubborn little fire, fed by a sticky, tar-like substance that resisted every chemical they had. At last they gave up the battle, and the dead professor's lights went out for good.

When Van Alen refused to reimburse them for the lost factory, the Roebling Company wrote the District off as a bad investment and withdrew. This was not as bloodless as it sounds. Pairs of Peacekeepers brawled on the Boardwalk, and gamblers whose debts the Roeblings considered irredeemable were found floating in the harbor for weeks.

As always, murder proved good business. Society deserted the District when the lights went out, but La Rocca saw to it that some of the saloons and gaming halls stayed open. Instead of selling style, they now sold danger and darkness and dirt—traditional exports of the Lower Westside—and they did well enough.

Marka would have hated it all.

Roy B. Sharp returned to the Eastside, but Screaming Minnie and her birds hung around. I sent her a note informing her of Mervyn Melody's secret, and she wrote to say I was welcome on her stage anytime—as long as I did not make a sound.

The police did not come for me. I spent months expecting their iron hand to fall on my shoulder, to be dragged to the Tombs and beaten lifeless for what I'd done to Koszler on the *Misery Queen*. Justice never came. Perhaps Van Alen exerted some of his failing power to protect me from investigation, or perhaps the Jersey cops lacked the wit to connect a charred corpse and a burned sloop with Gilda Carr. Whatever punishment I'd get, I would have to give myself, and that winter I gave plenty.

On a gray morning in January, I was watching the gulls drift on the river when I noticed La Rocca shredding a loaf of stale bread for the birds. When he saw me coming, he smiled like none of his friends had ever tried to kill me. I smiled too.

I stood beside him for a while, talking about closed saloons and dead friends, watching the birds fight over his scraps. Finally, I asked about Cornelia Prime.

"Ida Greene and I walked her to the fence ourselves, made sure she was put through all the channels. It was all very proper."

"Was she indicted? Will she be tried?"

"She wasn't even arrested."

"Why not?"

"What was the evidence? A scrap of paper on a boat in New Jersey? A confession made before unreliable witnesses? She wouldn't say anything, and they didn't care enough to force her, so they let her go."

"Where is she now?"

"Reassigned. Don't ask where—I wasn't told. Ida Greene found someplace for her in the Upper West. Quiet, she said. An easy assignment. I almost feel bad for her."

"Why?"

"For a woman like Cornelia, I don't know. All she ever wanted was a challenge. Quiet would be worse than death."

Maybe so. Maybe she was dead already. I never saw her on the Lower West again. But a few weeks later, I got a note from Ida Greene written in the soft lead of a Bishop's Blue Streak.

"You may have trouble believing this," she wrote, "but I should like to give you a job."

I went to hear the offer. I found I was only slightly surprised. After all, a woman is nothing without her work.

When I had left Cherub at the Boardwalk, I walked east toward Hellida and the town house, the dust of my old bed, the shards of my old life. I was three blocks past the Casino when I remembered what I was missing.

My house key.

I pawed through my bag. It was not there. I hurled the old sack over my shoulder and turned around. Each step was like walking on nails. And so I ran.

I don't know where I found the strength. I'd been pushed so far past my limit that day, come so close to breaking so many times, that it seemed impossible I had any fight left. And yet, when I cared, there was always a little more.

And I did care, I realized. I cared so much that no amount of pain could make me stop.

When I reached the Boardwalk, Cherub was gone. I looked south, toward the green expanse of the true Lower West. I saw no one. North, there were the last stragglers from the Eastside, the ones too drunk or broke or rude to find their way home. I charged through the pack, stomping on toes and eliciting all manner of "What's that?" and "I say!" and only wishing that I could hurt them all a little bit more.

I broke through the crowd. North of the square, the Boardwalk was empty. Cherub was not there.

Except, because once in a very long while the gods are kind, he was. He was two or three blocks north of me, strolling with his hands in his pockets, a man with nowhere to go.

I tried to run and found I no longer could. And so I limped, blood thudding against my ears, my legs so tired I could hardly lift them off the ground.

"Cherub!" I shouted. "Cherub, you beautiful idiot, turn around!"

The wind was blowing in my face. He did not turn.

I plunged my hand into my bag and withdrew a rock-hard dinner roll. I kissed it, reared back, and threw it as hard as I could. I was aiming for the top of his curly head. I missed by ten yards.

A dozen gulls swept down from the nearest saloon, squawking horribly as they fought over the roll. One of them buzzed right past Cherub's ear, close enough that he had to spin around.

He saw the gulls.

He saw me.

He waved and I probably waved back, and he was smiling as he loped toward me. The blood on his cheeks was smeared from where he'd wiped away his tears.

"Yes?" he said.

I bent double, my elbows on my knees, and fought for breath. When I'd finally collected myself, I wheezed: "Do you have my house key?"

Laughter bubbled out of him, shaking and painful and very much like a sob.

"What is it?" I said. "What's the joke?"

He pointed across the river, where the smoke from the *Queen* twirled across the soft blue sky.

"Oh god," I said. "That's right."

"They're in the cupboard under the bed. We put them there together, remember? We wanted to make sure they were safe."

There was nothing to do but laugh, to laugh until I was out of breath and tears and everything else, and when I didn't have the strength to laugh anymore, I grabbed him by the neck and kissed him hard, shoving him back against the railing. Probably the wood gave him splinters. I don't think he cared.

"And what did I do to deserve that?" he said.

"You stayed in the hallway. At St. Abban's, when everyone was screaming and fighting—"

"And that insane light was seeping out from under the door—"

"You did what I'd asked. You didn't come in."

"You had been quite specific."

"You were ready to let me die."

He brushed my cheek. His skin was so warm.

"When you say it like that, it sounds heinous," he said. "And yet, you smile."

"You trusted me. You didn't try to save me. You would have . . ."

I didn't have any particular idea of how I wanted that sentence to end, and so I let it go. I took another kiss. When I finally came up for air, he said, "Does this mean it isn't over?"

"Do you want it to be?"

It took him a long time to find what he wanted to say. My heart threatened to burst from my chest. Not once that weekend had I been so afraid. Finally, he squeezed his lips together and gave a single word.

"No."

For that he got kissed some more. There was blood on his lips and I'd never tasted anything so fine.

"If you don't want it to be over and neither do I," I said, "nobody else gets to decide."

"Well! How about that?"

He smiled, and I loved it and I loved him, and the sun was warm and the air was fresh and it was enough that, for a minute or two, I forgot that every part of my body hurt, and I was so very tired.

And so we left the Boardwalk behind. We crossed Spring Square, picking our way across the glittering glass and twisted metal. The ground was alive with seagulls fighting over last night's litter. None of them were our bird.

"It can't be like it was before," I said.

"Thank god."

"Today we're going home, to my home. You can stay as long as you want, but sometimes you will have to leave. I don't ever want to marry. I don't want children. I don't want anything binding us so tightly that we can't cut each other adrift the moment it makes sense. I will never forgo my work, no matter how dangerous or stupid it may become, because it's the thing that keeps me alive. If you can stand that . . ."

"If I can stand you, I can stand anything."

I kissed him again and we walked east. Before we turned the corner, I glanced back for one last look at the square, the water, the District, squinting at the gulls fighting over my stale roll. Grover Hartley was not there. I would never see her again. On warm days it was easy to believe that somewhere she found home.

ACKNOWLEDGMENTS

First thanks go to Sharon Pelletier, who has been with Gilda from the beginning, and David Pomerico, who ensures the tiny mysteries stay tiny. Thanks as well to the team at Harper Voyager. This book would literally be nothing without you.

Returning to Gilda's Westside in 2020 and 2021 was both a welcome escape and a challenge unlike anything I have ever known. I would have not been able to write a word if it weren't for Courtney Wilson and Lauren Crosby, who hung out with my kids five mornings a week during our long pandemic year. Thank you both. You are magnificent. My kids have no idea how lucky they are to have you in their lives.

Thanks as well to Patricia Woods, for reminding me that breathing is usually more important than work. If Gilda had you in her corner, she would be a happier person—and a lot less fun to write.

Thanks to Mom, Dad, Caldwell, and all my family back in Nashville. Your support is endless and very much appreciated. And thanks, most of all, to Yvonne, Dash, August, and Sonny the dog. When I first started *Westside,* Dash was not yet born. While I was finishing this book, he learned to read. It will be a long time before he's ready to tackle the stories of Gilda Carr. When he gets there, I hope they make him smile.

ABOUT THE AUTHOR

W. M. Akers is a novelist, playwright, and game designer. He is the author of the mystery novels *Critical Hit, Westside,* and *Westside Saints*; the creator of the bestselling games *Deadball: Baseball With Dice* and *Comrades: A Revolutionary RPG*; and the curator of the history newsletter *Strange Times.* He lives in Philadelphia but hasn't traded in his Mets cap yet. Learn more about his work at wmakers.net.

ALSO FROM W. M. AKERS

WESTSIDE SAINTS

A Gilda Carr Tiny Mystery, Book 2

"A masterpiece."

—*Library Journal*

Return to a twisted version of Jazz Age New York in this follow-up to the critically acclaimed fantasy *Westside*, as relentless sleuth Gilda Carr's pursuit of tiny mysteries drags her into a case that will rewrite everything she knows about her past.

WESTSIDE

A Gilda Carr Tiny Mystery, Book 1

A *New York Times* Notable Book of the Year!

"*The Alienist* meets *The City & The City* in this brilliant debut that mixes fantasy and mystery. Gilda Carr's 'tiny mysteries' pack a giant punch."

—David Morrell, *New York Times* bestselling author of *Murder as a Fine Art*

A young detective who specializes in "tiny mysteries" finds herself at the center of a massive conspiracy in this beguiling historical fantasy set on Manhattan's Westside—a peculiar and dangerous neighborhood home to strange magic and stranger residents—that blends the vivid atmosphere of Caleb Carr with the imaginative power of Neil Gaiman.